BOHEMIA BEACH

JUSTINE ETTLER

BOHEMIA BEACH

JUSTINE ETTLER

MELBOURNE, AUSTRALIA
www.transitlounge.com.au

Copyright ©Justine Ettler
First Published 2018
Transit Lounge Publishing

This book is copyright. Apart from any fair dealing for the purpose
of private study, research, criticism or review, as permitted under the
Copyright Act, no part may be reproduced by any process without written
permission. Inquiries should be made to the publisher.

Cover image: © Claire Morgan / Trevillion Images
Cover and book design: Peter Lo
Printed in Australia by McPherson's Printing Group
Author image: Kathlin Kippus

A cataloguing- entry is available from the
National Library of Australia: trove.nla.gov.au
ISBN: 978-1-125760-00-2

When Tereza came home, it was almost half past one in the morning. She went into the bathroom, put on his pyjamas, and lay down next to Tomas. He was asleep. She leaned over his face and, kissing it, detected a curious aroma...
—Milan Kundera, *The Unbearable Lightness of Being*

Heathcliff
It's me, I'm Cathy
I've come home
—Kate Bush, 'Wuthering Heights'

I just love Tilda Swinton's performance in *Julia* – it's absolutely dazzling. The older I get, the more I believe films and books can change people's lives. Watching her raise her glass, slug down liquor and then totter about in her slinky stilettos ... Swinton's compelling rendition of the female drunk makes even Meryl Streep's Violet seem a little heavy-handed. When she wakes up yet again with no idea where she is or how she got there, I realise how lucky I am to be alive. I try to hold on to the feeling but it doesn't last, so I pause the film, pick up my notebook and I write it down.

I go to the kitchen and fill the kettle with water. Sun slants in through the grimy window and lights a panel on the surface of the wooden table; traffic honks on the street below. The piano in the corner sits silent today. Recovering from a gruelling tour, I'm spending the day collapsed on the couch. I pour the water, add a dash of milk and, taking the tea with me, return to the couch and press play.

C.B.
West 9th Street,
New York
2018

LONDON

1

Light, incredibly bright – dying of thirst. I snap my eyes closed, head aching, then force them to open, struggle to focus. Everywhere around me, blinding sunlight, and in the distance, a headland at the end of an incredibly long beach. Where am I?

Dragging myself unsteadily first to my knees and then to my feet, I brush the sand out of my hair and shake out my damp, salt-encrusted clothes. I've lost my handbag somewhere along the way, though I've still got my mobile phone, and I discover a matchbox in my jacket pocket which seems vaguely familiar. Unsure what to do next, I stare closely at the image printed on the front of the matchbox: a palm tree and a sandy beach are superimposed on top of the Prague skyline. *Bohemia Beach* is written across the middle in red bubble letters, and there's an address and phone number in the Czech Republic I don't recognise printed along the bottom. Still gripping the phone, I return the matchbox to my pocket.

The morning sun warms the top of my head as a pristine wave breaks below me, cappuccino foam nibbling my toes. To my left the sky and sea meld into a grey-blue horizon with orange tints; to my right sand dunes sweep upwards, topped with tufts of grass like baby's hair. Up ahead the empty beach stretches away in a single undulating curve of white sand towards an indistinct headland. I take out the matchbox and dial the number on my mobile; the battery is low but hopefully it will last for a quick call.

'Tady je Odette,' a woman's voice answers.

'Hello,' I say. 'Do you speak English?'

'Yes,' the woman says.

'Is this the number for Bohemia Beach?'

'No, this is a private number.'

'Sorry to trouble you –' I say, but hesitate before ending the call. The woman's voice … It's not just the miracle of her near-perfect English, there's something about her voice. It sounds incredibly familiar, I'm sure I've heard it before somewhere.

'Sorry – what did you say your name was?'

'Odette.'

'Odette!' The coincidence is incredible. 'Did you used to live in London …?'

'Yes, for many years.'

'And you've a daughter named Catherine?'

'Yes, I do. Please, who is this?'

'Mummy!' I say, 'It's me, it's Cathy –' but just then the line goes dead. I try to redial the number but the phone's screen remains obstinately grey.

My mother – it must be my mother! How many other Czech women named Odette have lived in London and have a daughter named Catherine? I start to walk towards the distant headland. On the other hand it can't be my mother. It can't be my mother because my mother is dead. Unless – by some miracle …? Or else – more likely – somehow I'm also …? Is this a dream?

BOHEMIA BEACH

Shielding my eyes with the back of my hand – that sunlight certainly feels real! – I squint around me as I walk: crystal light dancing across the water; the sound of gulls circling above; the gentle slow sshh, ssshhh, ssshhhh of the lapping waves.

2

'Miss Bell?'

The doctor's voice drifts down from far away – such a lovely musical voice – pulling me back. I half-heartedly try to open my eyes but my eyelids are too heavy. I give up and resume my drifting, sinking down …

'Miss Bell, I'm Doctor – actually, you can call me Edgar,' he says. 'I need to ask you some questions.'

Not really wanting to answer any questions I find myself thinking about dying instead, about not fighting the pain, about letting the infection spread, eat me up, kill me. It would be quite nice, death, a release from all this –

'Miss Bell?' The doctor's voice is louder now, persistent. 'Miss Bell! Can you hear me?'

Why won't he just let me go? It's so difficult to climb back, even if I wanted to. Deep beneath the surface of the water, I'm slowly see-sawing down, well on my way to the dark sandy bottom. The grey London sky seems such a long way away.

'Miss Bell … Miss Catherine Bell?' he tries again, though I'm almost out of range.

But then a woman's voice, familiar, comes shooting down. 'Cathy? Cathy, can you hear me?' and jolted by it I struggle to open my eyes. Nelly – it must be Nelly? I try to speak but no sound comes out. Is there a mask over my face? I speak as loud as I can in my head. 'Yes it's me, Nelly,' I tell her. 'Can you hear me?'

A hand tugging sharply at my sleeve. There was something, something urgent I had to tell Nelly; now what was it? If only I could remember …

'I hope you don't mind me asking –' it's the doctor's voice again – 'but you wouldn't happen to be Catherine Bell the pianist, would you?'

How does he know? Has he recognised me somehow? Did Nelly tell him?

'I loved your last performance – what was it now?'

He has such a wonderful voice, so warm and kind.

'Rachmaninov?' Nelly says.

'Concerto No. 3, that's right,' he replies in dulcet tones.

'Beautiful.'

'But turbulent. Beautiful, turbulent and sad.'

'So sad.' Nelly's hand finds mine, wraps her fingers around it, warm and firm. *Nelly.* I must try again for Nelly. And her little girl – what's her daughter's name? Dragging myself upwards, I force my eyes open but when even this is too much, I let my left eye fall closed so just my right eye can narrowly see. This eye is stronger. Gingerly, experimentally, I peer into the light.

'There we go, well done!' It's the doctor again. 'Now, Miss Bell, you can understand what I'm saying, yes?'

For an answer, I open my eye a little wider, focusing on the dark patch in the middle of all the brightness. I concentrate on this shadow, letting my eye adjust, and meanwhile the light all around glows golden, making a halo. Inside that halo is an angel, a man with one of the most beautiful faces I've ever seen: green, almond-shaped eyes are set in pointy, fine-boned features and framed by a curly mass of light brown hair which fluffs up chaotically around his head, giving him a mad professor look. I blink one-eyed, just to make sure I'm seeing straight. How is it that after just one look at this man, death is suddenly much less appealing?

'Miss Bell?' he says, 'I have a couple of questions I need to ask you and then I can leave you to rest.'

I want to nod but I can't.

'How are you feeling?' he goes on. 'Are you in any pain?'

'I'm,' I begin and then, feeling stupid, because no noise comes out, my throat is too dry, I attempt a smile and open both eyes. A squeeze from Nelly's hand.

The beautiful face smiles back. 'It would really help us if you could answer a few very quick questions?'

For a moment or two I maintain a cheerful expression as our eyes lock, but then, remembering what happened the last time I let a handsome man into my life, I snap my eyes tightly closed. I'm sick of wanting something I can't have, a man I love who loves me back. Sighing, I let go of the golden light, and of darling Nelly – I just can't – and resume my slipping, drifting, sinking down …

But the doctor's voice follows me. 'Have you any idea how you got here, what happened to you?' and Nelly calls out, 'Cathy?', applying gentle pressure to my now lifeless hand. It's just too hard. Already they're too far away and I'm too tired. Anyway, I've been through it all too many times before and no matter what I do things always turn out the same. Even Nelly couldn't change that. I never get what I want. So what's the bloody point?

'All right, Miss Bell, it seems we've tired you out for today so we'll leave you to rest –' his voice is fainter now. 'But if you could just try with one more question – it's very important.'

My eyebrows twitch in an attempt to respond, but everything's already a dead weight on top of me. They've come to rescue me too late. Far easier to let myself go, to succumb to the familiar pull of the warm water, to drifting, and sinking down, and strange dreams …

3

Dusk. A chill breeze sweeps the beach. I build a little pile of driftwood and, using two crumpled electronic teller machine slips I find in my pocket and a match from the Bohemia Beach box, I coax the flames to life. I study the image on the cover again for a few minutes and then put it quickly away.

I'm just curling up to go to sleep when I hear someone calling my name: 'Miss Bell. Miss Bell – can you hear me?'

I shake myself awake. It's not someone calling my name but a cacophony of moaning noises coming from the water. All around me the beach is alive with belches, yups, screams and snores; grunts, thumps, knocks, pulses – chirps, whistles and clicks. I've never heard such odd noises before. I assume they're being made by some strange sort of singing fish. Or, more likely, by whales.

I sit up. Illuminated by the creamy light of the full moon I detect dark, distant shapes moving gracefully about in the water.

Wondering what the whales are singing about, I kick sand on the fire and strip off all my clothes. I creep down to the water's edge and walk out into the gentle waves. When it's deep enough, I begin a surprisingly smooth breaststroke, swimming far out into the inky darkness of the water. At one point I turn around and look back at the beach. The remains of the fire are a soft golden glow.

The closer I get to the whales, the louder their singing becomes. Soon the whole ocean seems to be vibrating in tune and I can't help joining in. At first my voice is soft; I find it initially quite difficult to swim and sing at the same time, plus the whole business of singing with the whales feels a little strange in itself, but gradually my confidence grows and soon I'm making my own moans, whistles and clicks.

I haven't been singing long when I notice a large dark shape moving towards me in the water. Unusually for me, I'm not frightened, even though the whale comes quite close – close enough for me to make out the oddly shaped bumps on its nose; if whales indeed have noses, that is – and feel the warmth of his thick breath rising above me in the air. I'm somehow sure it's a male. I wonder where the whales have come from – the Antarctic, the Arctic – and what drew them to Bohemia Beach. Suddenly tired, I rest by floating on my back. I point my toes at the beach, the coals of the fire still emitting a faint glow, and let my body relax.

Meanwhile, the whales have stopped singing independently and are singing a specific song in unison. I listen carefully to the strange-sounding words:

Tereza, jedině
Tereza
Měla by slyšet píseň mou
Ostatní prominou
Nestojím o jinou
Jen pro tu jedinou
Chci tady zpívat (píseň svou)...

It's a beautiful song, a love song. A little too showbizzy for my taste, it sounds like some kind of Frank Sinatra for whales, and I'm amazed at how human the whales sound, it actually sounds like they're singing in Czech, or some sister language, although I suspect this is not quite what whale singing normally sounds like. And just when I'm thinking how strange that the whales are singing in Czech, the scene shifts and suddenly I'm dancing by a river beneath a willow tree with a handsome man wearing black tie. I'm dressed in a red ball gown and as we dance he stares deeply into my eyes. He spins me around and around, and we dance all night together, our eyes radiant with joy.

'Miss Bell …?'

I recognise the voice instantly.

'Catherine?'

The golden doctor. Somehow I must have drifted up closer to the surface when I was singing with the whales. I can see his face, rippled with small waves, looking down at me where I lie beneath the surface of the water. He has such a lovely voice …

Still wary, I smile at him and am just about to dart quickly away again when he says, 'Catherine, can you hear me? This is important. I've just spoken with your father …'

My father? I'd completely forgotten about my father with everything else going on. Has anybody told him about my mother?

Changing my trajectory isn't easy but after a few awkward attempts I get the hang of it and soon I'm floating gracefully up towards him. When I finally surface into my narrow, standard-issue bed, Edgar is staring at me curiously. He's leaning down over me and studying my face, his clipboard forgotten in his hands, his hair askew. He reminds me of a romantic hero in a nineteenth-century novel; all he needs is a vast estate, a dark family secret and he'd be perfect. No doubt I should forget all about Tomas and –

'Miss Bell? Catherine?'

I open my eyes fully and look at him with all the attention I can muster.

Reaching for his clipboard he tells me, 'Glad to have you back on board, Miss Bell.'

Once more I notice the pretty green of his eyes and the fineness of his skin. 'How are you feeling?'

I try to speak, but my throat is too cracked and all that comes out is a painful, ragged cough. Unfortunately, once I start coughing, I can't stop.

'Whatever you've been up to,' he says, giving me a cheeky grin, 'you've managed to give yourself a nasty dose of pneumonia, on top of everything else. Won't be a minute,' he says, disappearing through the rubber doors and into the unseen corridor beyond.

Through watery eyes I see how pale my wrists look against the light blue of my hospital pyjamas. As the coughing fit subsides, I discover my upper torso is wrapped snug in clean white bandages – this is related no doubt to the pain that throbs intermittently from somewhere between my shoulder blades – my lips feel deeply cracked when I lick them, and there's a big scabbed cut on my forehead.

Reassured that nothing seems to be permanently amiss, I study my surroundings. The faded blue linoleum floor and the brilliant white of the sheets and blankets of the hospital bed make me feel like I'm drifting in a small sailing boat. To my left, blinds made of heavy tan paper coated with plastic frame a hazy view of modern hospital buildings, all glass and concrete and dotted with the occasional tree. Outside the sky is heavy and grey with clouds – it's been drizzling all day. Suspended from the ceiling above me hangs a child's mobile of a seagull. One of its four strings is broken so it's flying on its side.

Returning, Edgar hands me a plastic cup of water and I lift it cautiously to my mouth. Frowning, the water too icy on my still raw throat, my body stumbles on the seemingly forgotten magic of peristalsis and my eyes fill with tears as my coughing recommences with increased vengeance.

'Take small sips,' Edgar says, 'that's it.'

Following his instructions my throat soon relaxes and my breathing normalises.

'We've just started you on a different antibiotic, which should be more effective than the first one we tried,' Edgar says.

About to wipe my eyes and nose on my sleeve – 'Sorry,' he says, belatedly handing me a Kleenex – I manage a weak smile.

'We've – actually, *I've*; Nelly's made me promise to take good care of you – I've got some good news. I've managed to find your father. He said he'd try and pop by later today.'

I close my eyes on the fresh tears. Has anyone told him about my mother?

'Catherine, is that going to be a problem for you, seeing your father?'

I shake my head and clench my jaw.

'Catherine?'

I take a deep breath. Thinking of my mother reminds me of

Tomas and all that's gone before. '*I'm not Catherine*,' I manage, almost spitting my first words.

He frowns, then looks away. Looking back at me, a softness comes over his face. 'I don't understand,' he says. 'Nelly said – your papers say your name is Catherine Bell. Is that your name? Of course, I wasn't the doctor who admitted you, but I'm sure that's what it says on your admission report.'

I close my eyes, remembering, and retreat from any further interaction. Has anyone told him about my mother? I hear Edgar draw a breath as if he's going to call me back but a nurse arrives and tops up my medication and Edgar leaves. I reach for the chill numbness of the drug as it makes its way up my arm and around my body. I slip back down, into exhaustion, into sad memories, into strange dreams.

4

The smell of stale hospital food is pungent around me and I'm busy struggling through lunch when Edgar collapses loose-limbed into the brown vinyl chair next to my hospital bed. 'Me again,' he says, smiling up at me.

While it's too much effort to smile back I do manage to briefly meet his eye.

'I just wanted to let you know your father called to say he's running late.'

I nod, and let my eyelids close.

There's a pause, a rustle of papers from Edgar's clipboard and then Edgar's voice. 'You know, it would really help if you could tell me what happened to you.'

Tired, not wanting to go there, I turn onto my side so that my back is facing him.

'If Catherine …' he persists, climbing out of the chair and circling round the bed. 'You say Catherine Bell, the name on your admission report, isn't your real name? Then what is your name?'

I open my eyes only to find Edgar staring back at me, waiting. Such pretty green eyes. Unable to resist, I take a small breath in preparation, but when I speak my voice refuses to come. He pours water from the jug beside the bed and hands me a plastic cup.

'I'm not sure how I got here,' I rasp, sipping at the water. I pause, waiting for him to say something, but he just continues looking at me intently. His eyes, his beautiful eyes …

'There was water, a wall of water, and then …' I say, pausing again to sip from the cup. He watches me and frowns. 'Someone hit me, I think,' I say finally.

'Someone hit you?'

'Or maybe I fell and hit my head?' I continue. 'And after that, there was a beach – I was in Prague –' My eyes catch a glimpse of the seagull before they close.

'A beach! In Prague?' he prompts. 'Where?'

I try to stay with him but the urge to slide back down is too powerful.

'You were in Prague – on a beach?' Edgar says again, clearing his throat.

Yes, I tell him silently, succumbing to the exhaustion as it drags me back down.

'You mean a beach beach, with sand and seagulls and sharks and whales and everything?'

I want to say yes but it's too hard.

'You realise, Cathy, that we've been administering quite a bit of morphine for the pain in your back,' he says. 'Morphine is a strong drug, people often say they have funny dreams …'

He waits, then stretching, says, 'I'll let you get some rest.'

But just as he's leaving, I feel a sense of urgency and bursting back to the surface I force my eyes open and say, 'Tereza!' Then I repeat more quietly, 'My name is Tereza.'

He stops, turns, is about to ask me another question, when

an older man in a tweed coat and fine grey flannel trousers enters the room. He looks down at the bed and gasps, 'Cat – my darling girl.'

Cat? Then, recognising him, I smile, and hold out my skinny arms for a hug.

But my father remains at the foot of the bed. He drops the newspaper he's clutching to the floor as tears fill his eyes. 'Oh my God,' he says. 'First Odette, now this.'

I snap my eyes closed again. He already knows. It's only when Nelly arrives and places her palm gently across my burning forehead that I smile. Finally, finding the strength to resist the tug of the water as it tries to pull me back down, I let myself be washed ashore.

5

Prague, the beach. Just the mention of my trip to the Czech Republic has opened a door in my mind and now I can't get it closed again. Maybe this is what it's like to go crazy? I just want to sleep, but I can't, fragmented memories from Prague keep pushing their way into my mind causing my heart to race. It doesn't help that the woman in the bed beside me is still being monitored and the constant beeping is annoying. Also my back aches between my shoulder blades and I can't seem to stop grinding my teeth. They removed the butterfly yesterday afternoon, which means no more morphine, and the Nurofen has left my mind clearer but my body in pain.

It's just after one a.m. Last night I went to bed exhausted at eight after a light supper of tea, oatmeal cookies and cheese with my father, and I've been lying here unable to sleep ever since. I glance at my mobile on the bedside table and, my hand trembling, pick up the phone. Tomas. Heart racing, I dial his number and listen while the phone rings and rings until the line finally goes dead and I hang up. Now my heart is beating so fast I can hardly breathe. Is this a panic attack? I read about panic attacks once in a magazine – what am I supposed to do to calm down? Imagine I'm in a supermarket filling a trolley item by item? Take deep breaths? I try both but nothing works. I pick up the phone and dial again. This time I get his voicemail and hang up the phone. I close my eyes but my heart is still beating too fast to sleep. Fighting back tears, I look up at the seagull: please help me sleep, I tell it. I wait ten minutes and then give up. A sleepless night, the last thing I need on my last night in hospital. I dial Tomas's number again and this time leave him a message, asking him to call, telling him I don't understand. Gradually the panic attack starts to subside and my heart rate and breathing return to normal. Soon after, miraculously, I'm asleep.

I wake early and check my phone in case Tomas has called – he hasn't. I know I should forget about him, that's what Nelly would advise, but I'm not sure I can. Outside it's a sunny day though the weather report is predicting rain and a late storm. While the panic attack has stopped, my back is still aching and I'm completely exhausted. I drag myself out of bed and into some clothes – red knickers, a pink polo neck, beige tracksuit pants, red woollen socks, pink Moroccan slippers, and a camel cardigan – then, yawning with the effort, climb back into bed. The heating is up quite high making me dozy and my eyes alternate between staring blankly at the seagull for long intervals and closing involuntarily. My hair is completely matted and my lips dry and bitten. I pick up my mobile phone but when a sharp pain stabs my back, I put it down again. I need to get better ASAP so I can find Tomas.

Forget Tomas.

Remembering my father's reaction upon seeing me, I go to the bathroom in search of a mirror. The woman from the other bed has gone but I lock myself inside the cubicle nevertheless and study my face in the glass. What's wrong with me? How bad *is* it?

The left side of my forehead is deformed by a swollen wound, at the centre of which is a deep cut dotted with twelve neat indentations where stitches must have been. The bruising is light brown in colour and the scab mostly fallen away. There are dark circles beneath my eyes and my complexion is decidedly pale. Pulling my top up and turning so my back is facing the mirror, I see a thick wad of cotton bandage taped across the middle of my back. I sigh. I've clearly been injured during the flood and while my wounds aren't exactly attractive, they don't seem that bad to me.

Just then, I hear Edgar's voice calling, 'Hello? Mind if I come in?'

I exit the toilet and, seeing me, Edgar enters the room. I lie back down in bed and Edgar, angular as a crane, towers at its foot. He is dressed in black trousers and a red jumper, his rust-brown tweed overcoat slung carefully over one arm. For a second I imagine us running away together, getting married and living happily ever after like in a Gothic romance novel, but then I remember Tomas. 'Mind if I sit down?'

I nod and Edgar sits down in the vinyl armchair. 'So tell me, how are you feeling?'

'I'm feeling …' I begin but then stop. About to tell him I'm fine, I can tell that Edgar isn't after the social niceties, he's after the truth. I struggle with the words. 'I'm feeling a bit tired. I'm not sleeping well, and while the physio yesterday really helped there's a funny pain in my back –'

'What sort of funny pain?'

'A sort of sharp stabbing pain, although it seems a little better today.'

'Take two Nurofen whenever the pain gets too much, but let your doctor know if that doesn't contain it.'

'My doctor? Aren't you my doctor?'

'Nelly should be here soon,' he says, looking away, 'and your father, and then we can work out what to do with you.'

'But I'm still being discharged from hospital?' I say, giving him a look.

'Your father has ongoing commitments in Oxford and as much as he'd like to he can't get leave just now to be your full-time carer. I can't stress enough, you've been seriously ill and will need full-time care. Nelly offered to find somewhere for you in Berlin close to her rooms there,' he says and pauses.

'Berlin?' I wail.

Edgar nods and continues. 'On the other hand, I wondered if you might not consider a small private hospital in Surrey? I live nearby and could keep an eye on you, and Nelly and your father would be welcome to stay with me when they want to visit. You would be well cared for, they have a lot of experience with post-traumatic stress disorder, and I really think they might be able to help you. I hope you will consider it?'

I smile and look away, out the window at the gathering clouds, a blush rising to my cheeks. He really is incredibly nice, perhaps he *is* a romantic hero! (Though I suspect this whole set-up might be Nelly's idea.) 'But I hardly know you,' I begin. 'I mean, it seems too much.'

'Think nothing of it.'

'But I –' I say again, then stop when Nelly and my father arrive.

'Hello, Catherine, hello, Ed,' Nelly says, kissing me first

before kissing Edgar on the cheek. My father leans in to kiss me too and then shakes Edgar's hand.

Seeing my surprise at the kiss, Nelly says, 'Oh, didn't Edgar tell you? We're old friends from Edgar's practice in Chelsea.'

'We hadn't got that far,' Edgar says.

They all look at me and smile.

'Are you sure she's all right to go home?' my father asks Edgar. 'I really don't like the look of that scar.'

'Cathy, are you ready to go?' Edgar wants to know.

'I just feel tired,' I say, but thinking, *I told him I'm Tereza now, not Cathy, didn't I?*

'And will you go with Edgar to Surrey?' Nelly says. 'You'll be in good hands and your father and I will come and visit often.'

I look from Nelly, her dark eyes and hair, to my father's face creased with worry, to Edgar's beautiful green eyes staring evenly into mine. Finally, I smile at Edgar. 'If you're sure it isn't too much trouble?'

'No trouble at all,' he says, and smiles back.

'Good,' my father says. 'I'm glad that's all settled.'

Edgar gets up, suddenly all bustle. 'Let's see about getting you discharged then,' he says and leaves.

Outside the sky has grown suddenly darker. Following my gaze Nelly says, 'It looks like we might be in for some rain, though hopefully not before we get you down to Surrey, safe and sound.'

Nelly – there's so much I need to tell her, though now is clearly not the time.

Later, in Edgar's car, the shiny walnut of the dashboard and the low purr of the engine come as a welcome shock after the sterility of the hospital. We drop my father and Nelly at the nearest tube station and soon we're on our way, heading south.

At first we drive in silence, watching rain clouds assemble across the sky ahead, but after a while I turn to Edgar and look at him hard. 'You're a psychiatrist, aren't you?'

'Not exactly,' he says. 'I'm a psychotherapist and a psychiatrist and I'm particularly interested in trauma, although I tend to mostly work holistically these days.'

'I've gone crazy, haven't I?' I say, trying not to let the panic take over. 'For a while I thought I was dead, but probably this is just what being crazy feels like. Am I right?'

'No, I don't think you're crazy – I think you're confused, that's all.'

'Confused?' I study his beautiful face, his long elegant fingers loosely gripping the wheel, his fine features, his lovely lips. It's such a kind face. 'Confused about what?' I ask finally.

'You've just come out of a coma of several months' duration,' he says evenly. 'You were in a coma when you were admitted to hospital in Prague. Actually, you were in pretty bad shape all round – head injuries, severe bruising to the spine, your right arm was … Never mind about the details. After a while, you were transferred to the hospital here in London.'

'A coma!' It seems so incredible I don't know whether I can believe him. 'What date is it today?'

'November the twenty-seventh.'

'That's impossible. It can't be any later than the last week of August.'

Edgar shakes his head. 'You were admitted in August.'

'But that can't be!'

'I can show you a copy of your admission papers if you like.'

'There must be some mistake. I mean, *a coma*?'

'It's all in your case notes,' he says.

We stop at a red light. Trees line both sides of the road. Our eyes meet and he takes my hand and turns it so the palm is facing up. 'Look at the insides of your arms.' He points. 'See the needle marks?'

I pull up my sleeves and look at my arms. There are dozens of bruises on the insides of my elbows and on the backs of my hands. 'I saw those yesterday.'

'They're from all those months of life support. It was touch-and-go for a while whether you'd regain consciousness or not. It was only in the last two weeks that you really started to recover.'

'A coma …' I say, unable to take it in.

The lights change to green and we accelerate into the traffic. I frown at my arms and suddenly the thought comes, the first time since the flood: *A couple of vodkas would fix this*. Outside the window, the trees give way to houses, and the houses become a village. I check my mobile, nothing from Tomas, then close my eyes and collapse back exhausted in my seat.

I need to find Tomas ASAP.

Forget Tomas.

He's probably met someone else by now. And thinking this, I feel myself drift away and go sinking down into sad memories, and broken dreams.

'There's one other thing,' Edgar says, pulling me back. 'I'm concerned about something. The other day you said you're not Catherine. What did you mean by that?'

'Cathy's pathetic, I don't want to be Cathy anymore,' I spit. 'I want to be Tereza from now on.'

At which point, surprising us both, I burst into noisy tears.

PRAGUE

1

I text Hedley, an English expat living in Prague, and cancel lunch. A fellow pianist from my student days at the Royal Academy; I'm not sure I can stand his jolly optimism about the creative life today. Instead, I spend the day in and out of bed nursing my hangover and depression with hot cups of tea, blocks of dark Toblerone from the minibar and a handful of extra-strength Panadol. Come early evening, it's all I can do to drag myself out of bed and downstairs for supper at the hotel cafe – complete with grand piano, sentimental songs, and polished brass and crystal chandeliers. When the pianist launches into 'It Had to Be You', the song that was playing during my first date with Reed, I feel the tears start to well and the compulsion to drink becomes overwhelming but I force myself to my feet, sign the bill to my room and stumble out onto the busy square. I have to keep it together, at least until I get through tonight.

I wander fairly aimlessly, enjoying the gentle summer evening light, and follow the crowd. Eventually, I find myself standing outside Carpe Diem, a fashionable nightclub. It's so crowded I have to fight my way in. A man joins me at the bar: older, wearing black tie, and with salt and pepper hair. He has a strong, masculine face and a boyish grin. Our eyes meet and he smiles.

'What do you want?' the barman asks as my mind starts to spin. I've been on the wagon now for nearly two weeks but things have started to go crazy again lately and I'm wondering if I shouldn't get off and see if things calm back down. I've got to be able to perform tonight which means I should probably avoid getting completely plastered but I can't help thinking things might go better with a few drinks under my belt. Nelly, which is short for Nedjelja, my Bosnian refugee guru, said not to drink, that I need to go to AA, but I can't see the harm in just one or two to unwind, especially after the nightmare of yesterday. While my mind jams I scan the cocktail list, hoping it will convince me one way or the other. It only intensifies my confusion.

The barman asks the man next to me what he wants to drink and he says, 'I'll have …' in an American accent and then laughs and turns to me. 'I never know what to order in these sorts of situations.'

I smile uneasily, folding and refolding the belt of my floral print dress.

'I mean, should I order a beer, a glass of wine, or something stronger?' He looks back at the cocktail list. 'Should I order a Long Hard Screw, or an Old Fashioned, for example?' he says, gesturing at the cocktail menu and laughing again. 'Do you know what I mean?'

Our eyes meet although this time there's something more serious in his smile. I start to feel uneasy. The barman drums his fingers on the bar and the man looks back at the cocktail menu.

'OK,' he says, 'what about …? No, I know – I'll have a Flaming Orgasm!' he announces, causing my heart to pound.

I roll the belt into a tight ball and then shake it free. Vodka, just a couple of vodkas, then back to the hotel, change, taxi to the Rudolfinum by seven-thirty for eight – what's the harm in that?

Shaking his head, the man lights a thin cigar. He mutters something in a foreign language, I'm guessing he's speaking Czech, and gestures at me and then at the cocktail list. I don't respond. 'Not exactly subtle,' he says, and laughs again.

The barman places a colourful cocktail in front of the man and he smiles at me through his cigar smoke and offers to buy me a drink. With a shrug, I surrender to the inevitable and order a glass of champagne, trying to stay off the hard stuff for as long as possible.

When we next make eye contact he's staring at me blatantly. 'So,' he says, 'here we are then.'

He's quite sexy, I think, and look quickly away as my stomach flip-flops and suddenly I can't breathe. Nelly also said no sleeping around.

'Excuse me,' I manage, grabbing my drink and diving back into the crowd. A few minutes later I emerge on the street outside, the beautiful Art Deco apartment buildings lit pink in the fading dusk. I place the champagne carefully on the ground at my feet and, gulping mouthfuls of warm air, reach into my handbag and take out my mobile. *Nelly*, I'm thinking, *Nelly will help*. I search, dial and count the rings. Eventually, Nelly's voice answers, thank God. 'Hello?'

'Hi, Nelly, it's me,' I say, reaching for my drink while my heart continues to pound.

'Hi, I got your message earlier, sorry I haven't called back – are you OK?'

'Fine. I mean fucked. I've got the performance tonight and I'm freaking out, but it's good, it's all good.' The smoky sweetness of the champagne wafts beneath my nose and I lift the glass a little closer to my mouth.

'You're performing tonight? Cathy, you don't sound OK – have you been drinking again?'

I lower the glass so it's resting against my chest. 'No, I mean, I almost did, but I didn't. I called you instead, like you said, like we –'

'You remember what I said about staying off the booze?'

'It's not that bad, really, I –'

'Cathy, you've got to listen to me, I mean *really listen*. It's not just the alcohol, it's trauma, too. I mean, you know, we talked about this – I think that's why you drink. First there's your family history, you come from generations of trauma on both a personal and a national scale, and then there's your own history of relationships, all those addicts and abusive men. That whole Stockholm syndrome thing, remember? Cathy – are you listening? Because this is important. This could save your life.'

Nelly stops for one of her dramatic pauses but I interrupt. I've heard it all before. 'I know, I know,' I say, 'Alcoholism is a serious disease, I drink to relieve my PTSD, I know all that, but I –'

'Alcoholism is progressive and life-threatening and –'

'I'm sure it is, but – look, the reason I'm ringing is because my mother's gone missing from hospital. She left me a message saying she was coming to see the show and that she'd meet me in Prague.'

'She's in Prague? Where?'

'She said she'd meet me at the Grand Hotel Evropa. Also, I've broken up with Reed.'

'What?'

I start to cry.

'You've broken up with Reed?'

I sob, stop, sob, struggle to stop. Finally manage, 'He broke up with me.'

'OK. One thing at a time. When did you get the message from your mother?'

'Yesterday. I had the most horrible day,' I say, wiping my hand, which is wet with condensation from my glass, on my dress. 'First I had a massive row with Reed in which he told me our marriage was over unless I stopped drinking and then asked me to leave.'

'He wants a divorce?'

'He said, "If you need time out to go to rehab to sort yourself out that's fine but you can't keep going on the way you are." But you see, I hadn't been drinking. Not last week …'

'How many days has it been?'

'Ten days – I haven't had a drink for ten days.'

'You haven't had a drink in the last couple of days?'

'OK, I'm sober today. I had a drink before the dress rehearsal yesterday. But it was just to calm my nerves so I could –'

'Cathy, I –'

'Anyway, I took off my ring. I was so upset it was all I could do to pack my bags and get out of there. Then, when I checked my messages at Heathrow there was this strange message from my mother about Prague. I called the hospital and they confirmed she'd discharged herself and was coming to see tonight's performance.'

'OK, Cathy,' Nelly says. 'Sit tight. I'm going to try to sort this mess out with your mother ASAP. Let's keep in touch.'

'OK.'

'And no boozing!'

I look down into my glass, inhale the bubbles optimistically and then hold the glass up to my face. While I desperately need alcohol for the pain, Nelly's right, it's probably not a good idea. There's my show, for starters, but also I probably shouldn't sleep with this guy and I'm more likely to if I'm drunk. On the other hand, maybe it's OK to sleep with him seeing I've broken up with Reed? Then again, the last time I had a one-night stand I –

'Cathy?' Nelly's voice down the line.

'Yes.'

'This thing with Reed, it all sounds very sudden. Have you tried talking to him again now things have had a chance to settle?'

'No …'

'OK, well, I think there might be another conversation or two there … Anyway, how's our little friend?' Nelly says, changing tack.

I smile in spite of myself, return the champagne to the ground and reach into my handbag for the small cardboard box with the ventilation holes Nelly punched in it. I open it a crack and Mouse's nose and whiskers come peeking out: animal therapy, Nelly said. Reed gave me Mouse two weeks ago when I finally admitted I had a drinking problem.

'Any trouble with airport security?'

'No, it was fine. She just curled up in my pocket like we planned and went to sleep. She's such a darling,' I say, and kiss the baby brown mouse on the top of her head, closing the box.

'And what about the Janáček recording deal, any news?'

'Sarah still hasn't confirmed yet either way.' I close the box and put Mouse back in my bag.

'Can you try another record company?'

'Tried everyone else. Deutsche Grammophon is my last chance.' The pain rises up strong, the need to drink is now overwhelming, the champagne at my feet irresistible: I really need the money. *Please, God,* I beg. Then, mastering all my strength, I push the pain down. 'But I have a new idea, something completely different. I'm going to compose a symphony.'

'You see? One door closes and another door opens.'

'Listen, Nelly, I've got to go,' I say before she can begin another one of her spiritual lectures. 'I've got to get ready for the show.'

'OK, well, take it easy. This is your first big performance without alcohol. It's bound to feel a little strange. And don't forget our phone session: tomorrow at three.'

Christ, a phone session with Nelly; I'd forgotten about that. That's right – I know she needs the money for her residency application – I said I'd keep seeing her four times a week while I'm away, just by phone. I'm her best customer, after all. While she's a bit unorthodox she's very good, she helped me sort things out with Daniel, my emotional fuckwit ex, after just one session, although she's so bossy sometimes she's more like a PA than a guru. I don't think she's even started studying psychotherapy yet.

I struggle back to the bar and look around for the man, the memory of his hungry eyes strangely appealing, but he's gone, I can't see him anywhere in the crowd. Vanished! *Damn.* I empty my champagne – one can't hurt – and head back out onto the street and then on to my hotel to change. I really want to find that man. I check my mobile and see that Hedley has invited me to a recital tomorrow evening where his students will perform at the Loreta gallery. I return the phone to my bag without replying.

2

Dvořák's Symphony No. 9 blares from my portable CD player and I'm trying to decide between the black suit with the cream silk shirt with the bow at the neck or the midnight blue dress with the black Gucci shoes and fishnet stockings when there's a knock at the door and a folded piece of paper comes sliding into the room. I pick it up. The telegram, all but the message in unintelligible Czech, reads *Sarah says Janáček no go.*

What? Has the Deutsche Grammophon deal fallen through after all? How am I going to pay Nelly – pay for all of this? I mute the CD and sit down on the bed, my chest so tight it's difficult to breathe. I thought Sarah had everything under control? I was going to record 'On an Overgrown Path', a favourite of mine, as well as various other piano works by Janáček, all beautiful. I don't understand. I crack and rub my knuckles, one hand at a time, and then hold my hands out before me, palms down. They both shake, the left harder than the right, and, struggle as I might, I can't stop them. How am I going to play if I'm shaking like a leaf? Without Deutsche Grammophon tonight's got to be pitch perfect. I can't afford one more fuck-up.

No, *please no.* In two steps I'm at the minibar, the bottle of champagne open, the alcohol bubbling down my throat, bringing with it a familiar wave of bluster and grit. Somehow I just have to get through the show tonight. To do that I need a couple of drinks – nothing serious, mind, just enough to calm my nerves and get me through. Then tomorrow it will all be over and I can call Sarah first thing in the morning and face up to whatever financial nightmare awaits me in London. I'll have to go on the wagon all over again but that can't be helped.

Finishing the dregs of the champagne, the taxi waiting downstairs, I rub and crack my knuckles again and hold my hands out before me, palms downwards. My hands hover before me, steady, suspended midair.

'Please,' I say, 'I need you to step aside.'

OK, I admit it, I've had a couple of glasses – well, a bottle or so – since leaving the hotel, but I'm nowhere near pissed. Would bygones never be bygones? That damn Copenhagen concert and the damage it did to my reputation; the scandal that followed my tumble off the front of the stage at the end of the second encore, not a scheduled bow, mind you, a spontaneous one, and one I just slightly overdid, but still, when are they going to let me move on? Yes, it's true, waking up in the American ambassador's residence in bed with two guys I didn't know – one in front, the other behind – was a very bad look but God, everyone makes mistakes – right? Those gossip columnists need to get a life, then maybe they'd let me get on and live mine. Anyway, that stuff's all history – I'm getting sober, going on the wagon, don't they get it? All that drunk and crazy stuff is behind me now –

'OK,' the stage manager says, then pauses to listen to his

headpiece. The oboe plays an A above middle C and the violins make last-minute adjustments to their tuning, then the winds and brass all check they're in tune and blow air to warm up. 'You can play the Tchaikovsky with Krušina conducting. But any funny business and we'll cancel the rest, you understand?'

'You've made yourself perfectly clear,' I say, and, without waiting for his reply, stride out onto the vastness of the stage. The flutes stop practising thirds and the orchestra falls completely silent. This is going to be an absolute disaster.

The wave of applause that greets me nearly knocks me backwards but I've learned to filter it out and retreat to a place inside, a quiet room empty but for me and my music, until it's all over. I look for Ashkenazy, the musical director of the Prague Philharmonic, and spy him seated in the second row. No sign of my mother. A wave of booze rises up and I stifle a nervous titter. The rest of the audience look like pigs, pink-faced and overfed, and I swallow a burp as I gracefully acknowledge Krušina and take my seat at the long shiny sea of black and white keys. I rarely work from notes but I remind myself not to rush the opening, Krušina likes to languish a bit for my taste, or so it seemed at last night's dress rehearsal, but she is the conductor, after all.

A moment's silence, the audience holds its breath, and soon it's time to begin. At first it's business as usual as I sail away riding the sea of sounds in my quiet ship, but once the initial excitement of the opening is over I find myself curiously detached and my mind starts to wander. I watch helpless as my mind drifts off into the audience, scanning seats, and then starts churning fiercely with thoughts of Reed, the Deutsche Grammaphon deal, the phone call from my mother, and the next thing I know I'm in difficult waters. It's almost as if the piano is playing itself and I've become something of a spectator.

This sort of disconnection problem hasn't happened to me for a long time, not since my early fumblings on the big stage. I'm always completely switched on when I'm performing regardless of what's going on in my private life; I've always been able to completely lose myself in the music, especially in front of an audience. It takes everything I've got to force myself back to the piano and to stop this whole pianola charade before it's too late. In a long, drawn-out arm wrestle, which takes the entirety of the third movement, I battle with the instrument, but the booze has slowed my reaction times and made me sloppy. What's more, the pianola seems to be speeding up – I catch a worried glare from Krušina, and soon it threatens to leave the orchestra behind altogether. Finally, I shake myself from head to toe and force myself back into the concerto.

It's funny, but while every note has been perfect, my performance technically no different from any other, I just wasn't there. My only hope is that the audience hasn't caught on yet, but no sooner have I thrown myself into the closing section than suddenly it's interval. Christ. The Rachmaninov will have to be absolutely outstanding.

Standing up, I look out into the audience and find myself locking eyes with a gaunt-faced woman seated somewhere in the middle of the second row. I look away in order to acknowledge Krušina but when I look back I can't find her again. My mother – hard to mistake those pale, staring features. Can't deal with her now, must just get through the rest of the show!

One or two hangers-on have snuck backstage – 'Sensational!' one tells me as I rush past to my dressing room – where there's an open bottle of Vintage Moët, difficult to resist, in a bucket, on ice. The Tchaikovsky ruined, still the Rachmaninov to go and then the Ashkenazy duet for the surprise encore. The call of the champagne. I won't, *I won't*. Just get through the show. Must prove them wrong.

I recognise the piped music as Mozart's Piano Concerto No. 9 and scowl. I hate Mozart. So uptight; all I see when I hear his music are all those awful Hapsburg wigs … I need something that moves, although some of the sonatas can be quite soothing, and his Symphony No. 38, 'The Prague Symphony', is quite atmospheric. Give me Beethoven at least, Chopin's Scherzo No. 3, or Liszt; something beautiful like Debussy or complex like Scriabin. I reach into my handbag for Mouse, take her out of her box and, showering her with kisses, let her run up and down my arm and tickle the inside of my wrist with her cool twitching nose. But it's no good. That lapse in concentration … I rub my knuckles, then crack them, and hold my hands out palms down. I look up from their unsteady suspension to meet Krušina's eyes; she has entered without my seeing. She doesn't smile, just watches me lower my hands again, shaky, to my pockets. Mozart titters and ponces in the background. What on earth is my mother doing here, in Prague? Should I go look for her? Raise the alarm? At least she hasn't followed me backstage …

I sneak the first glass of the champagne without Krušina's noticing but the third is harder to hide. Krušina, then the stage manager, who is now standing in the doorway, both watch me empty a fourth glass and suddenly, their arms around me, I'm escorted to the stage manager's office.

I absorb the stage manager's wrath, agree and apologise

– stifling the urge to laugh and managing not to slur – I do everything to make them think I've repented and settled down, but really I'm just waiting for my next chance. The Rachmaninov can be bloody tricky, and I can't afford a shaky-handed wobble. In order to claw my way back into the running, this next part's got to be perfect. Truth be told, tonight's performance is the least of my problems, the question of the lost recording deal a mighty nightmare looming unresolved. I wipe my lower back – my hand comes away wet. Damn. The booze is making me sweat. That means sweat stains under my arms ... Desperation creeping in, I call Nelly, the stage manager is watching me from the doorway, leave a message and wait five minutes. But now it's only five minutes until I'm on again. The stage manager has gone. I slip out the door unobserved and head away from the backstage area, downstairs, and emerge front of house near a bar where I scull a glass of Moravian wine, then another, before someone raises the alarm. At which point I'm finished.

It wasn't always like this ...

A deep hush that's more silent than silence fills the auditorium as I rein myself in, pull myself back from all the sparkle, the glitter, the dazzle of the too hot lights, and prepare to begin. In the moment's pause, I reflect how Tchaikovsky himself conducted here at the inaugural opening of Carnegie Hall. Not the piano concerto, but the Festival Coronation March, his own composition but not as well known as the piano concerto. It never ceases to amaze me that Rubinstein, Tchaikovsky's composition teacher at the St Petersburg Conservatory, initially rejected the piece. Incomprehensible ... Even today, while some people find the piano concerto clichéd, I remain entranced by its robustness and complexity: the game of call and response that fires endlessly back and forth between the piano and the orchestra, between the piano and the strings, between the piano and the winds. But enough: I must concentrate.

I wait for the last faint rustle of a program to subside, for the man in the second row to finish clearing his throat, and then I close my eyes and retreat to a clear white space inside where my mind stills, the mental chatter ceases and I'm fully absorbed, ready to draw the sounds up through my feet, to listen with my whole body, as my first teacher always said, and then to play exactly what I hear. To follow, always to follow where the music wants to go …

With a force that's almost tidal I sweep up the room in a close embrace, and then, using the opening chords, I wash them clean away. I pour so much in that no-one can resist, no-one is left behind, and as I drag and entice and compel them to follow me on this strange harmonic journey to another land, this encounter with a parallel universe, as my favourite lecturer used to say, I know in my bones that I could never love anything as much, that I could never be anything else, and that nothing else could ever make me feel so fiercely free, so utterly alive.

Dom-dom-dom-dommm …

When I next surface into the auditorium it's to pause, to snatch just a millisecond of stillness, to listen and count until the winds have finished. Then, again, I leap into the fold.

Laa la la la la-la la laa la la …. More singing, apparently I have perfect pitch, not that anyone can hear me above this magnificent beast I alone must tame … And as I count and stamp my feet and sing to my heart's content I stare not seeing into the glorious abyss … Then finally, all too soon, I'm getting hot under all these awful lights, I'm striking the last note, and leaving everything hanging, leaving every soul in the hall waiting for the next note, the one *that would resolve the chord progression, but one which in this case never comes ... Because —*

— tomorrow will never come,
tomorrow will never —

Roses flying everywhere, a unanimous standing ovation. I mean, who on earth could resist such a big fat melody, the fierce rhythm of the chords? The directness of the modulation, the contrast, the repetition?!

And always, after such a big performance, the music plays on long afterwards inside my head, so that the applause only reaches me intermittently

(French horns:) CHORD CHORD CHORD CHORD / I stand / CHORD CHORD CHORD CHORD / look across / (Orchestra:) CHORD CHORD CHORD CHORD / the sea of up-turned fa-ces / (Piano:) CHORD CHORD CHORD CHORD / and bow / CHORD ...

In the end, joined and rejoined by Krušina and the first violin, I somehow remain standing alone, drifting on a sea of notes of my own fabrication as the applause pounds on, turning my face red, like a heavy downpour of rain.

CHODICI ZRANENI/WALKING WOUNDED, the theatre poster on Wenceslas Square reads in bold red letters. I stop to study it more closely, swaying slightly from side to side, an empty champagne bottle slippery in one hand. A dancer wearing a leotard and pointe shoes kneels in the foreground of the image, head in hands. Around her all is darkness except for the halo of light cast by a nearby street lamp. A man wearing black tie stands in the gloomy background. The play opened tonight. 'Walking wounded indeed,' I say out loud and bark out a laugh.

I tear myself away from the poster and toss the empty bottle, pretending not to notice as it misses the garbage bin and explodes onto the ground. Then, eyes not seeing, I make my way back to my hotel. Stumbling on the uneven cobblestones, my Gucci stilettos making an awful scraping sound and nearly tripping me over, I try to forget tonight's disaster. Thinking only of the hotel minibar, I hurry past the tourist shops and casinos, and push open the hotel's revolving glass door.

I call out to the porter for my key, he's not at his desk, but there's no reply and the office is closed. Stretched to the limit – can any more things possibly go wrong today? – I just need to get up to my room and my bottle of emergency vodka ASAP. I call out again, 'Hello?' When the porter still doesn't answer, I circle around the desk and grab the key to my room out of its wooden box myself. But then – damn – I drop it to the floor. I bend down and pick it up, slippery, then, gripping it in my hand, double check the box. There are no telegrams or messages from my mother and no sign of her in the lobby. Maybe I imagined her in the audience … ? I bet she never made it to bloody Heathrow in her condition. No doubt I'll get a call to say she's in an ambulance, someone's found her. I call out 'Hello' once more, I want to find out if she's checked in or holds a reservation. No reply.

Upstairs, I fumble with the lock – what is it with these double locks? – stumble into my suite, grab a bottle of local white wine from the minibar and collapse onto the bed. Taking a hearty slug, I reach for the novel I brought to read, *Wuthering Heights*, an old favourite, but the words swim senselessly on the page before me and I drop it to the bed. Tonight's performance a disaster, Janáček no go, my marriage in ruins, my finances desperate, my mother missing, sick, possibly roaming the streets of Prague ...

For a while I lie staring at the ceiling letting everything spin, but then I leap up and tear my suitcase open: where is my emergency vodka? But then I realise it isn't there because I took it out before I left. Bloody idiot! Guzzling the wine, anything to numb this fucking pain, I crash back onto the bed and try Nelly, even though she didn't take my call earlier, the one I made from backstage just before I was forcibly escorted from the Rudolfinum, and has not called me back. When I get her voicemail, I blurt, 'Hi, Nelly, me again, Cathy here. Bit of a disaster, where are you? You're never there when I need you.' I hang up and, hand shaking, swallow the wine. Nelly costs an absolute fortune, £150 a pop, the least she can do is call me back. Then I grab the rest of the bottle, and, swigging straight from it, fall back onto the bed. I don't read the half-dozen texts from the stage manager at the Rudolfinum, or the text from Sarah's contact in Prague. Finally, I call Sarah's mobile, she doesn't answer either, typical, and then let the phone slip between my fingers before crying long and hard into the pillow and passing out.

When I wake it's close to twelve. My head aches but things seem more stable. I take Mouse out of her box, dribble some water into the bottom of the bath, throw in the hand towel and then place her and her box inside the tub. 'Sorry, darling, only biscuit crumbs from the minibar for dinner tonight,' I say, as she sniffs up at me, her front paws resting against the side of the bath. 'This is all your fault, Reed,' I tell no-one in particular. I grab my bag and, taking one final slug from the wine, head out onto the streets once more.

I reach up and place my palms on the ceiling in a doomed attempt to stabilise. Below me Chapeau Rouge is a crowded smoky sea of faces, all staring up expectantly and calling out in a language I don't understand. Everything swims in a messy swill of beer and vodka, the surface of the bar is sticky-wet beneath my feet, and when the DJ starts spinning Kylie Minogue's 'Can't Get You Out of My Head', a woman I think I recognise from the jazz bar around the corner grabs me and starts dancing lasciviously. She's wearing a pink sarong and a hot pink sequinned top which clashes violently with my scarlet Chinese shift. It's not long before four men start writhing among the beer taps at our feet.

The woman I'm dancing with has the most gorgeous hair, long, dark and glossy. It shivers delightfully when, her back turned to me, she starts shaking her arse. Soon she's writhing against me making me giggle, and then she pulls me in close so my pelvis is bouncing against her roundly bobbing arse. Is she for real?

Without warning she moves away and starts waving at someone standing near the door. I look over her shoulder trying to see who but no-one seems to be waving back although I get the distinct impression someone is staring at me. Determined to find out who, I look away then, swivelling on my hips, I turn swiftly around – gotcha! – and lock eyes with an older man wearing black tie – the very man I met earlier at Carpe Diem! He looks quickly away.

As the music reaches its peak, the woman goes into a bend back: legs parted, dress hitched up and knees bent, shimmying the top half of her body sexily back down towards the beer taps. When she straightens up she reaches her hands around my bum and dances pressed against me. I giggle again and pull away but at the end of the song she brushes her lips lightly against mine in a stagy kiss. God, she really is quite wild. When one of the men starts licking my bare feet I think, *I don't care, I don't care, I don't care …*

Half climbing, half falling down from the bar, I look around for the mysterious man but he's gone. *Again!*

'Quick, in here!' the woman I've been dancing with says, leading the way into the ladies' toilets and leaving our four male admirers complaining loudly outside (the man in black tie is not among them, I note with a pang). I hurry after her into the end cubicle and lock the door as best I can – the lock only remains attached to the door by one last screw.

'I'm Cathy, by the way,' I say, trying not to slur.

'Anna,' the other woman says in an accent that could be Czech as she puts the seat down and starts chopping up some cocaine on the little white shelf above the toilet.

Soon I'm drooling over the four thick lines and thinking how I haven't done anything like this since I went on the wagon – what's that, two weeks ago now? Things are starting to blur. Anna snorts two of the lines then holds out a rolled bill and stares at my body in an intense way. I try to take the bill but she won't quite let me.

'Take your dress off,' she says suddenly, the rolled bill firm between her long fingers.

I'm a little taken aback but I really want the coke so I unbutton the top half of my Chinese shift and then undo the zip at the side. This is too much. Way beyond tipsy, I stumble slightly losing my balance as I step out of my dress but remind myself of the drugs that will soon be zooming around inside me.

Anna looks me slowly up and down, thank fuck I'm wearing my nice knickers, her tongue protruding along her bottom lip, and then loosens her grip on the rolled note. I wait for her to make room for me at the cistern and then, aware that she likes what she sees, I bend over and snort the two remaining lines of coke, one in each nostril. The rush removes the top of my head and I turn around and smile at Anna: that's better, clearer now. I step aside while she chops up four more lines. Too soon she reaches out for the note but I hold onto it fiercely and shake my head.

'Take off your bra,' she commands.

'No.'

She shrugs, turns around, snorts two more lines with another note and is about to snort up the two remaining lines when I exclaim: 'Wait.' I can't believe I'm doing this. I undo the clasp and, sniffing loudly – boy, is that stuff strong or am I just out of practice? – let my bra drop to the floor.

Anna moves aside and I do two more lines. She inserts a finger inside the waist of my underpants, toying with me. But when I turn to face her again, Anna's eyes zoom in on my lips. Then she looks up into my eyes and our eyes lock. 'Kiss me,' she demands.

I look at her lips, every inch of my body screaming no, but the idea of not snorting any more coke is not appealing. I don't move.

Anna looks at me, then at my lips and then at me again. She moves her face closer to mine.

Holy fuck.

I'm just closing my eyes, there's no such thing as too much coke – apart from anything else, it will extend my drinking time – when the door slams open and our male admirers burst into the cubicle, breaking the lock from the doorframe. Anna laughs, not in the least perturbed, and the men holler and whoop and stare. I reach for my bra and dress but it's too late, one of the men has grabbed me to him and pulls me outside. Meanwhile, Anna is standing on top of the toilet, still laughing, and the other three men are fighting over her. The cubicle door shuts by itself leaving me alone with the guy in the bright lights in front of the mirrors.

'No, stop,' I tell the guy, who's attempting to remove my knickers.

'Stop?' he echoes.

'Yes, please,' I tell him, and slip back into my bra.

He steps away and bows. But suddenly Anna bursts out of the cubicle, grabs me by the hand and drags me back out onto the dance floor.

'I love this song,' she says, and when we resume our position on the top of the bar, this time with me minus my dress, the room erupts into messy cheers and I holler back 'Woo-hoo!' with all my might.

At a quarter-past two the first DJ finishes his shift and the crowd rushes to the bar, the excess spilling out onto the street. Standing near the door is the man from Carpe Diem, the one in black tie. When he smiles at me my heartbeat quickens.

'Let's blow this joint,' Anna says, as we join him.

Outside on the narrow street, Anna links one arm in mine, the other arm in his, and leads us, chatting all the while to the man in what I guess must be Czech, through the eerie streets, dark and ill-lit, until we reach a cafe by the Charles Bridge. She selects a table overlooking the river and we sit down.

Quietly stonkered, the coke and booze buzzing around inside me in a satisfying way, Prague floats shimmering before me: the street lamps, the river, the trams, the quiet streets, simultaneously beautiful and remote like in a dream, all swaying, slurred, outlines blurred. Anna orders a bottle of Bohemia Sekt from the waiter, and although now I definitely need something stronger, I fail to protest.

'This is Tomas,' Anna says, introducing me to the man who leans forwards to take my hand. 'Tomas, this is my friend – sorry, I can't remember your name?'

'Cathy.'

Tomas kisses the back of my hand, then tells Anna, 'We've already met.'

'Isn't this a coincidence?' I say; he really is quite handsome. 'We met earlier at Carpe Diem. Did you two just meet too or —'

'We already know each other,' Anna says, smiling warmly and batting her eyes at Tomas, who is now smiling back at her.

Uncomfortable, I remove my hand, not really sure about any of this and hoping Tomas's expression may offer clues. But as soon as I attempt to study him, Tomas turns away and busies himself with the champagne bottle which has just arrived. While Tomas carefully pours out three bubbling glasses, Anna is meanwhile suddenly occupied with her mobile phone. I reach for my champagne and turn my attention to our surroundings instead.

The smooth, dark river with its beautiful buildings is so seductive it takes my breath away. On its far side towers the castle and on top of this rests the frou-frou Gothic spire of St Vitus Cathedral. Closer to hand is the Charles Bridge, lined with sculptures of saints, which connects the Old Town on this side with the New Town on the other. I sigh – Prague is just incredible. I take a long drink of champagne and sink into the soft lights twinkling on the water, the willow branches draping down to the river's edge and the golden glow of the castle.

'It's beautiful,' I say, turning back to my companions. 'It reminds me a bit of Disneyland, but the original Disneyland, if you know what I mean.'

'On a night like this it's quite magical,' Tomas says, now staring at me over the rim of his glass.

'It's nothing like Disneyland,' Anna says, snapping her phone shut. 'It's very vibrant here, artistically and socially. Things are really happening – they have been ever since '89, especially for the younger generation who've grown up in a free country, and who are doing some really interesting things now.'

I look at Tomas, who's still staring at me.

'What do you think, Tomas?' Anna says, smiling warmly at him.

'You've never been here before?' Tomas asks, ignoring Anna and speaking directly to me.

'No, it's my first time,' I say, sinking into his mesmerising gaze.

'And do you know much about the Czechs or their culture?' he says.

'No, not really,' I say, and then look away. 'I mean, Prague's obviously quite a fashionable place to visit right now but that's not why I'm here, and I know *The Unbearable Lightness of Being* – but everyone knows that. I only just discovered today reading my guidebook that the Prague castle once ran the Holy Roman Empire. I was quite surprised.'

'That's right, Charles was king of Bohemia and Rome, and he made Praha the capital city of the Holy Roman Empire,' Tomas says. 'And yes, Kundera's probably the most famous Czech writer today, but I'm afraid I have rather complex feelings about Kundera. Some other time, perhaps. But there's a lot more to the Czechs than Kundera and the Empire. A lot of famous people were Czech, although few people realise.'

'Famous people like who?' I study Tomas's face again, this time noting the excited sparkle in his eyes.

'Did you know Mahler was Czech, and so was Freud?'

'Mahler! I thought he was Viennese?'

'It's a fairly common mistake, but actually, he was born in Kaliště which is in Bohemia, in the Czech Republic. Even though the Czechs were part of the Austro-Hungarian Empire in those days and Mahler made his name in Vienna, he was born in the Czech lands. A Jewish Bohemian who grew up in a Germanicised society, but a Czech nonetheless.'

'I think that's stretching things a bit,' Anna counters. 'Mahler was Viennese, he just happened to have been born in Bohemia.'

'Now, Anna,' Tomas argues back, 'I'm going to have to disagree with you on this,' and turning to me he adds, 'John Lennon was living in New York when he was shot but nobody calls him American.'

The two have a brief argument in a fast foreign language, during which Anna touches Tomas on the arm. I empty my glass in one large gulp: just when I was starting to think he liked me, it looks like he's got something going with Anna.

But then Tomas shrugs dramatically at Anna and, turning back to me, tops up my glass. 'The Czechs break down into three tribes,' he says. 'The Bohemians in the west, that's where I'm from, the Moravians in the east, and the Silesians in the north-east.'

'And Prague is in …?' My hands clasp the stem of my glass as I look from Anna to Tomas and back again.

'Praha is in Bohemia,' Tomas says, and smiles. 'Actually, why don't I give you the grand tour sometime? How long are you staying? What about tomorrow afternoon?'

'Thanks,' I say, smiling back, thinking, *That's definitely a pass*. 'I'm half-Czech,' I add, 'but I don't know anything about the country.'

'Half-Czech! But you should have said so from the beginning,' he says, taking my hand again and clasping it tightly. 'I was thinking before, about your lovely eyes. Now it makes sense – they're Czech!'

'Yes, I guess they are!' I say, blushing.

'And do you have family here?'

'I have some cousins, though I've never met them before. My mother's younger sister and her children,' I say and shrug. 'Everyone else left or is dead. My grandfather Karel protested against the communists in '48, was shot at by Russian mercenaries hired by the communists and then escaped to Australia to avoid imprisonment. As a result the regime punished the rest of the family, which is why my mother left.'

'Yes, unfortunately that happened quite a bit,' he says, shaking his head.

I smile and loosen my grip on the stem of my glass as the blush fades.

But Tomas is staring at me intently and leaning forwards across the table. 'And where did your mother go?'

'London.'

'London!' He knocks his glass over, splashing the table with champagne.

'We went to Australia too for a while but my father's work drew us back to London,' I say. Then add, 'Are you all right?'

But Tomas just apologises, mops up the spilt champagne and pours himself another glass.

There's an uncomfortable pause – Anna taps the keys on her phone and Tomas stares down into the bottom of the bubbles. Then, suddenly, Tomas upends the glass and empties its entire contents down his throat.

Wondering at Tomas's behaviour – I mean, he's obviously pretty pissed, but still, why did he react like that to my mentioning my mother? – I let my eyes be drawn again by the river and the reflected lights on its surface. While Anna tells Tomas about her recent holiday in Croatia, my mind starts to churn obsessively, but Tomas's loud, 'Eight!' brings me back to the conversation.

'I don't want to bore you with the details ...' Anna is saying.

'What details?' I say, looking from one to the other and noting the way Anna's hand rests on Tomas's thigh.

'Anna was just telling me about how she was pursued by fourteen naked Italians on a naturist beach in Croatia,' Tomas says.

'First there were eight naked Italians on a boat,' Anna recounts, 'and when I ignored them they drove off and came back with *six more* naked Italians, obviously their friends. They dropped anchor again, swam ashore and suddenly I was surrounded. There were fourteen naked Italians in all,' she repeats and then pauses. Tomas laughs loudly but I don't laugh at all. One minute he's flirting with me, the next minute she's all over him and he seems to be going along with it. Anna leans towards Tomas, showing ample cleavage, and adds, 'Then they swam ashore. I was trapped!' and laughs again. Tomas stares down the front of her top and then half falls off his chair. Still laughing, he rights himself and meanwhile, I stare down into my empty glass. Maybe it's time I went back to my hotel?

When I look up, Anna is flashing her sarong open and closed at the thigh and asking Tomas to guess what colour knickers she's wearing and Tomas, laughing back, says, 'Well, red, I guess.' Anna's just inviting him to come and see her at the club one night when her mobile starts to ring and she hurries away from the table. Almost immediately, Tomas starts staring at me again, deeply, sadly, and I look determinedly away across the river towards the castle.

'Hey, guys, I've got to go,' Anna says when she returns, breaking the awkward silence.

'Where are you off to?' Tomas says, standing up to air-kiss Anna goodbye.

'Some friends of mine are playing at the Akropolis,' she says as she starts to leave but Tomas grabs her arm.

'Listen,' he says, a mischievous glint in his eyes, 'why don't we all go back to my place for a nightcap?'

But Anna ignores him, and instead tells me pointedly, 'You're both welcome to come along, though I'll have to meet you there. I need to change first.'

I look from Anna to Tomas, uncertain. 'I can give you a lift if you like,' Tomas tells me.

I'm not sure I want to get a ride with Tomas but the prospect of going back to my hotel and facing the disaster that is my life at present is not attractive. Finally I mumble, 'I wonder where I can get a cab?'

'Come see the band,' Anna says, the tips of her fingers momentarily resting on my arm. Then, leaning closer, she whispers in my ear, 'He's harmless, you know. He wouldn't hurt a fly.'

I look at her and frown. It's almost as if she's setting us up.

'OK,' she says, stalking off before I can reply, 'I'm late.'

Suddenly we're alone, standing not speaking beneath the haunted street lamps. I watch for cabs but there are none, while Tomas jiggles loose change in his pocket. Should I walk back to the hotel or go with Tomas? Then, remembering about the absence of emergency vodka, I say, 'Actually, I wouldn't mind a lift if that's still OK.'

'Yes, great,' Tomas says too soon. Leading me off into the dark streets of Prague, things are becoming increasingly wobbly. Tomas prattles on about what a coincidence it was to run into Anna and what a wild raconteur she is, and I tell him how I met her at the jazz bar and how she gave me drugs in the toilets. We fall into another awkward silence until we reach his car: an elderly white Skoda.

Tomas is about to get in first when, seeing me waiting on the other side of the car, he changes his mind, apologises and walks around, a little unsteady on his feet, and opens my side, gesturing dramatically for me to get in.

'Thanks,' I tell him, and meanwhile he walks unevenly back around the car, fumbles with the lock, then opens his door and climbs in beside me. But once inside the car, Tomas can't fit his key into the ignition.

He attempts to insert the key a few times, laughs and then says, half to himself, 'God, I think I'm a little bit drunk. I must be drunk! I can't get the key –'

I'm about to suggest we look for a cab when suddenly the key turns in the ignition and we lurch out into the narrow lane. Reaching for my seatbelt, I watch the road ahead – Tomas spends more time smiling and looking at me than he does looking at the road. When I can't find my seatbelt I watch the road even more closely than before.

'So what are you doing in Praha?' Tomas wants to know.

'Well it's part holiday, part business.'

'And what kind of business are you in?'

'I'm a pianist mainly, but I also compose music.'

'A composer *and* a pianist? You must be very talented …'

'Oh, thank you. I mean, you know, I was in a show earlier tonight at the Rudolfinum –'

'The Rudolfinum – what did you play?'

'Some Tchaikovsky actually, and then –'

'Wow. So what's your surname? Have I heard of you?'

'Bell. Actually, I'm here to research a symphony. I'm particularly interested in Janáček –'

'– *Janáček*,' he corrects, 'with a soft *J* –'

'– Smetana, and of course I'm doing lots of research on Dvořák.'

'Of course,' he says, patting my knee with his hand. 'Dvořák is a must!'

'I'm only here for a few days,' I say. I start to add, 'Then I'm off to New York,' but my words are cut short when we skid to a halt, narrowly avoiding a collision with a tram turning into our street from the left.

'Shit!' he says, laughing again and pulling over to the side of the road. He removes his hand from my thigh. 'I really think I might have had a bit too much to drink. I've been at a premiere …'

'Maybe we should get a cab?' I suggest, but he doesn't answer.

Instead he takes out his packet of thin cigars, offers me one, lights us both up and blows smoke in a steady stream out the car window. 'So, a symphony,' he says. 'You should meet my friend Franz, he's an expert on the whole Czech classical music thing. He used to play first violin for the Czech Philharmonic.'

'I'd love to meet him.' Then, relieved the car is stationary for the moment and curious about his accent, add, 'Are you American?'

'No, but I studied there in my early twenties.'

'What were you studying?'

'You ask a lot of questions,' he says, giving me a quick look. 'Dance. I was studying ballet.'

'*Ballet?*' I say. The theatre poster flashes into my mind. My mother was a ballet dancer in Prague when she was young … I want to ask him if he knew her but Tomas suddenly tosses his cigar out the window, starts up the car again and accelerates back into the traffic. I stare at the road ahead, concentrating on Tomas's driving.

We spend the rest of the trip in silence – Tomas driving carefully, and me thinking about the coincidence of Tomas and my mother and remembering his earlier reaction when I'd said my mother had moved to London: could they have known each other? It would be quite incredible, and I think about asking him but we've gone off topic with Tomas now pointing out buildings and explaining their history, and reading out street names, his mouth caressing the complex sounds, somehow making the impossible language less difficult. Speaking his native tongue, his voice is strangely reminiscent of my mother's: I wonder …

Soon we reach the Akropolis. When our eyes meet this time he's all smiles. His eyes find my lips and I watch him, frowning and wondering, *Is he going to kiss me?* Because I'm not quite sure if I really want him to just yet.

'Are you coming in?' he says at last. 'It's pretty late but we might just catch the second half of the main act. You can see some bona fide post-communist Czech pop music.'

I nod and follow him inside. While he pays for our tickets, I check my mobile. There's a missed call and a text from Reed apologising and saying we need to talk. Oh bugger him, and, remembering Nelly's advice, I decide he can wait. I ignore the message and, wondering what's happened to Tomas, hurry downstairs into the club.

3

The Akropolis is a complete catacomb, full of small cavern-like rooms, a whole labyrinth of them, and somehow I've lost Tomas in the crowd. I order a glass of Czech champagne at the bar and gulp it down quickly. Then, carrying a fresh glass with me, I attempt to find Tomas in the dark maze. Eventually I find him tucked away at a corner table covered in newspapers.

'Hi,' he says, standing up and kissing me perfunctorily on each cheek. He smiles without looking me in the eye, introduces me to everyone, pulls up a chair so I'm seated next to him, checks that I have a drink and then, snatching up the newspapers, leaves. I watch him join another table in one of the nearby rooms. When he sits down he has his back to me.

I frown into my glass, take a gulp of my champagne and swallow hard. That's it. Time to get wasted. After a few more sips and when Tomas still hasn't returned, I decide to stay for this drink and then if he's still acting like a weirdo, to leave. Coke clarity fading fast, I remind myself I really should start thinking hard about New York. Big one tonight – tomorrow to recover. I empty most of the rest of my champagne in one gulp. I'm about to leave – to get something stronger, or to go somewhere else, I don't know – when the woman beside me starts talking.

'Most critics shouldn't be allowed anywhere near creative projects, don't you think?' Originally seated on the other side of Tomas, the woman, whose name I think is Libuše, moves into Tomas's now vacant seat.

I smile vaguely. Libuše wears her hair in a messy bob and her velvet and silk clothes have an aura of the twenties about them. 'There are certainly a lot of very average critics out there, if that's what you mean,' I agree, studying her dark, elfin features.

'Take Tomas's play *Walking Wounded*, for example.'

'Is that his? I didn't know he'd written a play.' I glance over into the other room where Tomas is still sitting with his back to me. The theatre poster on the square, what a funny coincidence.

'Oh, Tomas is incredibly creative. He writes plays, he does all sorts of things. Anyway, poor Tomas. *Walking Wounded* just opened and the first reviews came out tonight and they're the most small-minded, mean-spirited rubbish I've ever seen. I'd like to see one of those pathetic reviewers write a play,' she says vehemently. 'All they know how to do is to tear other people's work apart.'

I nod, letting Libuše's words slowly sink in. Maybe that explains Tomas's strange behaviour? This time when I look up, Tomas is looking vaguely in my direction, although there are too many people standing between us for me to be really sure. 'So where are you from? You don't sound Czech,' I say, draining the last drops from the bottom of my glass, instantly wanting more.

'I was born in the US but my mother's Czech,' she says. 'I arrived in Prague after the Velvet Revolution and never went back.'

'And what do you do?' I ask, standing up in preparation for a trip to the bar.

'I'm a gallery curator.'

I nod, 'How interesting,' and offer to buy Libuše a drink. She accepts. On my way back to the bar I glance across the room in Tomas's direction and stop dead. Anna is draped all over him, her face pressed to his ear. When she's finished at his ear she straightens and gives him a look. Tomas looks up at her as she playfully twitches the hem of her black skirt. Finally, just as he reaches for her skirt she sneers at him, snapping her skirt away, and stalks off. Tomas sits motionless, his hair messed up and eyes lowered. Then he stands up and disappears.

Head spinning – this doesn't make sense – I stumble on to the bar. While everything continues as normal all around me – people order drinks, wait to be served, and the bar staff are busy behind the beer taps – my mind jams with thoughts of vodka and how a couple of vodkas would fix this. I'm actually just about to order a vodka martini but then, remembering Nelly's advice, I change my mind at the last minute. Do I actually have time for any of this?

Tomas reappears, one, maybe two champagnes later, sans Anna, and sits down beside me, smiling shyly. After a pause during which neither of us speaks, he moves his chair closer to mine. 'How's it going?'

'Fine,' I say, wanting to leave, wanting another drink, wanting to ask Tomas about Anna, doing nothing.

I look away and shake my hair from my face, jaw clenched tight. Is this guy weird, or is it me? I turn around and give Tomas a hard stare, but my face softens as my eyes trace his features. His strong jaw and greying hair contrast nicely with his boyish haircut, long and wavy at the neck with a floppy fringe at the front. Eyes dark beneath dark bushy brows, his mouth is bow-shaped, his lips a pink red, and his cheeks glow with wine above a shadow of dark stubble. Maybe it's the slight lack of focus to his gaze, or a certain looseness to his lips, I'm not sure, but I suddenly realise that he also seems quite drunk. That makes two of us.

Suddenly everyone at the table including Tomas gets up and starts moving inside. I rise on unsteady feet and follow the crowd. When I next look around I can't see Tomas anywhere. I'm completely surrounded by chain-smoking Czechs and, gasping, I wave the smoke away from my eyes. Soon the MC introduces the main act, The Czech Underground, and the band come on to wild applause. Four are old hippies and the fifth is a younger guy in John Lennon glasses and black leather pants. I look around again for Tomas. Not seeing him anywhere, I decide to leave after the show.

The piano starts to play an opening riff that sounds like bells and then the drum joins in, just the bass drum on the first beat of every bar. I instantly recognise the song, it's an old Velvet Underground song called 'All Tomorrow's Parties'. It's such a great song! All around me young Czechs start clapping and calling out but I don't understand what they're saying. The guitars have just come on when the band blow a fuse and the entire auditorium blacks out. Whispered conversations erupt all around me, punctuated by the odd wolf whistle. Poor dears, nothing like this has ever happened to me in all my years of performing, although once the mike broke during a live broadcast at the BBC, but that wasn't nearly as bad. After a few minutes of confused silence the band start up again and play without amplification. Soon, magically, the power comes back on and then a Czech Nico comes out and sings the lead. Suddenly, something about it all – I've definitely had too much to drink – has tears welling up in my eyes. Oh fuck, it feels like my heart's going to explode.

A little distance away Libuše has started to dance, and then right in front of me two young Czech girls in black start dancing too and when they play 'Sweet Jane', which is one of my favourite Underground songs, I can't resist any longer and soon I'm dancing too, not caring that things haven't worked out with Tomas, not caring anymore about any of my other problems, because I'm having fun. I'm having fun and that feels perfectly wonderful.

That's when Tomas pops up out of the sea of dancers, hair all messed up, lips wet, eyes dark, dancing towards me. I look away – what? – and suddenly zero in on a familiar face, all gaunt, staring eyes. Tomas starts kissing me, and all the time I see her staring hard. Then when the kiss ends she disappears.

What on earth is she doing here? And what to make of that look of horror on her face when Tomas gave me a kiss?

Tomas disappears as soon as the band stops playing and I find myself talking to a tall, dark-haired man with startling blue eyes; I recognise him as one of the people from the table Tomas went to sit at just after I arrived. I let him buy me a drink. He says his name is Bohumil, however you spell that, and he tells me all about Czech poetry and music. I find myself unable to concentrate and watch the crowd, looking for my mother, half expecting her to appear in front of me at any minute and tell me off for kissing in public. She must have come to see the concert – if so, what's she doing here? I'm just about to go and search for her, even though I sense she's already gone, when Anna appears. What the hell does she want? I empty the last of my champagne.

'What did you think?' Anna says. 'I have to say I love this band, but they're a bit of an acquired taste.'

'What are they called again?' I ask, scanning the room for Tomas, my mouth sucking all too soon at the empty glass.

'The Czech Underground.' She evidently already knows Bohu-whatever because she nudges him and says, 'You know all about The Underground, Bohumil – why don't you tell her?'

But at this Bohu's expression hardens and he leaves. What? I'm not following what's going on. Anna's voice cuts through my confusion: 'Most of the members are from another band, The Plastic People of the Universe. Did you know they were banned during the communist times?' Anna's eyes flash darkly in her face as she speaks. 'The Plastic People of the Universe were very popular during communism and now, amazingly, reformed as The Czech Underground, they're popular again.'

Not knowing how to respond to her little history lesson, I clasp my glass, needing another drink.

'The original Velvet Underground was really big in the dissident movement here.' Anna still seems to be talking. 'You know, Charter 77 and the samizdat – do you know about all that? The Plastic People of the Universe are all good friends of Havel's – the Czech president, the first after the Velvet Revolution? And Havel, of course, is friends with Lou

Reed – anyway, everyone here in Prague knows the Velvet Underground songs, even younger people really like them.'

'The first song, "All Tomorrow's Parties",' I say, my mind awash with Anna's jumble of words, 'that was the best one, I thought – it was incredibly atmospheric.'

Anna nods, studies my face. 'So how's it going with Tomas?'

I shrug. She waits.

'Actually,' I start and then stop. I look directly at Anna and she looks directly back. 'I'm not sure.'

'You should have an affair with him,' Anna says, placing her hand on my arm.

'An *affair*?' I choke. 'But –' I gulp at my empty glass, eyes finding the bar across the room. 'I don't think he's really interested in me,' I manage. 'He's interested in –'

'What? I just saw him.'

I start to tell her, 'No, that's OK –' but Anna brushes me away and disappears into the dense crowd.

Damn. I order more champagne from the bar and take a large gulp. When I look up my head is spinning slightly and Anna is talking animatedly to Libuše in the next room. I hurry on rubbery legs to find Tomas before she does, but by the time I find him he's with Anna and they appear to be having an argument. They're standing face to face and Anna is shouting at him. I should probably just turn and leave, but for some reason I decide to say goodbye instead.

'I just came to say goodbye,' I say, barely managing to keep it together.

'You're leaving?' Tomas says and frowns.

'You can't go just yet,' Anna says, removing my empty glass. 'Let me buy you another drink.'

'Well, I –' I begin but Anna links her arm with mine and Tomas links his through my other arm and we walk in formation back to the bar. I look from Tomas to Anna and back and shake my head, stumbling slightly.

'Have you tried Becherovka?' Anna wants to know.

'No, what's that?'

'You have to try Becherovka!' Tomas explains. 'It's delicious, it's the Czech national drink.'

Anna orders three shots and Tomas passes them round. Our hands touch slightly when he hands me mine – wow – God, that was so sexy.

'*Na zdraví!*' Anna says, downing the golden contents in one savage gulp, and Tomas copies her but I sip mine slowly. It tastes a bit like herbal cough mixture.

'No, no,' Anna bosses loudly. 'You've got to drink it straight down.'

When Tomas nods I do as Anna says and involuntarily pull a face. 'Very medicinal.'

'Would you like another one?' Tomas wants to know, full of boyish charm.

'No thanks,' I say, suddenly needing vodka, suddenly wanting to leave. I'm not supposed to be doing this.

Tomas orders two more but Anna slips wordlessly away. Now it's just the two of us and he's staring at me again, and after he sculls his next drink I return his look, my eyes sinking into his and the room starting to swim. After a while I find myself smiling, but his face remains sad, his expression doesn't change.

'Look,' I say, finally downing the other Beche-something-or-other, unable to leave it behind undrunk. 'It's been great to meet you, but I gotta go. Rehearsing tomorrow…'

'Yes, it's late,' he agrees, snapping out of it. He taps his pockets, looking for his cigars. 'If I'm going to the opening night party, I really ought to make a move.'

While he didn't invite me, I'm too sloppy to protest. I say goodbye and give him a wet kiss, one on each cheek.

Then, his eyes sliding into mine and tugging hard, he says, 'So what are you doing now? Fancy a nightcap?'

My stomach lurches but I pretend not to notice. Half looking at him, I surprise myself and say, 'Why not?'

Stumbling into a cab – thankfully Tomas is happy to leave his car – I stare out the window and force myself to think straight. Right. We'll just have this one drink at my hotel and I won't invite him up to my room. I should really spend tomorrow practising for New York but it wouldn't be the first time I've done that half-pissed on no sleep. Should be all right … I check my mobile: a missed call from Nelly. I text her, *Please call me. Urgent.* Then I see the time. Shit. Three-thirty a.m., way past her bedtime. I put the mobile back in my bag.

'Grand Hotel Evropa,' Tomas says as the taxi turns into Wenceslas Square. 'I can't believe you're staying there. Are the rooms nice? I never come to this part of Praha any more – Václavské náměstí has been ruined, too many tourists and the horrible casinos, I can't bear to walk along it anymore.'

'It's true,' I say, 'there's a lot of tourists, but Wenceslas Square is still great – right? And the hotel's amazing. The furniture's all mixed up, Louis the Fourteenth rip-offs, communist-era kitsch, bits of Art Nouveau. My bathroom's huge and it's all marble.'

'Do they still have the old cafe?' he says. 'Not that I can stand all those awful cheesy songs.'

I look away, thinking about Reed and how he loved precisely such 'awful cheesy' songs. Then, as the taxi pulls up, I push Reed away and we climb out. We fumble through the revolving doors only to find the lobby bar is closed. 'Maybe we can find somewhere out on the square?' I say, thinking on the one hand this is probably one of those signs Nelly's always going on about that says I should call it a night. On the other hand, I'm always up for a nightcap.

Tomas shrugs and looks pointedly at the stairs. 'I never come to this part of Praha,' he repeats, starting to walk towards the stairs. 'It's a bit of a tourist trap. Do you have a minibar?'

The pocket-sized bottles of vodka in the freezer, I put them there this afternoon … I check my mobile in the unlikely event that there's a message back from Nelly – there isn't – and tell myself I shouldn't be doing this, and then straight after, ask, *But what's wrong with a bit of company and fun? Reed rejected me after all.* I lead Tomas past the glass cabinets filled with Bohemian crystal, up the grand staircase and through three floors of faded Art Nouveau splendour to my suite with its balcony overlooking the famous square and close the door.

'You have one of the suites!' Tomas says, walking around, touching things. 'No wonder you like it here! This must cost an absolute fortune.'

'It's not too bad,' I say, en route to the minibar, circling the room and switching on lamps. 'A hundred and thirty pounds a night for the two rooms.'

'A hundred and thirty pounds a night? You must be rich!'

'No,' I tell him. 'By London standards it's not that bad.

Would you like a drink? There's beer, wine, or vodka in the freezer?'

'A glass of wine would be great,' he says.

I don't really want wine, I *need* vodka, but I open the bottle of Moravian wine and pour two glasses. If I really need it, the vodka's always there …

I hand Tomas a glass and he takes it and sips at the wine, avoiding my eye. Then he picks up the *Prague Post* from the end of the bed and starts flipping the pages. Right. So he's not interested in me after all. I slurp my wine. He's still reading. I slump, what the hell, and walk into the other room. But Tomas doesn't take the hint. Damn. When I go back out, Tomas puts the newspaper down and looks at me. I smile. Suddenly Tomas appears right beside me, staring hard. There's nowhere else to look and so I stare back but I can't keep up the poker face and I crumble into a smile. The next thing I know he's dragging me back into the bedroom and my heart's pounding double time. Shit. Now what to do? My wine's over near the minibar … But Tomas's hand is warm and his eyes fierce. I swallow hard.

There's the slightest hesitation from Tomas, and then he's kissing me so sweetly, so gently, I'm surprised. He pauses, leans away to look at me, his eyes are focused on my lips, and then he kisses me again: talk about chemistry. Soon he pulls me into a hug and cradles me in his arms. He smells faintly sweet, of cologne, and the frightened flirty look he gives me before kissing me again is an electric blink that goes straight to my heart.

We kiss again and again as he inches us over towards the bed. I go over backwards, landing giggling on the soft puff of the duvet, and he tumbles lightly on top of me. He fondles my breasts through my shirt, then unbuttons the buttons and slips his hands inside. He kisses my breasts and my hands hold his waist and when he pulls me to him I close my eyes. Everything's blurry and warm. Don't think.

'So you're from London?' Tomas runs his hand through my hair and smiles. Light from the square outside seeps in through a gap in the curtains, illuminating the bed where our bodies lie wrapped in the crisp hotel sheets.

'Yes,' I say, my mouth tasting completely foul. I reach for what I think is water but when it turns out to be more wine I drink it down, washing the stale taste away.

'So your mother's Czech,' he says, studying me closely, a strange smile twisting his mouth sideways, 'and your father's English. Which makes you half Czech.' He draws a line down the centre of my body between my breasts. 'So let's see – which breast is English?' he says, sucking my left nipple, 'and which one is Czech?' He plants a wet kiss on my right breast.

'The nicer one, obviously,' I say, giggling. Then add, 'I have a Czech middle name, or at least I think it's Czech.'

'What's that?'

'Tereza.'

'Tereza,' he repeats, rolling the *r* in the Czech way.

'It sounds great the way you say it.'

'I'll call you Tereza from now on.'

'Thank you.'

'*Tereza,*' he sings, '*jedniné Tereza, Měla by slyšet piseň mou …*'

He stops, laughs.

'That's lovely – what is it?'

He shakes his head.

'Sing some more!'

Again, the shake of his head.

Later, sweating, legs tangled together in the clear warm soup of the bath, Tomas smiles at me through the blur of steam. I smile back and sip at my wine, no longer pissed but solidly drunk, the wine keeping my hangover at bay. But when Tomas asks, 'So tell me about your childhood?' I eye him over the rim of my wineglass and take a large gulp.

'Why do you want to know?'

'I want to know all about you.'

I look down at the surface of the water. It's so still I can see Tomas reflected upside down. From this angle he looks older somehow and heavier. 'I don't know what to say.'

Tomas shrugs, sips his wine and smiles again. 'Were you always musical?'

'When we lived in Australia, I was always singing songs in my head, but it wasn't until we moved back to London that I started to learn the piano properly. Then, later, I won a scholarship to the Royal Academy, although I didn't actually finish my degree, I –'

'And what do your parents do?'

'My father's an academic, and my mother –' I break off. Do I imagine it or do his eyes brighten at the mention of my mother?

'And your mother,' he says, 'her name is …?'

'She's … not well.'

'Not well?' he says, jolting upright.

I frown. 'Are you OK?' The mention of my mother, his reaction … But surely he'd say if he thought he knew her?

'Yes,' he says, his face hardening into a mask. Then he adds,

'I'm sorry to hear she's not well.'

'That's OK,' I say. 'She has cancer.'

Avoiding my gaze, he closes his eyes and sighs. After a while, he repeats, 'I'm sorry.'

I wait for him to say more. When he doesn't, I prompt, 'She's much too young.'

'How old is she?'

'Forty-six.'

'That *is* too young!'

'How old are you?' I ask.

'Fifty, and you?'

'I'm twenty-five.'

'So she was twenty-three when she had you?'

'Twenty-two.'

'And Czech, you say?'

'Yes.'

He 'hmms' vaguely at this, and looks at me from far away.

How strange, all those questions about my mother and me thinking I saw her in the crowd — it couldn't have been her, surely? At some stage I'm just going to have to ask him point blank if he knew her. I find my thoughts drifting to the mini bottles of vodka in the freezer and decide to text Nelly when I get out. She'll know what I should do about seeing my mother.

'And what was she like when you were a child?'

'What do you mean?' I say, instantly needing the wine to be vodka.

'Was she happy?' Tomas asks, peering at me through the steam.

'For a long time after I was born,' I tell him, 'she did nothing …' I pause, unsure.

'Go on.'

'I suspect she was depressed. In spite of all the material comforts, my childhood was miserable. It's hard to explain.' I try catching his eye, but now he avoids my gaze. 'My mother seemed pretty depressed,' I continue, 'and my father was rarely at home. I always blamed her childhood here, in Prague. Growing up during communism can't have been easy. I guess I always thought communism was the reason for her being so unhappy. What do you think?'

'And do you have any brothers or sisters?'

'No,' I say. 'Why do you ask?'

But Tomas doesn't reply. Instead he gazes, wincing, at the surface of the bath, before slumping down into the water, his eyes closed and his jaw clenched tight. When I remain silent, he drags himself upright and out of the bath, wrapping himself in a freshly laundered towel. 'If it's any consolation,' he says, resting his damp hand momentarily on the top of my head, 'I don't know anyone who had the fairytale.'

'Is that your guitar?' Tomas asks, nodding his head at my electric guitar and amp in the corner.

Frowning, I up-end my glass and, wrapping myself in the white terry towelling hotel bathrobe, get out of bed. I pick up the guitar and flick on the amp. 'Now, I like it to sound …' I say, fiddling with the settings. 'There.' I strum a distorted G6 chord. 'Like that.'

'That sounds great,' he says, sitting up, his eyes flashing, excited. 'So you take it round with you?'

'Just for fun.'

'Play me something!'

I think for a few moments and then turn the reverb and distortion up to full and strum the first few chords of the Tchaikovsky. I'm almost too drunk to play, my fingers feel slow on the strings, but I somehow manage to keep it together.

'It's a bit loud, isn't it?' he says.

But I keep playing, undeterred, occasionally getting a chord wrong. His face crinkles in a mixture of admiration, humour and dismay. 'That's awful. You can't do that to poor Pyotr, you're crucifying it.'

When I still don't stop he says, 'I've never heard it played on the electric guitar before.'

'Evidence of a misspent youth. I heard it played on the spoons once.'

'You're kidding?'

'No.'

'You look so fucking sexy in that bathrobe playing your electric guitar I could eat you alive,' he says.

I flick my eyebrows at him but don't stop playing.

I'm just through the opening when suddenly he leaps out of bed and joins me, saying, 'Let me have a turn!'

I play a few more chords then hand him the guitar.

Shouldering it he starts to play 'Hey Jude', but his fingers stumble on the strings. 'I usually play a steel string,' he says, struggling valiantly on.

I nod, wait while he starts the song again at the beginning, and this time sings the words in Czech. The song sounds quite interesting like this and I smile.

Smiling back, Tomas misses a chord. 'Oops,' he says, his fingers all mixed up.

When he reaches the chorus I sing along in English and Tomas laughs, hamming it up, exaggerating the Czech even more. And singing like this, having fun together, I think, *Home, I've come home*. Then, quiet again, I listen while he muddles through the next verse, and notice how Reed has somehow miraculously become someone I used to know. I make a silent wish that Tomas is going to be in my life for a long, long time.

Just as I think this, Tomas says, 'Shit,' and gets another chord completely wrong. He puts the guitar down, breaking the spell. Catching my eye, he tries to hand the guitar back to me and says, 'Sorry.'

I shake my head at his offer of the guitar so he leans it against the wall. As soon as he turns around I hug him tight, but Tomas's body stiffens at my touch and he leans away, talking about his guitar playing. I close my eyes and squeeze him tighter, trying to make it right, but all that happens is that Tomas pulls even harder away, and then, disentangling himself from me completely, he picks up the guitar and plays the opening chords of 'Nowhere Man'.

'I think I'm falling in love with you,' I say.

'I'm not very good at relationships,' he answers.

I check to see if he might be joking, but he isn't. His mouth is pulled tight and he avoids my gaze. Great. Over at the minibar, I reach for one of the mini vodkas but end up snatching a bottle of wine at the last minute. The phone rings and it's the concierge with a complaint about the noise. *Something's wrong with me,* I tell myself, *I keep going for the wrong sort of guys, guys who have serious problems, although Reed was different, but now he's left me too.* Almost immediately after I've emptied the bottle the room starts to blur. Of course, if you've been drinking solidly for twelve hours or more, chances are you'll eventually –

I jolt awake, not knowing where I am at first, but slowly the events of the previous evening come back to me: Anna, Tomas, the strange conversations about my mother – vodka, that's right. I was dreaming about drinking vodka … I look around, just bottles of wine. Thank God – if I'd gone back to the vodka Nelly would have been really angry with me. Champagne and wine are bad enough. In fact, if this looming hangover is anything to go by, I'm going to have to have a glass of wine right now just to stabilise. Unable to go back to sleep – now I think of it, the practice room is booked for nine a.m., I'll have to call and tell them I'll be late – I'm counting the cars swishing in the light rain on the street below when Tomas switches on the light. I check the time. It's 6.10 a.m. I pour myself another glass of wine and top up Tomas's glass.

'You OK?' he says.

'I keep thinking about Anna.'

'Anna?' He props himself up on the thick feather pillows waiting for me to say more, but I avoid his gaze, wanting him to speak, and study the room instead: the large red rug with the gold flowers in the centre, the bed and wardrobe with cream and gold painted flowers, the matching round table with the glass top, the stained red velvet curtains, the gold and brown floor-to-ceiling porcelain stove in a flower mosaic pattern, the incongruous orange plastic phone. 'What about Anna?' he says finally.

I sigh. 'Is Anna straight or lesbian? Because when I first met her the other night I was sure she was flirting with me, and then –'

'Do you fancy her?'

'Not really. I mean, I don't know. I've never been with a woman.'

'Would you like to try?' he says, frowning.

'I'm not really interested in being with women.'

'She might be bi,' Tomas says, frown fading. 'I don't know her that well.' There's a pause and then he says, 'Have you ever had a threesome?'

'Is that why you invited us both back to your flat?'

'It wasn't my idea, it was Anna's. First she was all over you, and then she was all over me. I think she fancies us both.'

'Do you fancy her?'

'Not really.'

I sigh, relieved. 'She seems a bit strange to me.'

'Does she? She seems all right to me,' he says, then adds, laughing, 'For a Ruske!'

'But she speaks near perfect English?'

'That was Sven, her Swedish ex-boyfriend – he taught her English. She was a sex slave, you know. She arrived just after the Revolution in '89 and worked in a brothel full of sixteen-year-old sex slaves.'

I look at him in horror.

'The sex slaves are mainly for the German tourists – we Czechs can't afford them. Anyway, now she's working as a lap dancer. She's quite good, actually. She's always on at me to come and dance with her. We should go and see her one night.'

I nod, and then frown into my glass, something not quite adding up. 'Did you see us when we were dancing together on top of the bar?'

'I ran into Anna outside,' he says, looking down into his

glass. 'She was leaving just as I arrived. Anyway, enough about Anna – tell me more about your music,' he says. 'Where are you up to with the symphony?'

'I'm just at the beginning, really,' I say, a little thrown by the sudden shift, sensing he's lying about something and wondering why. 'I'm just researching –'

'A symphony, though,' Tomas says, turning from me to drink his wine. 'That's impressive.'

'But I've also got a big concert coming up in New York,' I tell him before pausing. Then, fishing, I ask, 'What about you? Tell me about *Walking Wounded*.'

'Well, it's partly autobiographical, and partly a play about ideas.'

'And the storyline?'

'Basically,' he sighs, 'it's a love story between two dancers. The hero is the lead of a famous ballet company and the heroine is the new female lead, only she's married and they're having an affair. He really loves her but he messes things up. She's ready to leave her husband but he chickens out.'

'So what happens in the end?'

'She leaves him and once she's gone his life completely falls apart. He struggles on for a while, has an affair with an erotic dancer, but eventually he collapses, he can't sustain it. It ends with him getting into bed and not getting out.'

'God, that's quite bleak.'

'That's what my agent said.'

'I'm sorry – I mean, you're obviously quite fascinated by the dark side?'

'It's not that exactly, it's more like that's just how my life's been. That's what feels true-to-life to me.'

We sit in silence for a while, Tomas staring out through the window at the facades of the buildings on the other side of the square, me studying his face while my head starts to pound. Up close, I notice there are vertical lines on either side of his nose which run down to his mouth; they're quite pronounced. There's something about the way he holds his jaw that makes me think he's clenching it, even now.

Just after twelve we raid the minibar for breakfast, our conversations from last night making tape loops inside my mind. While Tomas attacks the dark Toblerone I reach for one of the mini vodkas, making Tomas frown. I put the vodka back and use bottled water instead to wash my handful of Panadols down. Tomas starts to complain about me drinking vodka for breakfast but I change the subject by telling him, 'You have great legs – do you still practise every day?'

'I used to dance professionally,' he says. 'I told you that, didn't I?'

'You mentioned you studied ballet.'

'I was the lead of the Czech National Ballet!' he corrects me, then, showing off, he pirouettes on the shiny strip of parquet floor in the kitchen part of my suite.

Watching how wonderfully he moves – it just seems like too much of a coincidence – I sneak the mini bottles of vodka into my handbag. Finished, I ask him if the male character in his play was based on him and when he answers yes, I feel the blood rush to my head. 'And what about the female ballet dancer, was she autobiographical too?'

But Tomas just ignores my question and resumes dancing, leaving me to stare, my cheeks red. I'm about to ask him outright if he knew my mother when his mobile phone starts to ring. He walks that dancer's panther-like walk to answer it, and exclaims 'Libuše!' into the phone. He soon disappears into a conversation in Czech. After a while, he begins to argue and then, holding the phone away from his ear, he surprises me.

'Libuše is insisting I invite you to the castle. She's offering us both a lift.'

'What castle?'

'*My* castle.'

'*Your* castle?'

'Yeah, I have a castle,' he says. 'Come, you'll really like Libuše, you'll meet some really interesting people,' and before I can answer he tells Libuše in English, 'Yes, Tereza is coming,' before the conversation disappears back into Czech.

It registers that he didn't actually say he wanted me to come and that he pushed me away when he was dancing just now. Am I just being paranoid or is something strange going on? If he knows my mother, why doesn't he say — unless there's some weird communist angle? I remove one of the mini vodka bottles and hold it to my lips — I know Nelly said I absolutely shouldn't, that I should definitely stay away from the hard stuff, but I can't resist, it's all too hard. Heaven in an instant, pain anaesthetised, all my problems solved … But the familiar bitter burn of the liquor doesn't come. Somehow in my desperation I've forgotten to remove the lid. Ready to throw it somewhere hard, I hold the bottle in front of me — it is only Smirnoff, after all. Laughing, I toss the bottle on the bed.

A castle, I reflect, running the shower. *A castle!* Unable to believe my good fortune. A playwright/former ballet dancer who lives in a castle and has a colourful history with the communists – not to mention a bit of a wild side to keep things interesting ... Oh, to hell with it. Not waiting for the water to warm up, I climb straight in, the water washing away my problems, and meanwhile another part of my mind is busy composing alternating ascending and descending passages, from the left hand to the right and back, up and down the keyboard, a messy kind of bliss.

When I get out I notice a text from Reed. It reads, *Cathy, I need to talk to you ASAP. Where are you staying in Prague? Happy to come to you if need be. Reed.* I switch off the phone and hurry into clean clothes. Sadly for him, Reed's text has come too late.

On a brighter note, I suddenly realise there's one very good thing about going away to Tomas's castle: no more Anna. It's only once I'm in the car, speeding west out of Prague into the Bohemian countryside, that I realise I've not only completely forgotten to call the Rudolfinum, I'm going to miss my scheduled call with Nelly. Oh well, she can just charge it to my account and I can catch up with her next time.

ROSSBACH CASTLE

1

The need for vodka increases every minute. The castle turns out to be little more than a dilapidated hunting lodge: a large rectangle of buildings clustered around a weed- and rubble-filled courtyard. Great. Treading carefully, I pass through the remains of a gate on one side – there's no actual gate, just empty hinges – with an uneven stone wall on the other. To my left is the faded grey-brown grandeur of a three-storey Baroque building – I notice a whole row of windows are boarded up and quite a bit of the rendering has fallen off – and to my right is a pile of partial ruins. I look at Tomas, and then at the building. Not quite what I expected …

'That's where the old kitchens used to be,' Tomas explains, joining me and looking straight ahead at a low, single-storey structure whose roof has partly collapsed, as Libuše continues on without us, disappearing inside. Then, gesturing towards another structure he adds, 'There used to be some stables there, and servants' quarters, and an old theatre.'

Making up the fourth side of the rectangle is another single-story structure which ends at the gate. With the exception of the last section, which has been partially converted into a cottage with a small garden bursting with gnomes and flowers, its roof has also collapsed.

Tomas turns to face the Baroque building once more and I follow his gaze. 'The hunting lodge was built in the early 1700s,' he says, 'just before the original castle was abandoned. The Nazis used to lodge their SS brass here during the occupation, and then the communists seized Rossbach in 1949 and converted it into a storage space for grain. Later, they housed peasants in it and everything about the house was just let go. That whole section there is on the verge of collapse,' he says, indicating the boarded-up windows, 'but I can't afford to fix it at the moment.'

'So you inherited this as part of a restitution claim or something?' I say, wondering about his past.

'Something like that. It's a long story.'

Thinking aloud, I say, 'And your parents, they were members of the "corrupt" bourgeoisie, I assume?', eyeing the rubble outside the front door, where a circle of chairs that look like they're on their last legs are scattered around two upturned wooden crates. When I look up Tomas has turned his back to me. Ooops, clearly on shaky ground here. 'It's so great,' I back-pedal, 'you've got to save it somehow.'

'It's very expensive to fix' is all Tomas says. Then, not quite looking at me, he adds, 'Not forgetting, of course, that curiosity killed the cat,' and stalks off towards the double wooden doors.

At his rebuff, I reach into my handbag and check the minibar bottles, which are exactly as they were the last time I looked, ready for an emergency. I really want a shot – the Panadols are barely holding back my hangover and the beer in the car has left me craving something stronger.

Arms folded pensively across my chest, I follow Tomas across the courtyard, and when I catch up he's smiling at me again. I check my mobile – a missed call from Nelly and a text from the Rudolfinum – and send two hurried replies, telling the Rudolfinum I'll be away for a day or so but back soon, and apologising to Nelly and asking her to charge the session to my account, which hopefully has enough money in its overdraft facility not to bounce or incur a fine.

Noting the faded hall with its battered occasional table, a vase of dead meadow flowers and an empty bottle of Stoli, I consider the house with renewed interest: hopefully there'll be some wine inside.

'Franz?' Tomas calls out. Then adds for my benefit, 'Want me to show you around?'

'OK,' I say, noticing that the chandelier above us is completely devoid of light bulbs. 'Actually, I could do with a drink.'

'In that case we'll make our way to the kitchen. But first, the ballroom.'

Tomas opens the first door to our left and gestures for me to enter. I emerge into a room of vast proportions whose high, dirty domed ceiling is lit from either side by dozens of lamps. White marble fireplaces adorn both ends of the room; a floor of battered parquetry is covered with an assortment of ragged rugs in varying designs and colours. The walls are painted mustard yellow and the improvised-looking vermilion velvet curtains droop in places from the curtain rails.

'The Nazis were the last to use it as a ballroom,' Tomas says, and with his words the room suddenly comes to life and I see it as it must have been then: brightly lit, a band playing at one end, Nazi officers dancing with beautiful Czech women …

'It must have been amazing,' I say and frown. I can picture

my mother here; she would have loved the Old World splendour of its former incarnations. Thinking about this starts Janáček's 'Reminiscence' tinkling in my mind, but Tomas remarks, 'We had a bit of a party here last weekend,' and brings me back to the room in its present incarnation. Tidied up, it would be an amazing place for a recital.

At the nearest end, two nondescript couches with torn upholstery face the fireplace. Wooden crates serving as tables are littered with beer bottles-turned-candle holders, overflowing ashtrays and glasses partly filled with a bright green liquid. If Tomas would only turn his back I'd slug one down, but Tomas doesn't. He's looking to me and then around the room and back and smiling. The other half of the room is empty except for hundreds of folding chairs stacked against the far wall.

I cross to the curtains and pull them open. 'It's such a great space.' French doors open onto a paved area which leads out to wild woodland.

'We'll be having another party soon.'

I turn around and smile. 'Sounds fab.' Letting the dimensions of the house slowly sink in, I calculate the length of the room. 'How many people *live* here?'

'That depends,' Tomas says. 'Come on.' He nods his head towards the door.

I walk back across the vestibule and follow Tomas down the hall, past the dining room and one Tomas refers to as the 'rehearsal room' but which looks more like a musical junk room (though I notice there's an upright in there which I might be able to use to do some practice), and into the kitchen. I'm just eyeing the fridge hopefully when I'm startled by a tall, bulky man who appears in the doorway, speaking Czech. When he sees me, he stops.

'*Ahoj*,' I say in my only Czech so far and hold out my hand, eyes slowly taking in the yellow, knee-length walking socks, the too-short grey tracksuit pants and a black T-shirt with a red sword emblazoned across the chest. Blue-green eyes are framed by shorn, blond hair and sunk deep into a jowly, round face.

He smiles, takes both of my hands in his, kisses them and tells me 'Hello' in a German-sounding accent. 'How do you do?' He shakes my right hand firmly and for too long.

'I'm well, thank you,' I say and, when he still doesn't release my hand, raise my eyebrows to Tomas.

'Tereza, this is Franz,' Tomas says, gazing sharply at Franz, who finally cottons on and lets go of my hand.

Tomas and Franz begin speaking rapidly in Czech and I slink away in search of the liquor cabinet. The kitchen is enormous with a beautiful Cornish blue porcelain stove in one corner, but there's no booze in sight. When Tomas beckons, I join him at the foot of the stairs.

Wanting to remind Tomas about that drink, I swallow this question and replace it with another. 'Is Franz German?' We begin to climb.

'He's what we Czechs call a German-speaker. His family live here, but they speak German at home.'

'And is he your flatmate?'

'One of them.'

'He seems a bit odd …'

'He's completely obsessed with Anna,' is his only whispered comment.

Anna? Curious about this, I try to catch a glimpse of Tomas's face but he hurries ahead so I can't see.

The circular staircase would be lovely except that the

wooden balustrade has been painted dark grey and the walls are a dirty turquoise – it could still be the original colour, given the darker rectangular patches where paintings must once have hung. We pause on the first-floor landing, where Tomas points to a door to our left and says, 'That's my office.' Then we turn right and Tomas invites me into his bedroom.

'It's huge!' I blurt.

Tomas smiles and raises an eyebrow and I smile back, my cheeks turning a brilliant red. I look away across the room, taking in the bed, which is a super-king, the dusty chandelier, this one filled with candle stubs, and the two large windows, looking out over the rectangular courtyard. One window is cracked and taped up with gaffer tape. A door leads to an ensuite with a giant-sized white tub and a rust-stained cream marble floor.

'It's amazing,' I tell him.

'The Presidential Suite,' he declares, taking my hand in his and pulling me close. 'I hope Madame will be comfortable here.'

We kiss, deliciously, but when the kiss ends, I open my eyes and spy half a dozen or so photos of Tomas with various beautiful women taped to one of the windows. My chest tightens and I step away. I know next to nothing about this man.

'What is it?' he asks.

I take a deep breath and open my mouth to speak, but then shut it again. Finally – I really need a drink – I say, 'What did you mean about not being very good at relationships?'

Following my gaze to the photos, his face freezes cold in reply. He turns from me and starts walking towards the door.

'I mean, I hardly know you,' I call after him. 'I'd love you to tell me all about your past, you know, who you are, really, and …'

He only pauses to say 'I'll show you to your room' over his shoulder before walking out.

What? I follow Tomas down the long, winding corridor, past three smaller rooms and a bathroom, until we reach a large room decorated in communist-era laminated wood and burnt-orange acrylic. My heart sinks.

'It's the only free room left,' Tomas says. Then, 'I'll go get your bags.'

When Tomas's mobile rings and he says, 'Anna!' the sinking feeling intensifies.

'How's it going?' he continues. 'That's crazy – you're completely naked, did you say?'

I close the door to my room, take Mouse out of my handbag and lie down on the bed.

'Christ,' I tell Mouse. 'This is all a bit strange. Maybe we shouldn't have come here after all?' I kiss Mouse on the top of the head. He's flirting with bloody Anna again! Suddenly I'm incredibly depressed. Thinking of alcohol but trying to save the vodka for an emergency, I return Mouse to her box and hurry back downstairs.

For dinner at the local pub – this is growing tedious, Tomas remains distant throughout – I have a champagne (at last!) and peppers stuffed with some kind of meat, while Tomas, Franz and Libuše have roast chicken with paprika and caraway seeds. At one point during the meal, tired of being ignored, I follow Libuše into the ladies' room and ask her how I would go about getting back to Prague under my own steam, mentioning something about a practise session for New York.

'You'd need someone to give you a lift to the station,' Libuše says. 'Or perhaps you could call a taxi from the castle, although the service isn't great. When do you need to go? I can give you a lift if you like – I'm driving back to Prague the day after the party.'

'I might need to go sooner.'

'I'll ask around about a lift for you.'

After Libuše leaves I give myself a stern talking to in the mirror: no matter how difficult, I've just got to stay off the hard stuff somehow till I've got through my performance in New York. Right?

Back at the table we finish up and then pile into Libuše's car. Soon we're hurtling down the narrow country roads to Plžen, the nearest big town.

'It's great, Bohemia Beach pub,' Tomas announces to the car in general.

'Bohemia Beach,' I enthuse, attempting to catch Tomas's eye. 'Isn't that Shakespeare? *A Winter's Tale*?'

But Tomas doesn't answer.

'Isn't that Shakespeare?' I repeat, raising my voice. 'The seacoast of Bohemia? No-one was really sure if it existed.'

'It existed,' Libuše says. 'The Czech Kingdom used to rule right down to the Adriatic Sea.'

'I thought Bohemians were French?' I say.

'Actually,' Tomas says, addressing Libuše, 'the word "Bohemia" is originally Celtic. The Germans drove the Celts out and the Celtic word "Boii" became the German word "Bohemia". When the Slavs drove the Germans out, the name stuck.'

'But "Bohemian" means an intellectual, doesn't it?' I say, looking at Tomas.

'It does, but it only started to mean that in the twentieth century, when Prague came to rival Paris as the intellectual capital of Europe,' Libuše says, when Tomas again refuses to respond.

'Bohemians were artists as well as intellectuals, though, Libuše,' Tomas says finally, but the conversation is cut short when Franz suddenly erupts, the front seat groaning beneath his bulk, gesturing and pointing at something we've just passed and speaking excitedly in Czech.

Tomas answers him in Czech and Libuše realising I can't understand, translates.

'They're talking about the one thing about the post-revolution Czech Republic that really makes me sick,' Libuše says. 'The sex industry. Everyone is hoping the EU will put a stop to it, but the Russian mafia is so strong here.'

'The sex industry?'

'You mean you didn't notice all the sex venues in Prague?'

I shake my head.

'Prague has become the sex industry capital of Central Europe. Franz's telling Tomas how we just passed this brothel he went to once that was full of Russian sex slaves. It's run by the mafia and there are two hundred and fifty rooms the size of shoeboxes, filled with two hundred and fifty girls, all sixteen-year-olds. You can go there and bargain with them and get a girl for two hundred crowns.'

'That's horrific. How much is two hundred crowns in sterling?'

'Two hundred crowns is a lot of money on the average Czech salary,' Libuše says, not answering my question. 'It's mostly for tourists, you know – Czech men like to be married and have a mistress on the side, so who needs a prostitute?'

'Which means *The Unbearable Lightness of Being* is a true story?' I say, and remember that both Smetana and Janáček had mistresses (though Dvořák appears to have been faithful to his wife). Just then Franz mentions Anna's name and Tomas laughs loudly, snagging my attention. Tomas and Franz continue talking in Czech.

'What are they saying about Anna?' I ask Libuše.

But Tomas intercepts. 'That was such a funny night,' he tells Libuše.

'You were so drunk,' Libuše answers.

'That club – it's just outrageous,' Tomas says.

Then Franz says something in Czech and they all laugh.

'What's he saying?' I ask.

'He's saying that deep down he knows Anna really *does* fancy him,' Libuše translates, laughing still.

'Does she?' I ask, not following.

'No, I don't think she does,' Tomas answers my question. Then talking to Libuše, he says, 'Anna's quite a good dancer, though, don't you think?'

'Is she coming up for the party tomorrow?' Libuše asks.

'God, I completely forgot to mention it, I was just talking to her,' Tomas says, taking out his mobile.

I stare out the window at the narrow cobblestoned streets lined with shabby apartment blocks. Anna coming up for the party, Tomas ignoring me, me trapped at the castle? My face hardens and suddenly all I can think about is getting really drunk, on vodka. Fucking Anna – great! Pointless trying to delay the inevitable anymore.

Then Tomas says, 'Her mobile's switched off,' and we lurch to a halt outside Bohemia Beach pub.

Checking my own mobile, I see there's a text from Nelly which reads, *Are you OK? Call me if you need to. I'm worried about you. Nelly.* I switch the phone to silent and tuck it back in my bag. The last thing I need now is one of Nelly's lectures. Besides, she really is a bit of a quack. No formal degree and all that psychic hypnotherapy shit … I mean, I know she needs the money, and that's fine by me. But save me the bullshit. When the going gets tough, the tough get … well, a real drink. Pronto.

'*Na zdraví!*' Tomas, Franz and Libuše cry, clinking their James Bond 007 Russian cocktails.

Libuše hands me a cocktail and I clasp onto it tightly. A small part of me knows I shouldn't start, knows that once I start on the hard stuff there's no going back, but this is an emergency. Being stuck here with Tomas and Anna is the proverbial last straw. I take an exploratory sip and gasp. 'What *is* this? It tastes like pure alcohol.' All through dinner I was desperate for a real drink but this tastes like rocket fuel.

'It's basically fifty per cent vodka and fifty per cent Noilly Prat with a couple of ice cubes and a skein of lemon,' Libuše explains. 'I first had them in Moscow.'

'My God, it's so strong,' I say in faux complaint, taking a larger sip this time. Fuck, that feels good. 'No wonder this country has lost its way.' I even manage a smile. That's more like it: booze! A real fucking drink at last.

'Tereza is horrified by the corruption here,' Libuše explains.

'Everywhere it's the same, though,' Tomas says, 'even in London.'

'She means the brothel with the two hundred and fifty sixteen-year-old Russian sex slaves.'

'There are sex slaves in London too!'

'Not to the same degree,' I counter.

'Well, it's the police – the police here are totally corrupt,' Tomas says.

'That's true,' Libuše agrees. 'My American friend, Jay, he always drives around Prague with five hundred crowns on the dashboard in case he runs into the police.'

'Why?' I want to know.

'Because the police pull you over for no reason and hassle you about nothing until you say something that pisses them off, or admit to something you haven't done, and either way they come up with a spurious fine. How much they fine you depends on the conversation, on what you say to them. So Jay would just say, "Here's five hundred crowns, I don't want to talk to you," and hand it to them and drive away.'

'But how can they do that?'

'They just can.'

'But that's so corrupt.'

'Yes, it is. We're hoping becoming part of the EU will change things.'

'But it probably won't,' Tomas says. 'It will probably all just go further underground.'

My head is already humming slightly from the Russian cocktails when a guitar and a bottle of something called slivovice appear and are passed around the room until they reach Tomas. He tries to pass the guitar on to Libuše, but she says, 'No no, you play,' and hands it back to him. Then, standing up, he hands the guitar to me and announces, with a bow, 'She's famous, she's from London.'

I laugh, 'No,' and push it away, but he pushes it back.

'Anglicky' cry the drunk crowd. 'Kiss me, baby.'

Tomas hands me the slivovice to swig – which I grab gladly – and leans close and whispers, 'Do you know any Karel Gott?' in my ear, the closeness of his lips making my heart leap.

'Who?'

'Never mind. In that case, just play, "You've Got To Hide Your Love Away".'

I hold the bottle to my lips again, ready to suck it hard. My mother's favourite song. Strumming the guitar a couple of times, yep, it's in tune, I pause. God, this reminds me, I've really got to start getting ready for bloody New York, the Rachmaninov can be a fucking nightmare. When I look at Tomas he's all smiles and looking at me intensely. I swallow the slivovice in one mammoth swig.

I give the chords a rough run-through, make sure I've got it right. Converting the chords from the piano as I go, half laughing, I start singing but I'm almost too drunk to play. Libuše and Tomas start singing too, though one of them sings 'Here I stand' while the other sings 'How could she', but no-one seems to care and I keep going regardless. Soon half the pub is singing along and someone starts to play the accordion, which gives the whole thing a vaguely gypsy feel. I finish to loud applause and try to stand up and take a bow but when the room starts to spin I quickly sit back down.

Tomas is busy telling me, 'I once heard it played by Karel Gott,' when Franz leaps to his feet. He's been moaning incoherently into his beer for the last thirty minutes or so, but now starts to recite Byron's 'She Walks in Beauty Like the Night' line by line, first in English, then translating into German, and then into Czech – 'In honour of Tereza,' he slurs. He's so drunk I'm surprised he can stand, let alone recite and translate poetry.

Tomas hands me another cocktail and one of his thin cigars and I place the cigar between my lips and light up, then remove the cigar to take a large gulp from my glass. I'm pretty pissed now myself – how many Russian cocktails have I had? I've lost count. I swallow the slivovice Tomas hands me and smile when Tomas takes my hand to hold beneath the table. No-one's listening to poor Franz and when he finishes Libuše and I are the only ones who clap.

'He's a poet,' Libuše says.

'He's so drunk,' I answer.

'Any time, you come my room – I show you poetry,' Franz tells me, leaning across the table and reaching for my hands.

'OK,' I say, pulling my hands away.

'Any time,' he repeats. 'You can come. You have husband?'

I shake my head, immediately regretting the way this makes the room spin.

'It's not possible,' he says.

'Franz is a poet,' Tomas tells me, frowning.

'I know, I know.'

Franz sits unsteadily back down but, suddenly changing his mind, he staggers over to the bar. I don't understand what Franz is saying, it's all in Czech, but I gather the barman is refusing to give him another drink because he shakes his head and Franz's voice gets louder and louder.

'He's a complete drunk,' Tomas tells me.

Franz has started to thump the bar when a pretty girl

approaches. Leering, he springs forward, cupping one hand over each of her breasts. The girl screams and pushes him away, and in the ensuing struggle – the barman tries to pull Franz off while Tomas goes to the aid of the girl – Franz tears the girl's shirt off and she goes crying, hands clasped over her bra, to the ladies'. Tomas and the barman forcibly drag Franz outside, as he shouts unintelligibly. What a complete bloody psycho.

'I think it's that time,' Libuše says, emptying her glass.

'I must practise some piano tomorrow,' I tell no-one in particular and, finishing my cocktail, stumble out into the fresh air.

'Look, a full moon,' I say, forcing myself to sit upright.

Tomas and I share the back seat as the car hurtles through the darkened countryside, taking turns to drink from a bottle of vodka. Franz snores heavily in the front.

'It's so hot,' Libuše sighs. 'Does anyone feel like a swim?'

'There's a pool?' I slur.

'No, a lake,' Tomas says.

'What lake?'

'It's below the ruined castle, on the other side of the lodge.'

'You haven't seen the square tower?' Libuše asks.

I shake my head, slump. My eyes start to close again.

'You can see it from the front of the castle,' Tomas says. 'It's just beyond the main courtyard.'

'I think maybe I saw it from the road?' I say, opening and then closing my eyes.

'I'll show you,' Tomas says, and I smile without opening my eyes. Meanwhile, the car falls silent as we circle the perimeter of the castle. This time Libuše drives right into the courtyard instead of stopping outside the gate. As the car pulls up, I straighten and look out the window at the moon. Beneath it, I notice, is the ruined tower, its jagged contours just visible above the far side of the hunting lodge. 'There it is!'

We all crane our heads to admire it, desolate and beautiful and somehow enduring, a witness to the new era and all that has preceded it. Then Libuše switches off the ignition, breaking the spell.

'I think I'm too tired for a swim,' Tomas tells Libuše, who shrugs and wanders inside, leaving Tomas and I on opposite sides of the car and Franz noisily asleep in the front seat. I hold on to the car to stop myself from swaying.

I think about asking Tomas about Anna and the party, but just thinking about Anna makes my head spin. I'm just about to suggest we grab a nightcap when Tomas walks around to my side and takes hold of my hand. I can't help smiling.

'Come on,' he says, his eyes two dark wells. 'I'll show you the original castle.'

Holding hands, we stumble across the courtyard. My shoes come off somewhere, and it vaguely registers that my feet hurt on the uneven stones but I don't stop to look for them. We pass through an arched passage in the third wing, the one Tomas said had an old theatre in it. Tomas takes a swig from his vodka and passes it to me and I swig it and pass it back. Soon, the square tower rises up ahead in jagged sections. In some portions the tower is four metres high, in other areas the walls are much higher. The moon is white and full and high in the sky. I look at Tomas and smile again as we ascend a steep ridge leading up to the ruined tower along a path of uneven stones and gravel.

'The tower, which is part of the original castle, dates from 1346,' Tomas says, playing tour guide and stepping into the centre of the tower, waving for me to follow. 'It was built by the Rossbach family and later became a Jesuit monastery. It was finally destroyed in a fire in the 1700s and construction of the hunting lodge began shortly after.'

Tomas moves to stand in front of a neat rectangular opening, gazing out, and I join him. A few metres in front of the tower wall, the promontory ends in a sharp cliff, the lake and pine forest visible below. I take one more swig of the vodka, then, realising it's empty, hand it back to Tomas, who places the bottle at our feet.

'How beautiful,' I sigh. In my mind I hear a slow ascending melody, right hand only, in a major key, and commit it to memory. Maybe I can use it for the symphony?

'The tower would have protected the original castle,' Tomas says, nodding in agreement and pointing to the adjacent rocky mound. 'There was a drawbridge and a small moat at the front, while this side of the castle was protected by the sheer drop in the rock face. This is all that remains.'

The whole scene is completely magical: moonlight shimmers on the surface of the water and a breeze scented by the pine trees below rises up from the valley. Blurry, I picture myself as a princess in a castle surrounded by a moat, a prince approaching. Do I or don't I lower my drawbridge?

'You can see the tower for miles around,' Tomas says, and, pointing below us, adds, 'On hot summer nights we often go swimming in the lake.'

I squeeze Tomas's hand. 'Feel like a skinny dip?'

'Not really.'

The moonlight on the lake loses some of its glow at his no, and my doubts about Tomas and Anna return, as does the need for another drink, but when Tomas grabs me and pulls me close all is wonderful again. 'Come here, you,' he says, and kisses me up against the roughly hewn wall. He lifts my T-shirt and kisses my breasts, one at a time, and then unzips my jeans and inches them down.

'Wait –' I say, he's going too fast, but for an answer he tugs down my knickers, loosens his belt and plunges his fingers inside.

'Wait,' I repeat, not wanting but needing to know; grasping hold of his fingers in mine, I force myself to focus. 'Is there something going on with you and Anna?'

'What?'

'Are you sleeping with her?'

'With Anna? Would I be here with you if I was?'

'I don't know, maybe.'

'She's a dancer, we're both dancers. That's it. Stop being so jealous and insecure.'

Why is it that guys are always accusing me of being jealous? I let him continue, numbing out. Our lovemaking is athletic, passionate; after we finish I try kissing him but he pushes me away. I search his eyes. 'What are you feeling?'

'What do you mean?'

'Right now – what are you feeling?'

'Nothing. I mean, OK, I guess.'

I flinch, stagger back, instantly at sea. *Nothing?* I look at him, hard. Is this what he meant when he said he couldn't have relationships?

Watching my face, Tomas reaches for my hand and says,

'Come on,' and, softening his voice, 'let's go to bed.'

I push him away, fumble for my jeans; it's a struggle to do them up. Nothing? Nelly says this panic is my fear of abandonment. I don't really understand what that means, I only know that I'll do anything to make it stop once it starts. Craving, urgently needing booze, something – the sense of home from the Grande Evropa is fading fast. Crashing, dissonant chords, the thunder of timpani. When my teeth start chattering, I'm no longer thinking about a nightcap, I'm thinking about a few vodkas, maybe even a whole bottle of vodka. Time to raise the goddamn drawbridge and barricade the gates!

My head hangs low as we make our way back down the hill, across the courtyard and into the hunting lodge. When I can bring myself to look again, Tomas's face is lost in darkness. Pain growing stronger, I've gotta keep it together. Making an excuse, I let Tomas walk upstairs alone. I enter the kitchen looking for grog and am busy studying the fridge, nothing but beer, when Franz enters the kitchen and offers me a shot of schnapps.

'Thank you,' I say, holding out a glass and leaving it there while he fills it up. I drink it straight down – Tomas, Anna, the anonymous sex – and I'm about to ask for more when Franz starts up with Byron again. I begin to move away but when his eyes head south, I give him a vague wave and run upstairs, snatching up and emptying a bottle of unidentified liquor I find on my way.

I pause outside Tomas's door. I just never seem to get it right with guys; music's the only thing I've ever been any bloody good at.

2

I look up and groan, surprised to find myself in Tomas's bed, and hold my head in both hands. Christ, a killer hangover, that's all I need.

'I'm not too bad, actually,' Tomas says, handing me a mug of sweet tea and pecking me on the cheek.

So now he's being nice to me again – well, well, well. I prop myself up in bed so that I'm resting on one elbow and take an experimental sip of tea. As I do, the room starts spinning one way, and I start spinning the other. I moan again – this is really bad. I'm wondering why it's so very bad, and then I remember: those Russian cocktails, the slivovice, the endless shots of vodka … 'Have you got any painkillers?' I croak, but Tomas shakes his head. Christ, I'm back on the hard stuff, the real deal: this is not good. And when uninvited memories of the pub, the ruin and Tomas's 'Nothing' start ping-ponging around inside my head, I stagger out of bed and feel my way to the bathroom cabinet. Fuck. I need painkillers, or better still, I need a shot of something fast – but there are no Panadols or painkillers of any description. I check my handbag – zilch, just a text from Reed that begins, *Come on darling, we used to love each other …* and which I don't bother to finish reading.

Back in the bedroom, Tomas says, 'How about some breakfast?'

I'm about to agree when I realise breakfast probably won't involve alcohol, so, thinking about the glasses of green liqueur I saw downstairs yesterday, I say, 'Is it OK if I check my emails first?'

'Why don't we get breakfast and then you can use my office when we get back?'

'Don't you have anything here?'

'We've got some bread, cheese and salami.'

'For breakfast! Don't you have anything civilised, like toast and marmalade?'

'You're not much of a Czech, you know.'

'Maybe not,' I agree, struggling into my clothes, a blue silk sarong and a turquoise and brown singlet top. 'It's so hot,' I complain.

'What about a swim and a picnic by the lake later on?'

'OK. So, can I use your computer?' Tomas nods and I lean over and kiss him goodbye.

The desk in Tomas's office looks out through a large window onto a tangle of tree limbs, and overflowing bookcases line the walls. A battered biography of Nureyev balances precariously on top of Čapek's *RUR*. I scan the shelf. Havel, Klíma, Kundera, Hrabal, more Čapek. Where are the Czech women writers? I scan the next few shelves but there are none. Not even Němcová's *Babicka*. How disappointing. I tug out the Nureyev and, opening the book to a random page, find a faded letter. It looks like a love letter. Don't go there. I snap the book closed and replace it on the bookcase. I empty the first of the two glasses of green Pernod-like liquid I brought upstairs with me and pull a face. Tasting like Pernod, only stronger, one glass is enough to take the edge off my hangover: brilliant.

I log on to Tomas's computer and check my emails. The first message is from Reed. *For goodness sake, Cathy,* he writes. *If you can't even manage to return my texts, I honestly don't know if I can be bothered. Just don't say I didn't try. R.* It's immediately followed by an email from Sarah, my London agent, demanding I call her ASAP. What? After this is an email from New York asking me to confirm my flight details and the upcoming dress rehearsal at the Lincoln Center. Feeling somewhat under the gun, I drop my head to the desk, rest it on the backs of my arms and close my eyes. Oh God … Momentarily setting aside Reed's veiled threat, I decide to focus on Sarah's email instead. Why does Sarah want to speak with me now? She knows I'm in the Czech Republic en route to New York.

I pick up my mobile, search for Sarah's number and dial. Sarah's 'Hello?' is all business and clipped consonants.

'Sarah? It's Ter–' oops, 'I mean, it's Catherine here.'

'Yes.'

I wait but there's nothing more. 'I just got your email –' I begin but Sarah cuts in.

'Good girl, can you come in today? I heard about the Rudolfinum and we need to talk damage control if we're going to try to save New York.'

'But I'm in the Czech Republic …'

'Then get on a plane ASAP,' she says. 'I'll be blunt. I don't have room on the books for people who aren't pulling their weight.' She launches into a tirade about pressure from investors and the new era that's begun and concludes with:

'There's no room for crazy boozing in the new business environment. Increased concentration of ownership, tighter production costs, the corporatisation of the industry have all changed the way things are run. I just can't afford cancelled shows ... But you know all this already.'

'That's right, Sarah.' Bloody hell. I rub my brow, change the phone to the other ear and struggle to think clearly. There were at least three more glasses of green stuff downstairs ... I drag my mind back to the problem at hand. We've been through tough times before, Sarah and I, but somehow we've always managed to come out heads up. But there's something I'm just not getting in all of this ...

'If you need time out to go to rehab and sort yourself out, take it,' Sarah is saying. 'But you can't keep going on like this – you'll ruin what's left of your name and reputation and I won't let you drag me down with you.'

I let Sarah's ultimatum register and meanwhile think, *If you need time out to go to rehab ...* Now where have I heard that before? Bolt upright. Rigid in my seat, my eyes lock onto Sarah's email.

Reed! His words exactly.

No, surely not?

But my mind forms the links before I can stop it and suddenly things start to make sense: Reed ditching me so suddenly; Sarah practically firing me a few days later. And then something else, last year's Christmas party: Reed and I saying goodbye to Sarah and Sarah tucking Reed's business card into her bag and telling him, 'I'll be in touch.'

'Sarah,' I say. 'I'm going to have to call you back.'

'I'm assuming that's a no then. In that case, you've got

twenty-four hours to cancel New York or I'll cancel it for you –' is the last thing I hear before the dial tone.

Sucking the dregs from the first and immediately emptying the second glass, I dial Reed's number wrongly twice before remembering I have it programmed into my phone. My thumb stumbles on the letters of his name. *R-A*, dammit. *R-E*, there it is! *Enter.*

The number rings and rings. I picture him struggling to find his phone amid the chaos of his desk, and then his voice.

'Cathy! I was just thinking about you …' he says, his voice papery, familiar, deep.

'Really? Why's that?'

'My last email –'

'I was just speaking to Sarah,' I say. Then cold, 'So when were you two planning on telling me?'

There's a pause and then a sharp intake of breath. 'Listen, Catherine, it's not what you think.'

'Not what I think?' I say, my mind jamming.

'Cathy, please. I really care about you, and I know Sarah does too. We just can't stand to watch you do this to yourself –' is about as much as I can take before I hang up the phone. Bastard!

As if getting fired by my agent isn't enough, Sarah appears to have stolen my damned husband! Gasping as the pounding in my head returns with full force, I dial Nelly's number, log out and head downstairs towards the ballroom, noting that my battery is getting low and counting the rings before Nelly picks up. When she does I burst into tears.

'Cathy, darling – how are you? I've been worried about you. How're you going in that big old shithole, New York?'

'I'm not in New York.'

'What?'

I stifle a moan unsuccessfully.

'Cathy? What's going on?'

'I'm still in the Czech Republic.'

'What are you still doing there? I thought you had to be in New York by now?'

'No, I'm in a castle somewhere just out of Prague.'

'What?'

'I'm with this guy …'

'Oh.' In the ensuing pause I can hear Nelly's mind ticking over as I stifle another groan. 'What's going on?'

'Well it's just that …' I start then stop. Where to begin? 'Look, is there any way we can bring tomorrow's phone session forward to today?'

'Tell me what's going on and we'll see, OK?'

'Well – OK. It all happened quite suddenly … I guess after what happened with Reed, I –'

'Have you spoken to Reed yet about what's going on?'

'Sort of.'

'What does that mean?'

'Look, it's complicated,' I continue. 'There's this other woman and –'

'Reed's seeing someone else?'

'Yes, I think so – I'm coming to that. But actually, I'm also having problems with this new guy.'

'Right.'

'It's hard to explain –'

'Look, Cathy,' Nelly jumps in. 'I really think you need to put this new guy to one side and just concentrate on New York, OK?'

'I guess ... But Sarah's threatened to cancel it after the disaster the other night.'

'Leave Sarah to me – OK? But tell me – what happened at the Rudolfinum?'

'I'd rather not.'

'I'm assuming it involves alcohol ... Never mind. The first time doing something's always the hardest. But for now, you need to stop drinking again, and I mean yesterday.'

'OK.'

'Good girl. Now in the meantime, you said you had cousins in the Czech Republic. Can you check to see if your mother is with them?'

'I'll try, but my phone credit is low. Maybe you could try them too? You speak German and I'm not sure how good their English is.'

'OK, text me the details. Speak soon. And try to talk things through with Reed – it doesn't seem quite finished to me. Let's talk again tomorrow at three – actually, on second thoughts, sit tight. I'll call you back.'

I mumble goodbye and text Nelly my cousin's details. As I do, a loud beep confirms my credit has finally expired, which means I won't be able to text her again or make our phone session tomorrow. I'm on my own.

After vodka, leek and potato soup and rye bread for breakfast at Bohemia Beach pub, Tomas is strangely distant again and complains about my drinking vodka for breakfast even though he's drinking beer. I find myself alone in the castle – I can't seem to find Tomas, Franz or Libuše anywhere. I'm just about to – finally – sit down at the piano when I remember Nelly's advice and I take a beer to Tomas's bedroom and dial the number for my cousin Háta from his landline. (Tomas said it was OK to use the phone if I needed it, which means I'll be able to call Nelly tomorrow after all.)

'Hello?' a heavily accented female voice answers.

'Hello, is that Háta? It's Cathy, Odette's daughter from London.'

The voice hesitates and then says something in unintelligible Czech.

'English?' I try.

Again I'm answered with a jumble of Czech.

'Háta?' I say, speaking slowly. 'I am at Rossbach Castle, I am Cathy, Odette's daughter. Is Odette there with you?'

The woman says something in Czech but Rossbach is the only bit I recognise.

'My mother,' I repeat, 'Odette. Is she with you? It's important. I'm worried about her, she's very sick …' When the woman again answers in Czech I tell her goodbye and that I'll call her back later. Hopefully Nelly will call and explain or else I'll have to find someone here to act as my translator and call back.

There's a confused silence and then I say, 'Bye,' and hang up the phone, hoping the woman will understand. At least one thing's clear, my mother can't be at Háta's – if that was Háta – otherwise Háta would have put her on the phone. Maybe it wasn't my mother in Prague after all.

No-one is able to give me a lift until this evening, when Libuše is going to the station to collect some party guests arriving from Prague, and meanwhile Tomas's invitation for a swim in the lake has turned into a group excursion. In the rubble-filled courtyard, Tomas and I are joined by Franz, Libuše and Anna, who has just arrived from Prague with Krasava in time for tonight's party. Great. As they follow the winding path through the pine forest, Tomas and Anna touch each other constantly. I look away, stare at the soaring branches above, the matted pine needles below, the tree trunks to either side, but it's no good. With only two mini vodkas in my handbag, I hold on tight to my mobile, my only link to sanity and the outside world.

Up ahead a fallen log blocks the path and Tomas helps Anna to climb over. As Libuše and I approach I catch Tomas saying, 'OK, so she's talented, but she's incredibly insecure, and she drinks like an absolute fish.'

When he sees me Tomas stops talking abruptly, jumps over the log and hurries away without waiting to help Libuše and me. Was he talking about me? Second mini vodka at my lips, I stumble over the log and meanwhile Tomas and Anna disappear around a bend in the path.

While there's no sign of Tomas and Anna when we reach the bend there's a break in the trees ahead and soon Libuše and I emerge into a desolate empty field which borders onto a lake. Up ahead Tomas and Anna are standing together in the middle of a grassed area with a jetty and a rowing boat. Nearby is a small changing shed.

'The fields seem really empty,' I say, forcing myself to speak.

'Ever since Pilsner Urquell was sold to a South African firm, most of the fields around here have been fallow,' Libuše says. 'The South Africans don't buy the local hops anymore. They buy their hops from Japan. The hops aren't as good, but they're cheaper.'

'Has it changed the taste of the beer?'

'Some people say it has. I don't know, I'm not much of a beer connoisseur.'

Apart from the fields, the setting is incredibly picturesque. To the left lie small cottages with upturned V-shaped roofs. To the right, a dirt path runs among willow trees along the shore of the lake. We head towards it and soon our feet go sinking into the lush grass.

'Isn't it beautiful?' Libuše says, but I'm incapable of responding. Tomas has his arm around Anna's waist and Anna's head is resting on his shoulder. Emptying the second vodka, I reach for a third knowing there is none. Fuck. I can't do this anymore. I check my mobile for messages. Nothing from Nelly, dammit.

I mumble something vague about having a headache and turn back to the castle.

'Is it because of Tomas?' Libuše wants to know.

I sigh, unable to meet her eyes.

'Oh, screw him,' Libuše says. 'Why not stay for the party and have some fun?'

I shrug, a kind of mute acquiescence. Despite the dancing sunshine all around, the idea of a lonely train ride back to Prague sends me running straight back to the castle and hopefully another bottle of vodka. The dark water is everywhere around me, taunting me, pulling me quickly down.

I'm up in my room, a glass of wine in one hand, my mobile in the other and Nelly's number glowing from the screen, and meanwhile my thoughts circle around Tomas. If he wants Anna, then why does he chase me? If he can't have relationships, why start one with me? If he just wants sex, why doesn't he say so? Unless he's lying to me, in which case he's an arsehole. Nothing adds up or makes any sense, which means he probably is an arsehole, a throwback to my pre-Reed days ... When I start to cry, I get up and close the door. I thought I'd finished with those kind of guys. Suddenly my mobile glows green with life and starts ringing. Nelly! At last.

I snatch it up and am about to jump straight in, but somehow she's already talking.

'I'm catching a lunchtime flight to Prague,' Nelly says, without asking if I'm OK. 'I should be there in time for dinner. Things have reached a point where – look, I think we need to talk in person, OK?'

I try to take this in through the cloud of my obsession about Tomas but I fail to respond: dinner, with Nelly, in Prague, tomorrow?

'I'll meet you at your hotel, the Grand Evropa, at six p.m. OK?'

'OK,' is all I can manage.

'Sorry to rush, but I've got a client ...'

There's a pause during which I don't speak.

'Look, I don't mean to worry you unnecessarily but I had a call from your mother's surgeon, your father passed on my number when he couldn't get hold of you. He said that if she has this next operation she may have another six months, but if she doesn't, it might be as little as a week or two. We need to find her and get her into surgery ASAP.'

'One week? But wait, I think I saw my mother in Prague – I told you about that already, didn't I? I mean, she looked OK –'

'You saw your mother in Prague?'

'She didn't look like she was on her last legs or anything –'

'After speaking with the surgeon, I checked and your mother definitely boarded the plane. I haven't managed to get Háta on the phone yet, but I'll keep trying.'

'OK. But –'

'Sorry, Cathy, I really need to keep this brief. Now quickly, have you heard anything about the Lincoln Center?'

'The thing is, everything's really messed up, and I –'

'Let's just try and concentrate on one problem at a time, OK?'

'Look, I'm still going to New York, it's just that I can't bear it. I'm pretty sure Sarah's ditched me and gone off with Reed. It's all just a complete mess.' As much as I struggle not to, a whole string of sobs leak out at this point. After a while, I realise Nelly is talking but I can't hear what she's saying. I'm just forcing myself to take deep breaths and asking her 'What?' when the door opens and Tomas is suddenly right there, catching me crying on the phone to my guru and holding an empty wineglass. God.

'Nelly,' I blurt, 'I'll have to call you back –'

'No, it's OK –' Tomas says and leaves.

'Was that the guy?' Nelly wants to know, and meanwhile I'm thinking about how Tomas was looking at me kindly again.

I'm about to tell Nelly it was nothing and that I have to go when I hear her voice booming from the handset '– just concentrate on New York, OK? Forget about that guy till after your show.'

Finally, I manage to cut her off with 'OK, bye, Nelly,' but before I hang up I hear her say, 'And that means no chasing that guy in the meantime, OK?'

I put down the phone, dry my eyes and, having emptied all the remaining glasses strewn about Tomas's bedroom, am heading back down to the kitchen in search of alcohol when I run into Tomas, who's waiting for me outside.

'Libuše sent me to see if you're OK.'

'Libuše?'

'She thought I might have offended –'

'Look, I think we should just forget it,' I cut in, grasping at Nelly's advice. 'I can't do this right now. Is that OK?'

But Tomas doesn't answer. Instead, he looks at me intensely with dark eyes and then hurries away, disappearing into his room. Feeling slightly better, I realise I've now got to get my drinking back under control, at least until I get to New York.

3

There's no hard liquor in the kitchen. Krasava is so busy stirring saucepans at the stove she looks like Nigella Lawson on speed and Franz's round, sausage-finger hands arrange food in large irregular mounds on mismatched serving plates. Muffled conversation drifts in from the ballroom where guests from Prague have already started to arrive.

'Look, I found these.' Dressed for the party in a beaded black sleeveless top and baggy black velvet trousers, Libuše appears brandishing two dusty bottles of red wine. 'I think it's quite good, Moravian – God only knows how old it is. It could be vinegar by now. We'll need to decant them.'

'Decant them! We're only going to drink them later?'

'You're supposed to decant all red wine,' Libuše insists as she opens the first bottle. 'Especially if it's any good.'

I watch the wine trickle into the crystal decanter. What an incredible waste of time. 'Maybe we should taste some first, to see if it's any good?'

But Libuše ignores me. 'Is this your first trip to the Czech Republic?'

'Yes, although I'm not exactly a tourist – I have family here.'

'Really? Where? You should pay them a visit.'

'I'm not sure how good their English is.'

'And you don't speak any Czech?'

'No, I hardly know anything about the Czech Republic or my family. I mean, my great-grandfather was arrested and sent to Auschwitz.'

'Was he Jewish?'

'No, he was in the resistance.'

'Few people realise how many non-Jewish Czechs and Romani also suffered at the hands of the Nazis. Did he die there?'

'No, but when he came out he was very sick.'

'Like in the Maus comics.'

'Mouse comics? As in "squeak, squeak"?'

'They're these comic books about the concentration camps. Maus as in *M-A-U-S*. Anyway, while you're here, you should really get in touch with your family, you know. Apart from anything else, if your family had property seized by the communists, you might be able to make a restitution claim.'

When laughter erupts next door, I catch myself listening for Tomas's voice and force myself to stop. 'I know, it's just …' My voice trails off. It's silent next door. None of this nonsense with Tomas would be so bad if it hadn't happened so many times before. The more I think about it, the more he reminds me of Daniel, and Daniel was a complete emotional fuckwit. 'Most of my immediate family have left or are dead. My mother never really talked much about those who remained behind and now she's sick I can't really ask her about it. My father always said my mother couldn't see the point in talking about her family because of the regime – it was like there wasn't any point, it was as if the whole country didn't exist for her under the Russian occupation, as if it was dead.'

'Yeah, my mother was the same. She never wanted to talk about the past, about communism or the war. Most people don't like to talk about it.'

'I think my mother might actually be here, in the Czech Republic, though I haven't managed to meet up with her yet. She escaped from hospital to come see me at the Rudolfinum.'

'And she's sick – wow. You really must try to meet up with her then,' Libuše says as she finishes pouring the first bottle.

I nod. 'It's finding her that's proving difficult,' I say, admiring the decanter full of wine.

But Libuše doesn't smile back. 'So here's a good Czech story,' she says, beginning to decant the second bottle of wine. 'Did you hear about what happened when Havel went to the White House?'

I shake my head, wondering what she might mean by a 'good Czech story'.

'During communism Havel was friends with The Plastic People of the Universe,' Libuše says, pouring me a half glass of wine as a taste test. 'They were this band that used to play secret concerts out at Havel's country house when the communist police were arresting them for playing everywhere else.' Libuše looks at me intently, and while I return her gaze, the wine is everything – it can take away my pain, and I drink it hungrily down.

'Anyway,' Libuše continues, 'Clinton held this special reception for Havel when he was elected president. So Clinton says to Havel, "Hey, who do you want to invite to your reception?" And Havel says, "Lou Reed." And Clinton's aides are like, Hmmm, not really very politically appropriate, so they say no. But Clinton says, "Hey, if Havel wants to have Lou Reed, we'll have Lou Reed." So Lou Reed came to the White House and played a gig with Mejla, the lead singer from The Plastic People of the Universe.'

'Havel and Lou Reed were at the White House with Clinton?' I say, the glass suddenly empty, my eyes glued to the decanter. 'That's actually quite funny.'

'Yeah, and then Lou did an interview with Havel when Havel was first elected.'

'Incredible,' I say, and smile as I pour myself another half glass and try not to gulp.

'You see,' Libuše continues, 'the Lou Reed connection was formed when Havel smuggled a Velvet Underground album into communist Czechoslovakia.'

'Right.' The wine is going down too quickly. I would drink less overall, I reflect, if this were vodka.

'The album was passed around and everyone here listened to it,' Libuše says, watching me watch her decant the wine. 'It helped inspire the Czech Underground movement. Lou kind of became a symbol for everything that was against the regime.'

'The Plastic People of the Universe?' I say, clasping my empty glass. 'Was that the gig I saw with you in Prague?'

'Re-formed into the Czech Underground, yes,' Libuše says, finishes decanting the second bottle and then carries the two ruby-coloured decanters into the dining room, talking to me over her shoulder. 'OK, so did you know the founder of McDonald's was a Czech?'

'This time I really don't believe you!' I say, following behind with a chuckle, instantly relieved to see a row of wine bottles down the middle of the dining table.

'It's true! Ray Kroc, whose parents were Czech immigrants bought a diner called McDonald's and expanded it into a chain. But the biggest irony is that after the Velvet Revolution they built a McDonald's on Václavské náměstí, and there was a huge public outcry.'

'Actually, now I think about it, I do remember hearing something about that at the time.' My glass is empty.

'People didn't realise he was just a local boy made good.

'And then there's Frank Zappa…'

I nod, switching off. I feel like I'm playing some kind of Czech Trivial Pursuit and coming last. I look around and notice the room looks quite lovely in an art-school kind of way: the table and sideboard are covered with white sheets; candles line the centre of the table, and flowers are scattered among the candles; an odd assortment of clean, scrubbed-looking plates and cutlery are carefully arranged at each place; and serving spoons lie on the sideboard among more flowers and candles. 'I didn't realise it was a dinner party,' I say, thinking I've probably got at least an hour to rehearse before dinner starts, though the chances of the piano actually being in tune are another matter.

'I think it started as a regular party but then turned into a dinner party. It was Anna's idea.'

'Ah,' I say. Anna's idea! Here we go. How on earth am I going to get through this thing without vodka?

Libuše pours herself a glass of wine and tops up my glass. I grip the glass in my hand as an image of Tomas and Anna walking together in the forest flashes into my mind, and empty the wine in one gulp.

'Hey, shouldn't you go a little easy on the pedal?' Libuše says.

'It's just so delicious,' I say, and while I change the subject, I ask her if she can help me get through the party. Libuše doesn't offer me any more of the Moravian wine.

4

I avoid the dinner party by holing up in my room with a bottle of wine and by the time I go downstairs and peep into the ballroom, lots of new people have arrived and the party is in full swing. I spot Peter and Betty, a couple of English expats, and Libuše, and quite a few members of The Czech Underground dotted around the room, but no vodka. Czech Beatles booms through the enormous space. In Czech, 'From Me To You' sounds something like '*Stodne Stohe Stodne*'. I pick up a CD cover and study it, recognising the name of the singer, Karel Gott, as the one Tomas wanted me to play at the pub. The party seems to have morphed into a fancy-dress party. Spying a half-empty bottle of wine next to the stereo, I snatch it up and pour myself a refill.

A tall, athletically built woman with long dark hair and olive skin joins me by the stereo. Dressed in burgundy and black, she is wearing a shawl, gold loop earrings and a head scarf – I realise she's come as a gypsy. Before I can say anything, she swoops on the CD, plucking it right out of my hand, and exclaims, 'Karel Gott!'

A man appears at her side – tall and dark he's dressed in a black suit and smoking a pipe – and says, 'Do you know Karel Gott?'

'I vaguely know the name,' I say, and give him a big smile.

'Mařenka,' says the woman, holding out her hand to shake. 'And this is Jenik.'

'I'm Tereza.'

'Quick,' Jenik says, as the song ends, '"Jezebel".' He skips the CD till he reaches the right track.

'No, "Tereza"!' Mařenka says, pushing his hand out of the way and skipping tracks again.

On cue, muted whaa-whaa trumpets and strings play a jazzy opening riff, and a smooth male voice starts to sing, '*Tereza, jednině Tereza …*'

Recognising it as the song Tomas sang to me that night in Prague, I ask, 'But *who is* Karel Gott?' wondering what the lyrics mean in English.

'Just don't mention the zombie word,' Jenik titters. I look from him to Mařenka and back again – are they together?

Mařenka explains: 'Karel Gott's a popular singer from the sixties. Actually, he's still big now, especially in Germany.'

'He sold out to the communists, if you'll excuse the tautology –' Jenik says.

'What do you mean about not mentioning the zombie word?' I want to know.

'The zombie word?' Mařenka says, rolling her eyes. 'OK, well, in the sixties, Karel was this popular singer, he was very famous. Kind of like the Czech Frank Sinatra – they used to call him the Singing Nightingale. But he didn't like communism, he wanted to defect to Germany, and when the communists found out they "offered" to get behind his career, to make him the "official party singer", but really they didn't want him to defect because he was so popular. Anyway, Karel Gott ended up staying and becoming a communist pop star and singing a lot of really terrible songs. Ooompa-boompa, "Roll Out the Barrel"-type Socialist Songs of the People. Then after the Velvet Revolution he relaunched his career, and he's just as popular now as he was before communism.'

'And there was this big event recently,' Jenik adds, 'Expo in Germany, and Karel Gott was invited to sing. Anyway, the press here, free at last to criticise Gott, because all the time under the communists no-one could criticise him, the press here finally criticised him. They said they didn't want the Czech Republic to be represented at Expo by "that singing zombie".'

'I get it now,' I say, finishing off the wine with a laugh.

'And Gott had a total breakdown about it, he was just like a little child, because he'd never been criticised before,' Jenik continues, trying not to laugh. 'But the funny thing is, Gott's German fans, and there are a lot of them – but you know the Germans, their taste can be a bit kitsch – his German fans took to the streets in protest demanding that Gott come to Expo.'

'It's quite a saga,' Mařenka says, deadpan.

'So Gott went.'

'But you know, he's really disgusting,' Mařenka says harshly. 'He's always in the popular magazines with a different young girl – the girls are always twenty-five or thirty, and he must be sixty by now.'

Jenik rolls his eyes at this point and I wonder about Tomas and his affection for Gott: he's an older man and I'm a younger woman. I try to remember if my mother ever mentioned him but nothing comes to mind. I never did ask Tomas point blank if he knew her …

'So how well do you know Tomas?' I ask Mařenka.

'Quite well, we've been friends for a while. He and my husband both work in theatre.'

'Was Tomas ever involved with the Communist Party?' I ask, looking around for Jenik who has suddenly disappeared.

'Tomas? I don't think so. He had some problems with his –'

I want to ask Mařenka with what but a woman dressed as a hippie has already called her away.

A man wearing a red silk satin shirt with billowing sleeves, black pantaloons and, accompanied by a Russian wolfhound, joins me and fills my glass from a tall green bottle with something that tastes vaguely like Pernod. He says his name is Edvard and when we shake hands his long fingers linger cool in mine. In a deep, smooth voice he tells me, 'It is a delight to meet you.'

I toast him and empty my glass, savouring the rush to my head. What is this stuff? It's so strong.

I'm now swaying slightly and laughing to myself but things only get more bizarre when Wolfhound guy and I are joined by Jan, a Czech revolutionary poet wearing a purple shirt with black jeans, whose hair is so long and bushy it's started to form dreadlocks. I count twelve dreadlocks, most of which are so long he wears them tucked into the back pockets of his jeans. He waves a video camera at me and smiles. Both Wolfhound and Dreadlocks have travelled up from Prague especially for the party.

I try to concentrate on what turns into a rather convoluted discussion about national identity and history. While Wolfhound makes an argument for geography as destiny – 'A nation's geography is the fundamental building block of its psyche. Therefore if you are the Czech Republic, a small landlocked country with big powerful neighbours like Germany and Russia, you are always going to be fighting off attacks from invaders and struggling to create national identity,' – Dreadlocks argues in favour of forging one's own destiny, and meanwhile, I wonder what on earth I'm drinking. It really packs quite a punch.

My glass empty again, I leave Wolfhound and Dreadlocks to go in search of more alcohol. Discovering Krasava manning a cocktail blender in the kitchen, I ask her what she's making.

'Is absinthe cocktail,' Krasava says in heavily accented English. 'You put absinthe with lemon, with ice, add sugar, and blend.'

'Absinthe!' I say and laugh. That explains the funny Pernod taste.

'Or,' Krasava is still talking, 'You can drink straight, like French way. You put absinthe in glass, put sugar cube on spoon, and pour water onto sugar cube. Or you can drink Prague way, with flame. You would like?'

'Yes,' I say, although I only manage to say 'Yes' again to Krasava's 'First way?' I'm just lifting the absinthe to my mouth when Anna walks in, her lipstick all smeared and minus her shawl.

Seeing me, she stops. 'Be careful,' Anna warns, 'it's very strong. I had to stop drinking them because my head felt like it was coming off.'

'I've never had absinthe before,' I say, struggling to focus my eyes as Anna stalks off …

… I'm not completely certain but I think the person standing next to me has walked straight out of the Bible. He's wearing a billowy white shirt, a felt waistcoat with a matching cropped coat and pantaloons, and seems to be speaking in tongues. I wait for him to stop swaying and then I realise he's telling me, 'I am Bulgarian shepherd,' over and over. Confused, I turn away and crash straight into some kind of 1920s vamp in a full-length green dress with a fishtail and a plunging velvet neckline; she's smoking a cigarette from a cigarette holder, her hands encased in long, black satin gloves topped with feathers. Somehow Shepherd and Vamp seem to be talking about Czech composers, or rather, Vamp's talking and Shepherd and I are listening.

'Czech classical musical flowering,' Vamp says, 'It was very brief time …'

'I always wondered about that,' I slur. 'What the fuck happened to all those fucking great Czech composers?'

'Well, partly it was communism, but also we Czechs were bad with promotion. Cultural trends at time did not help. On one hand, Czechs were nationalistic, but on other, they were cosmopolitan. Someone like Janáček he is interesting because he lives in Praha but then goes to Brno, so Praguers ignore him when he is in Brno. Firstly because he is international composer with many overseas commissions, but also because of nationalism, he was in Brno not Praha. Crazy, no?' Vamp shakes her head sadly. 'For Janáček, it's like catch 22.'

I nod, sway, drift off. *Catch 22* – wasn't that a film? …

… Suddenly – Karel Gott has been blaring indistinctly from the stereo in the ballroom again – the sound cuts out.

'Typical,' says Franz, who is somehow by my side.

We're joined by two more guests – a man dressed in a black beret, a black polo and trousers, and with a pencilled-on goatee beard, and a woman wearing flared jeans, a white embroidered hippie shirt and a large peace pendant. I smile encouragingly, but am unable to follow their conversation: are they speaking English? Just then, a woman in her fifties wearing a white smock dress appears. She's tall and has long, thick burgundy hair. Staring intently into my eyes – her face soon creases with concern. 'Don't worry about him,' she says.

I shake myself, forcing myself to concentrate. 'What?'

'This kind of man, he's no good for you.'

'I'm not sure what you mean,' I manage.

She reaches for my hands and holds them in hers. 'You're stronger that you think.'

I try to pull my hands away but she won't let me.

'You're OK, you don't know it, but you're OK right now. Everything's going to be all right.'

A warm feeling floods through me as she says this and for just a few moments I start to wonder how it would be if what she is saying were actually true.

She keeps staring deeply into my eyes. Uncomfortable, I try to look away, but somehow her eyes keep pulling me back. She frowns. 'What kind of fruit do you like to eat?'

'Fruit?'

She nods.

'Well, I guess, I like grapes and –'

'Too much sugar, you are full of sugar, your body, your energy is all over the place, spilling out of you. You need to eat apples and pears, these two fruits are good for you, not grapes.'

I nod, stupidly. 'Apples and pears.'

She holds me for a few moments more and then gives me back my hands. 'Your power is with you, not outside of you.'

I look away – she reminds me a bit of Nelly – and she's

somehow gone when I look back. Just melted away into the crowd.

Seeing Jenik heading towards the kitchen, I follow him in search of another absinthe cocktail. On my way I glance sideways into the dining room. I stop abruptly and double back, failing to compute. I stand, gaping, in the doorway, trying not to sway too obviously.

Tomas and Anna are dancing together on top of the dining table. Their pelvises are pressed together and Tomas has his hands around her hips. Anna, now minus the black lace singlet and dancing in her bra, does a bend back, but when Tomas pulls her up into a kiss, his eyes slide over to find mine, his hands on her breast, on her arse. Fuck, I can't … is he? – I leave. I run stumbling outside, but then head back into the kitchen and grab the bottle of absinthe. I'm just heading outside again when Tomas catches up with me and grabs hold of my arm.

'Tereza, wait –'

'What's fucking wrong with you?' I spit, pushing him roughly away. 'You sleazy bastard, you two-timing –'

'It's not that,' he says reaching for me again. 'Tereza, please –'

'Fuck off,' I say, messy. 'It's finished.'

He stands there, watching me sadly, and meanwhile I glower back. There's a lengthy pause.

'It's just that …' he tries again. 'It's just that I don't want a relationship. With you or with anyone else.'

'You're pathetic,' I slur, before turning around and careening off into the darkness. This time he doesn't follow. Outside, huddling in some wretched ruin, sobbing uncontrollably, I suck down the absinthe until … things start to crawl… all thoughts, obliterated. Time fuses, and ... I don't know what any of this has to do with fruit. Later, it starts to rain –

– footsteps! I half turn, expecting it to be Tomas come to grovel, but it's only Franz, slipping in the rain. As I watch he goes down in the mud. He picks himself up and then disappears into the night, calling, 'Cathy, Cathy?' I sink down, everything is swaying, and I close my eyes. All goes black and quiet and, bottle empty, I lose track ... the water dark around me ...

I force my eyes open when a woman's voice calls, 'Cathy?'

It's Libuše, I know that voice. I try to move my mouth but I can't. 'Stoo lay,' I slur.

Eventually ...

... and finally, out of the dark, comes a half-remembered song. At first I'm kind of moaning, then singing too loud,

Two or three girls has he
That he likes as well as me
But I love him ...

... All my life is just despair
But I don't care ...

... What can I do

5

The BBC interviewer has lovely hands, small with dainty pointed fingers, and startling blue eyes. They've just finished filming me playing the Piano Concerto in G minor – all I could think about was my dress and how the neckline is too low and that all anybody will notice is my breasts wobbling as opposed to my musicianship – and now they want to ask me about Tchaikovsky, the man, from the point of view of a performer of his work.

The sound man adjusts the microphone one final time and then Charles smiles across at me and the interview begins.

'So, can you tell us a bit about Tchaikovsky, the man – what is your sense of him as a person?'

'I think he was incredibly sensitive, I think I read that somewhere,' I say, still feeling ridiculously self-conscious in this damn dress and silently hating the young twit in wardrobe who insisted I wear it. 'I don't think he ever really got over being sent away to boarding school, and then, when he was still just a boy, the sudden death of his mother. That's something I think a lot of creative people will relate to, that sense of being as fragile as glass …'

'Is that something you relate to as a performer and composer, being as sensitive as glass?'

I pause, thinking. 'Yes, it is,' I say eventually, knowing without wanting it to be true.

'And as a composer? What's your sense of Tchaikovsky as a composer?'

'His immense popularity made his work difficult to assess – critically, I mean. Personally, I find his music irresistible, but then –'

'You're a romantic?'

Again, my slow, reluctant reply. 'Yes.'

Incredible thirst, disgusting taste in my mouth, throbbing head … When I wake up the sky is stained an orange-red and everything is quiet. Something smells disgusting – God, is that vomit? Trying not to gag, I get out of there, fast. Where the hell am I? I stand jittery in the doorway to the kitchen, knowing I have to leave – leave the castle, leave the Czech Republic – but head pounding so relentlessly and mouth so dry I'm unable to manage the basics: do I need alcohol or water? I'm just reaching for the door to the fridge and the bottle of vodka I hope to find there when Franz leaps up from behind the kitchen table.

'Be careful,' he says, making me jump and closing the door to the kitchen behind me. He grabs my forearm with one hand and indicates the floor with the other.

I peer around the wooden table and study the floor where Franz was sitting but fail to detect anything unusual. I let my gaze drift over the contents of the kitchen: the laminated benchtops, the shabby cupboards in need of paint, and finally the beautiful porcelain stove. I shrug my shoulders. I don't know what he's talking about. I reach for the fridge door.

'You see,' Franz says, restraining my arm with one hand

and pointing at the floor with the other, 'I'm cleaning the cages …'

Cages? There are no cages as far as I can see. I remove Franz's hand from my forearm, open the fridge door and look for alcohol. There is none.

'Please, I don't know how to say in English!' Franz says, opening one of the cupboards and handing me a half-empty bottle of vodka.

I start to pour myself a glass but change my mind and, hands trembling slightly, hold the bottle directly to my lips. Relief floods through me as the pounding in my head says thank you. Lowering the vodka, I'm still wondering what could be down on the floor when a brown mouse with enormous pink ears crawls around the back of Franz's T-shirt, sniffs the underside of his neck and stares at me, its nose twitching hard.

I smile and tell him, 'Mouse,' remembering my own Mouse and wondering when I last fed her. I hand him the bottle but Franz shakes his head. The mouse and I stare at each other and then the mouse sits back on its haunches and starts cleaning behind its ears.

'You are not frightened?' Franz says. 'You like mice?'

I nod, drink more of the vodka and tell him, 'I like most pets.' Then, starting to return the vodka to the cupboard before changing my mind and taking a third draught – this one stings as it goes down – I nearly tread on a large grey and white mouse with a white dot on its back.

'Svatopluk!' Franz says.

This time when I look down I count over half a dozen mice scurrying across the floor.

'Be careful, Svatopluk,' Franz says, bending down to pick up the grey mouse and placing it on one of the benchtops.

'Svatopluk?' I say, stifling a laugh. What an unfortunately named mouse.

'Svatopluk is a very popular Czech name, many parents give it to their children. It was name of Czech king.'

'Really?' I say, taking another swig from the vodka and struggling to choke back another laugh as the vodka meets up with the absinthe and I start to feel human again.

'You are not afraid?' Franz says, smiling. 'An elegant lady like you?'

I take one more swig of the vodka before returning it to the cupboard. 'I have a mouse myself, in my room upstairs.' The pain is now mixed with a seesawing light-headedness. 'She's called Mouse,' I say, with a short laugh.

'I make them ladders,' he says, showing me the miniature ladders he's building out of twigs, previously hidden behind the table but spread out over the floor. 'The mouses –' he begins.

'Mice.'

'The mice live in my room. You would like to see? Maybe after we can see your mouse?'

At Franz's invitation, the memory of his behaviour at the pub flashes into my mind and I hesitate, but when Franz picks up a fat white mouse and hands it to me to hold, the image fades. 'She's so pretty,' I say as the mouse freezes, trembling in my hand. 'OK.'

I hand the mouse back to Franz and he places it with the other mice inside a small plastic cage, and then I follow him upstairs. But as I climb, an image of Tomas and Anna dancing on the table flashes into my mind, only to be replaced by an image of Reed and Sarah. *That vodka in the cupboard…*

'Hang on, Franz,' I call, reversing my steps until I'm standing in front of the cupboard. When I open it, the vodka bottle peers back invitingly: just one more, one more for the road, it says, and I wonder, is one more really going to make much difference either way? I pick it up and hold it to my lips, letting the fiery liquid burn my throat. Head spinning, then settling, I tug the bottle away and return it to the cupboard. But the thought of leaving it there hollows my guts and I reach for the vodka again, hurrying after Franz, the vodka at my lips, half tripping as I climb the stairs. At the top, I turn away from Tomas's room and follow Franz, but when I reach Franz's door I hesitate, swaying just a bit. I start to laugh, but then stop and force myself to focus. I'm not completely sure but I think the blur of Franz's bedroom walls is covered from floor to ceiling with posters of Liz Hurley: from the early days, through the Hugh scandal, right up to the present. I want to keep laughing but something about the way Franz is looking at me stops the laugh short in my throat.

What was the name of that film again, the one about the serial killer? I go straight for the vodka, lifting it up, then, hand shaking with the effort, lower it down. Maybe it's time to slow down? 'You like Liz Hurley?' I'm just managing to say when Franz pulls me inside and closes the door behind us. I remove his hand from my arm and step away, back towards the door. Crikey.

'I hear about fan who was so obsessed,' Franz says, placing the mice on the bed, 'he would change address on mail so it looks like it is for Liz but with house number incorrect. He would pretend to live at the incorrect address and go to her door, give the mail and probably he would see her.'

'That's crazy,' I tell him, placing the vodka on the bedside table. I look from the posters to the odd assortment of mouse aquariums and cages spread across the table beneath the far window and back again.

'You know her work?' he asks.

I nod, trying to stabilise.

'When I meet Liz, I will be honest. I will ask her out to best bar in Praha, somewhere with river view, buying her best champagne.'

I force myself to look at Franz's face. His eyes bulge slightly and his round cheeks are shiny with sweat. I don't know whether to laugh or cry. Over on the bed the mice climb out of the little cage and start running around.

'I would just be natural, you know,' Franz continues, picking up Svatopluk and holding the mouse to his lips, 'asking about her day, how her new film is going, is she happy with agent or will she go elsewhere with business?'

'I see.' Evidently the subject was one to which Franz had given a lot of thought.

'I would tell her I am director,' Franz says, kissing the fat mouse's furry back, 'probably Liz would be asking me about my work, about my film, and soon she will look, how you say in English, closely into my eyes. She will know I am one for her.'

'Hmm,' I say, 'I don't think she's available at the moment,' my stomach turning slightly queasy.

'I would tell her all about first film,' he says, returning Svatopluk to the bed, 'one I shot on second-hand digital camera and which is about ...' He catches my eye, his face devoid of expression.

'Yes?' I say. My fingers twitch for the vodka on the nearby table.

'Probably it is Czech and German thing,' he says.

I raise my eyebrows; I have no idea what he's talking about.

'The Czechs are like the Germans on this, you know, our toilets ...'

'Let me get this straight – you plan to seduce Liz Hurley with a film about Czech and German toilets?'

'You have seen shelf? Probably English toilets have no shelf?'

'The shelf?' Is he talking about the shape of the fucking toilets here?

'When I was child,' Franz says, wiping sweat from his brow, 'my uncle would sit on stairs. Always we were eating dumplings and pork and cabbage. When we were ready he would ...'

I wait for Franz to continue.

'You know Czech national anthem?' he says. 'The fourth movement?'

'Not exactly.'

'The one with all the –' he blows a succession of raspberries, '– the ooompa-boompa, the tubas and the drums?'

I shake my head.

'So, my uncle ... would ...'

I wait, not sure I really want to know.

'... fart ...'

In spite of the very serious expression on Franz's face, a series of small, vodka-laced laughs pop out before I can stop them. I reach for the bottle and drink from it to stifle my laughter. When I lower the bottle this time I see that it's nearly empty. I really must *stop*: am I seeing things, or did the room just lurch to the right?

'Yes, fourth movement of "Má Vlast". We Czechs,' he says, quickly reaching down to prevent one of the mice from leaping from the bed to the floor, 'we are very expressive in this way. We have shelfs for same reason.'

'Very *expressive*,' I say, unable to prevent myself from laughing again, noticing that Franz isn't joining in.

'So!' he says, nodding his head for emphasis. 'My first film is about what it is to be real Czech.'

I stop laughing – his face is still serious – but soon erupt into giggles. 'I'm not sure I follow.'

He frowns. 'Love and Farting.'

'Love,' I titter, 'and farting?'

'Not *Laughter and Forgetting*, Love and Farting.'

'*Laughter and Forgetting* – that's Kundera, isn't it?'

Franz nods and stares at me hard.

I swallow my giggles, trying to keep a straight face, to keep things in focus, aware I'm starting to sway. 'But I don't see how the two are related,' I say, this time managing to stifle a guffaw into a cough.

But Franz continues, oblivious. 'Yes, it is good question. The story is about young Czech man and his first love. He is all the time wondering when he can be himself, when can he fart …?'

This time my laughter erupts unchecked but before Franz can respond there's a knock at the door and a woman's voice calls, 'Franz!' and then says something in Czech I don't understand.

'No, Krasava,' Franz answers in English, frowning at me and approaching the door. 'I am busy now.'

I deaden the rest of my laughter with some help from the last little dribble of vodka and think about getting away from Franz. While thoughts of Tomas and Anna and Reed and Sarah have faded to a dull ache thanks to the vodka, I'm not sure how much more of Franz I can take. Meanwhile, Krasava's voice increases in volume from the other side of the door and then the barrage of words ends abruptly. Franz grunts and opens the door.

'Hello,' Krasava says, smiling sweetly at me.

I tell her, 'Ahoy.'

But when Krasava attempts to enter Franz's bedroom, Franz waves his hand dismissively at her in a way that indicates she should leave, and then he starts to close the door, speaking in Czech all the time. The smile fades from Krasava's face as she resorts to pressing her foot against the door to stop it from closing. This time when she speaks there's a frantic edge to her voice and an even further increase in volume. Franz replies – they are both speaking loudly in Czech now – and the conversation turns into an argument.

I turn away. Perhaps it's time I made myself scarce? I study the cages on the table, the empty vodka at my lips once more. The table's made from an old paint-flaking door and two sawhorses. It's completely covered with mouse paraphernalia: I count six cages full of shredded newspaper, plastic wheels and cardboard tubes from toilet paper rolls.

At Krasava's yelp of pain I turn back to catch Franz and Krasava wrestling in the doorway. Franz is trying to close the door and shouting 'Schnell, schnell!' and Krasava is equally determined to keep the door open. I start towards the door with purpose but, seeing me, Franz removes Krasava's fingers roughly, kicks her foot away and slams the door hard enough to make the windows rattle. Krasava remains on the other side, knocking and calling Franz's name, but Franz yells at her brusquely and she falls quiet, her footfalls eventually fading away down the hall. Franz turns to me, sighs heavily and mutters beneath his breath.

'Listen,' I say, moving towards the door. 'I really ought to …' But just then the little brown mouse throws itself off the bed onto the floor, where it lands with a soft thump and freezes, looking up at Franz with startled eyes.

'Fish,' Franz tells it, bending down and placing his hand palm upwards on the floor just in front of the mouse. 'Come.' Fish looks at Franz's hand for a second or two but remains frozen to the spot. Suddenly Franz grabs at Fish. The tiny mouse makes a run for it under the bed but Franz, somehow faster, seizes the mouse by its tail and tells it, 'Nein.' He holds Fish up in front of me, Fish's legs scrambling at thin air.

'It doesn't hurt,' Franz says and looks at me hard. 'Picking them up by tail. Fish is part of experiment, you see. I will interbreed pet mice with indigenous Czech mice to increase intelligence – yes? You really like mice?'

I nod my head, watching Franz drop the mouse into the glass aquarium and close the lid, my fingers clasping, slippery with sweat, around the neck of the bottle.

'An elegant lady,' he says, then dropping his eyes to my chest adds, 'with such beautiful breasts – you *really* like mice?'

At this I begin to inch away. For a few seconds we both freeze, and then my eyes seize upon a strange object hanging from the back of the bedroom door. Franz follows my gaze and smiles a big smile.

At first it looks like grass but, stepping closer, I realise that it's some kind of plaited tree fronds. The thin branches are knotted at one end and dangle loosely at the other; the whole thing looks like some kind of crude whip. When I turn back to Franz his eyes are all lit up. *Blimey*. I make a desperate dash for the whip but Franz, moving with lightning speed, blocks my way and snatches the thing from the door.

'You like whips?' he says, brandishing it playfully towards me as my heart beats loudly in my chest.

'Probably not.'

Franz stands between me and the door, holding the whip.

'But you would like to try?' he says, flicking his eyebrows suggestively. 'It doesn't hurt, it's for special ritual, for Pagans.'

'A Pagan *ritual*?'

'Ja,' he says, 'it is Czech national fertility rite!' At this he starts moving determinedly towards me, levelling the whip at my thighs.

The whip tickling against my skirt, I back quickly away. 'A national fertility festival?'

'Yes!' he says, tickling more persistently this time.

'But what's it *for*?' I say, stepping further backwards still.

'How you say in English? Easter?'

'Easter? You Czechs whip each other *for Easter*?'

'We make sure you not drying up,' he says, laughing a deep, dirty laugh, but my laugh goes dry in my throat when I come up against the wooden table. There's a short pause before Franz flicks his eyebrows at me once more and then comes lunging towards me, but before he can catch me I snatch the whip out of his hands, dropping the vodka bottle to the floor, and skip away from his groping arms. My back to the door, I brandish the whip in front of me. 'So do women have whips too?'

'No, women give sweets,' he says, smiling, advancing towards me, his hands outstretched for the whip.

A little unsteady on my feet, I inch backwards towards the door. Then without warning, Franz snatches the whip, pulls me to him, and, completely overpowering me, clasps me in a tight bear hug, tearing my top from my shoulder and exposing my breast. I kick and hit out with both hands, digging my elbows into his chest, biting him, but it's no good – he just smiles and licks his lips; he's too big, too strong, I'm completely enveloped. Just then, I hear a heavy footfall from the hallway outside.

'Help!' I call, kicking him and hitting him again.

'Shh,' Franz says, squeezing the air out of me by tightening his bear hug. 'Shh, my lovely little English, my mousy.' He leans in again and swallows my entire breast whole in his mouth like a giant fish.

At this I scream, '*Noooo!*'

The footfalls stop just outside the door but Franz's palm over my nose and mouth is too strong as his arms around me squeeze tighter. I can't seem to get enough air and I struggle for a while before – maybe the combination of vodka and absinthe is kicking in? – I pass out.

When I wake up, everything hurts. I'm not wearing any clothes and I'm not in Tomas's bed. I don't know where I am until I see the mouse cages over near the window ... What the fuck? As I hunt the room for my clothes – underpants near the door, skirt under the pillow – the only sound is the quiet whirring as one of the mice runs in its wheel. Dressed, I rub my aching head and, unable to leave without noticing the bed – the depression in the pillows where Franz's head must have lain, his clothes from last night folded neatly at the foot, the stains on the sheets – I cup my hand over the trickle between my legs and, grabbing a half empty foil of Panadol from Franz's bedside table, run out the door.

6

Tired, not thinking clearly, Panadol barely touching the pain, I hurry first to Tomas's room, empty, bed unmade, black lacy bra hanging on the bathroom door, then downstairs as quickly as I can, but no-one is around, just Bohumil. He's sitting outside in the courtyard on one of the rickety chairs wearing a black felt cowboy hat. Hands trembling, pouring myself a glass of white wine, I discover a note addressed to me. It says, *Háta called*, and then something in Czech I don't understand. I check my mobile in case Libuše has texted me – wasn't she going to give me a lift? – but there are no new texts. A text comes through from Hedley asking me how I went at the Rudolfinum. I can't reply, but I think about calling him back from Tomas's phone – maybe later?

Pocketing the note, I go outside and approach Bohumil. 'Mind if I sit down?'

He looks up from his newspaper and fixes me with his brilliant blue eyes. 'Please,' he says, and then turns straight back to his newspaper.

I open my mouth to speak but Bohumil shakes the newspaper loudly and I close it again. I stare out across the mess of the courtyard – a patchwork of rusty dirt, stones and straggling weeds – at the old stable with the collapsed roof where I spent last night. I've got to get out of here – meet Nelly. My headache intensifies across my brow … I interrupt his reading. 'Do you know where Libuše is?'

'Probably she's at pub with Tomas and others,' he says, not looking up.

'Do you know when they'll be back?'

'No.'

Bohumil turns the page, snapping the newspaper loudly into shape. I watch him read, unable to resist staring uselessly at the pages facing me, powerless to decode the unfamiliar Czech headlines and studying the pictures instead. The wine is going down too fast. I'm about to go inside for a refill when he puts the newspaper down on the table and looks at me and frowns.

'So, what's happening in the world?' I ask, too brightly.

'Always it is same,' he says, 'Always same depressing stories.'

'Really?' I say. Then, thinking of the first topic that pops into my head, I say, 'So how do you think it will be once the Czechs become part of the EU?'

Bohumil sighs deeply. 'The EU?' he says. 'Probably we will hate it. Possibly there will be some changes, but probably it makes little difference.'

I frown, try a different tack. 'So are you one of those elusive Czech Underground people I keep hearing about?'

He gives a short bark of a laugh. 'I was. Not anymore.'

My attempt at levity a failure, I try again. 'So what did it mean to be a member of The Czech Underground? Did you ever go to prison?'

'Yes.'

'What was *that* like?'

'Horrible.'

I wait, hoping he will elucidate, but he takes out a packet of cigarettes and lights up instead. It's clear he doesn't want to talk about it.

I sigh, look at the empty courtyard and driveway. 'So, this pub, is it within walking distance?'

'You would need car,' Bohumil says, making no effort to blow his cigarette smoke away.

I turn my head and gasp for air. 'I don't suppose you're going that way?'

'I don't have car,' he says, exuding more smoke.

'So, Czech,' I say, fingering the note in my pocket. 'How difficult is it to learn?'

Bohumil shrugs and sucks hard on his cigarette. 'Grammar is very difficult,' he warns, 'you probably don't want to learn.'

'What's so difficult about it?' I say. 'Can you give me an example?'

Having translated the note, which says, *Háta will call back later*, Bohumil is busy explaining the complications of Czech grammar, the six cases and four genders, all of which unbelievably decline, and teaching me the basics in Czech – 'yes', 'no', 'hello', 'goodbye', 'do you speak English?', 'I don't speak Czech' and 'thank you' – when Libuše's car pulls up with Tomas in the front seat, and Krasava in the back. There's no sign of Anna or – thank God – of Franz. When Tomas smiles hello I look studiously down and he continues on past us and enters the castle. Just then my phone beeps as a text from Nelly comes through: *Háta's expecting you for lunch on the 1pm Nýrsko train. Ask her where else your mother may have gone. Catch 4.30 train back to Prague to meet me by 6. N.* I thank Bohumil and hurry upstairs to pack.

'I don't know why I bother,' Tomas moans.

To escape the heat, Tomas, Bohumil, Betty and I have moved inside and are sitting at the laminex table in the kitchen drinking locally brewed beer from a recycled plastic Vitel bottle while Libuše packs and gets changed upstairs. I wish she'd bloody hurry up. I also wish it would hurry up and start raining. I'm tired and on the verge of tears and it's unbearably hot and I don't want to be drinking beer even when it's this good. Bohumil puffs at his cigarette.

'What do you mean?' Betty says.

'There's no point in even trying.'

'Trying what?'

'What I do,' Tomas says with a fierce sigh, 'my work. No-one's interested in Czech culture here, just a few Czechs who are artists themselves, but less and less people all the time. Everyone just wants more and more Hollywood.'

'Tourists are interested in Czech culture,' I protest.

'Yes but *Don Giovanni*!' he spits. 'They have two hours to fill between breakfast and their coach trip out to Karlštejn and all they want to do is have a quick look at the famous theatre, Stavovské divadlo, just so they can see for themselves what a beautiful old building it is and marvel that it was the place where Mozart's famous opera was first performed.'

'Have you ever tried to get tourists to see your plays?'

'No,' he says. 'My work is in Czech and they can't understand it. But even if they could, they wouldn't be interested in it because I write about Czechs and they're not interested in

Czechs. Czech culture is such a fragile thing, the first Republic only had ten years between the wars and another fifteen years since the Velvet Revolution – and let's face it, the last twelve years have been little more than cultural and economic rape and pillage as the global multinationals have bought up big on everything that was valuable.'

'What about writing in English?' Betty says, looking at Bohumil and me for support, but Bohumil has taken out his newspaper again and is reading it studiously.

'I can't.'

'Or having your work translated?'

'I can't afford it. It costs a fortune to have something professionally translated.'

'Really, it's that expensive?' Betty says, before adding, 'I guess it takes practise learning how to write in a foreign language, but I'm sure you'd get there in the end.'

'Well, I've tried and it just didn't feel right. English is so different, the grammar, it's a language of empire. Czech only became a national language in the late nineteenth century. Before that, educated and refined people spoke German, another language of empire, for centuries.'

'Tomas has never forgiven the English for reneging on the Munich Agreement,' Betty says, for my benefit.

'We were the tenth richest nation in the world with the most technologically advanced munitions factories,' Tomas claims, 'and the English and the French gave us to the Nazis – stupidity! We could have stopped them right here, at the border.'

'What's that?' says Peter, who's just come in.

'Oh, this country's gone to the dogs,' Tomas exclaims.

Peter opens his mouth to argue but Tomas is too quick for him. 'Everyone hoped things would be better after the Velvet Revolution, but all that's happened is now we can see what we can't have, although we still can't afford it, as opposed to before, when we couldn't see it *or* have it.'

'But you can travel now, the country is growing richer. It will take time for the wealth to filter down,' Betty counters.

'It didn't take much time for the people with money to buy everything we had. And for nothing – boy, did they get this country cheap! Since the end of the First World War this country has been bought and sold I don't know how many times and now the state's nearly bankrupt. It's all corrupt. Completely corrupt. And of course, all the old communist cronies are still around, running everything and tunnelling out state resources for themselves and their friends –'

'That's not entirely true,' Peter says, interrupting him. 'Things are improving.'

'And what about all the yuppies, the disgusting Czech yuppies?' Tomas rants. 'The Czechs sure are lapping up the corporate life! I went into Oskar last week – the mobile phone company,' he adds for my benefit, 'and there they all were in their bright red uniforms. Praha is completely overrun by Czech yuppies. Things are improving for some, for the young yuppies, and for people like you it's good here,' Tomas tells Peter. 'You're paid in foreign currency, you can afford to live well. But I still get paid in Czech crowns, and not well even then, and that's a different matter. And you can go on and on about tourism but the reality is that the money doesn't go back into the Czech economy to nurture things here, it stays in the hands of the tour operators, the rich multinationals. Between the corporate west and the Russian mafia, a tiny near-bankrupt country like the Czech Republic doesn't stand a chance.'

'But you've got to fight,' Betty tells him.

'And do what? Work for nothing?'

'You sound so bitter.'

'The thing is that capitalism has all but succeeded in doing what Hitler and forty years of the totalitarian regime failed to achieve almost overnight: the eradication of Czech culture!'

'So what's the answer?' Peter wants to know, but before Tomas can explain, Libuše arrives, suitcase in hand, and says, 'Shall we?'

I nod, glance over at Tomas, whose eyes drill into mine, and escape upstairs to collect my bags. Checking my mobile, there's a text from Hedley saying I missed a great show at the Loretta and that we should catch up for a drink.

7

It starts to rain as soon as Libuše pulls up outside the station. She kisses me goodbye and tells me, 'Let's catch up in Prague, OK?'

I tell her, 'OK,' and board the train but my thoughts are circling so obsessively I can't decide where to sit. In fact, I'm so hungover and upset I keep forgetting what I'm doing. I'm showered and dressed in clean clothes but my brain doesn't seem to be working properly. When I reach the end of the carriage for the second time, I force myself to concentrate and end up sitting in a window seat. Outside the rain continues steadily.

The train, I vaguely notice, is full of Czechs, mostly women with small children. Panicking – I was hoping there'd be some tourists on the train just in case I needed help – I ask the mother nearest to me, 'How long till the train reaches Nýrsko?'

But she just shrugs her shoulders in reply. I look around to see if anyone looks like they might speak English but they don't. Aside from the families, the only other people in the carriage are an old couple carrying two large baskets full of blackberries. I close my eyes, spend a minute or two forcing myself to decide what to do about Sarah and my show in New

York before concluding I'd let Nelly handle it, and then drift off. When I open my eyes again – my heart is beating wildly as an image of Franz's sheets flashes into my mind – the sign for Nýrsko outside comes as a kind of aftershock. I manage to exit the train in time but the tiny station is empty when I alight. I'm just heading off up the unpaved lane in what I guess to be the direction of the town when a small blue car approaches and pulls up by my side.

'Cathy?' the woman driving asks.

Smiling in spite of myself, I climb inside.

Dressed in a plastic coat and a wide hat, the rain coming down heavily all around her, Háta plucks cucumbers and tomatoes from her garden while I wait patiently beneath the big umbrella on the wooden deck. Harvesting complete, Háta disappears inside her small cottage and reappears, minus the rain gear, carrying a plate of freshly baked apple strudel. 'Please,' she says, holding the plate out.

I take a piece and bite into its delicious warmth. Háta waits for me to finish and then takes the plate back to the kitchen. When Háta next appears, she carries two shots of Becherovka in small crystal shot glasses. Not exactly the champagne or vodka I'm looking for but better than nothing. While she doesn't speak any English, we somehow seem to understand each other so far.

'London,' Háta says as I swallow the Becherovka in one gulp. '*Anglicky.*'

I nod and say, 'Yo,' and Háta smiles her missing-toothed smile. I smile back and take a second piece of strudel and study Háta's loose floral dress which she wears with a blue, green and yellow headscarf and grey-white socks with slippers. She's a large lady and when she laughs her whole body shakes. I'm just wondering what to say about my mother when Háta's son, Antonin, arrives with his American friend Mark. Hopefully one of them will be able to translate when I ask Háta about my mother.

'I'm Háta's cousin,' I tell them, 'visiting from London.'

'Yeah, Háta's been telling us all about you, the English girl,' Mark says, his hand warm shaking mine.

We enter Háta's cottage. Spotlessly clean, the main room serves as both kitchen and lounge room and is completely filled by a nest of tables and chairs, and two old sofas covered with pieces of white lace.

Háta pours us all shots of Becherovka and we toast. '*Na zdraví!*'

I hold my too small glass out for an instant refill and, swallowing that down, say, 'So, Mark – would you mind asking Háta for me, has she spoken with my mother lately?'

Mark repeats the question in a slow Czech full of halts and pauses and Háta answers in rapid singsong. Then Mark turns to me. 'No, she hasn't spoken to Odette since last year.'

I nod, damn. 'She was in Prague a couple of days ago, at least I think she was, but now I don't know where she is. Do you have any idea where she might go?'

Háta shrugs sadly after Mark translates, and we down a further round of Becherovka. Then Háta asks a question in Czech which Mark translates for me. 'How's Odette?'

I shake my head. 'She has cancer, she's very sick.'

When Háta understands, she frowns. Then she moves her chair closer to mine and takes my hand, speaking in rapid

Czech. 'It was so sad,' Mark translates. 'Your mother had such a difficult life. Like many people, she didn't like to talk about it, but I thought you might like to know some of the family history. Your great-grandfather, Václav, was part of the Czech resistance during the German occupation. He passed on information about the progress of the war he obtained by listening to illegal BBC news bulletins to other members of the resistance. In 1939 he was caught by the Nazis and spent the war in Auschwitz. Then after the war – he survived Auschwitz – the Russian communists took over the country and your great-grandfather was rewarded as an anti-fascist and given a castle near the German border. But when your grandfather, Karel, protested the communist regime and its illegal elections in 1948, the communists punished the family by taking the castle back and Karel was sent to prison. When he came out he was unable to resume his studies and later, when your mother was born, she was unable to dance professionally. We were all blacklisted at school.'

I nod. While I know some of this already, I didn't know about the castle or that it was the communists who stopped my mother dancing.

'You might be able to make a restitution claim for the castle in Germany,' Mark adds. 'I could help you, if you like.'

Háta falls silent and Antonin offers her some more Becherovka but she shakes her head. '*Ne, ne.*'

I hold out my empty glass. 'I'll look into it when I get back to London. Right now, I just need to find my mother.'

Háta shrugs and raises her eyebrows, and Antonin shakes his head. But when Háta turns on the stove and begins arranging the pans, Antonin and Háta start arguing vigorously in Czech.

Mark protests, 'Please, Háta, don't go to any trouble on our account. It's too early to eat.' Háta, however, is unswayed and produces roast pork, dumplings and tomato and cucumber salad, which is incredibly delicious, though the bottle of Becherovka is empty much too soon.

8

The train to Praha pulls into Plzeň just before five. My heart beating hard, I can't keep the image of the stained sheets out of my mind, and the next thing I'm thinking about buying a bottle of vodka. I alight from the train but all I can find is a small bottle of Becherovka at a *tabak* on the platform. The rain noisy on the station roof, I buy two and reboard the train.

Soon the hard, grey concrete and puffing smokestacks of the industrial town disappear outside the grubby windows as we speed past, leaving no trace. The sky is dark with the rain. A swollen river, I don't know which one, not the Vltava, stalls under a modern bridge which is empty of traffic. I wonder where my mother is and hope she's all right. Somehow I must remain seated on this train for an hour and a half, which feels like an impossible feat in my current state. I'm feeling very Beethoven's 'Pathétique' – all sad, lonely and lost. I open the Becherovka and swig it greedily down. I want the pain to stop. Thoughts like *This is fucked, completely fucked* circle obsessively. Taking deep breaths, I notice someone else has entered my booth, a young executive. He takes his shoes off and opens a thick business report. I remove my coat and hang it on the hook behind me.

Outside, dark forests flash past the dirty windows – the teeming rain, sudden fields of dead-looking grass, the slow, winding, overflowing river. A farmhouse and a barn, their roofs shaped like upturned *V*s. Inside the carriage, my heart is all fast triplets rollicking, up and down in waves of brilliant but terrible scales. The Becherovka has me pulling faces as I drain the small bottle.

Oh screw this. You're such a sorry drunk.

The female conductor is talking angrily in Czech. I tuck the Becherovka inside my handbag and wipe my tears on the back of my hand.

'*Nevím Český,*' I explain in my pigeon Czech. '*Anglicky?*'

The conductor is shaking her head and focusing hard.

I hand her my ticket, not understanding. 'Praha?' I ask.

The conductor hands me my ticket, pointing at it and talking angrily. Then she gestures to the young man, and leaves.

After she's gone I turn to my companion and hold out my ticket for him to look. 'I don't understand,' I say.

He takes my ticket, and, smiling, speaking slowly and carefully, he explains. 'This seat, here, first class. Ticket, second class.'

'Oh,' I say, 'but I asked for first class – there must be some mistake.'

But he shrugs and repeats, 'Ticket second class.'

'Thank you,' I tell him and gather up my bags.

From my second-class window I spy the dark snaking girth of the Vltava, swollen with the heavy rain, the water threatening to burst its banks. Soon after, the train stops in a tunnel just out of Praha hlavní nádraží. I jump up, impatient to get off. Standing beside me is a woman, both of us close to the door. Cradling a bunch of roses, she looks quite old and wears a scarf tied around her head. She starts talking to me in Czech and her wrinkled, kind face looks at me intently, waiting for me to reply.

'*Anglicky,*' I tell her. '*Český nevím.*'

She nods, and keeps talking for a while. Then she hands me the roses and says, 'Please.'

But just a few minutes later, alighting from the carriage into the dark, dome-ceilinged station, *I can't cope* becomes a mantra. With the remains of the Becherovka I push the thoughts away.

It's six-thirty and I'm late to meet Nelly and I hope she's waiting for me at the hotel. I climb into a cab and tell the driver, 'Grand Hotel Evropa,' as an image of Tomas and Anna dancing together at the castle forces its way into my thoughts, followed by an image of my underpants on the floor of Franz's room, and a wave of nausea fixes me in its grip. Wondering whether I'm right or not about Reed and Sarah, I punch out a text to Reed, forgetting I still don't have any credit on my phone. Hopefully Nelly will know how to find my mother. I've missed Sarah's deadline for London but hopefully I'll still be able to make New York. It's only then I reach inside my bag for Mouse and I realise I have no idea where she is.

THE PRAGUE FLOOD

1

I'm pushing open the heavy circular door to the Grand Hotel Evropa when Nelly's text comes through. *Where are you? Am waiting up in room. Love N.* I stand for a few moments in the foyer staring at the empty porter's station, then check for messages at reception – hoping there's something from my mother. Finding no message, I empty the bottle of vodka I bought as soon as I arrived in Prague, and, leaving my suitcase with the porter who has just returned, hide the empty bottle behind a potted palm, grab my handbag and guitar, and start dragging myself upstairs. No sooner have I reached the first landing, though, than I'm forced to stop. Sweating profusely – is it hot in here or is it just me? – I'm unable to keep the cabinet full of cut glass in front of me from spinning out of control. I reach out for the banister but –

Christ! – Nelly is towering over me, shaking me and then – aaarrgghh! – pouring a glass of water over my face. At first I want to slap her – *What the hell?!* – but her look of concern just melts me inside and then I feel more like crying.

Nelly sits down on the side of the bed and takes my hand. 'Cathy,' she says in her serious voice, 'this is an intervention.

Do you know what that means?'

'A what? An inter-what?'

'Your drinking has spiralled out of control,' Nelly explains, squeezing my hand. 'I'm here to help you get things back on track.'

'No, Nelly – I'm OK, I just … On the train – I guess I missed a couple of meals, or something …'

Nelly looks at me but says nothing.

I struggle to sit up, to focus. 'So, what – you think I'm – what?' I try to stare Nelly down but her warm eyes won't look away and it's me who caves. Damn.

'Cathy, I'm concerned about your show in New York – I don't think you really want to ruin your career.' Nelly's voice is quiet, steady. 'You've worked so hard. Now, we need to get you through New York and then we need to find your mother.' She pauses, pours me a glass of mineral water. 'And to do that, you need to forget about that guy, whoever he is, because at this point, he's only going to drag you down …'

'No,' I sit up, ignoring the water. 'I left him already.'

Nelly raises her eyebrows.

'I did – and I texted Reed, like you said.'

Nelly shakes her head. 'No men for now. Forget Reed, forget about this new guy and concentrate on your music.'

'Forget about men – what? This is my marriage we're talking about!' I start to climb out of bed, fall back down.

'Where are you going?'

'This is bullshit – no men?' I stumble, struggle into my clothes.

Nelly watches me but when I make a grab for my handbag – I was sure I had another mini bottle of vodka in here somewhere – she stands up. 'Come on,' she says, holding out her hand. 'Let's go get you something to eat and talk this thing through.'

Somehow, miraculously, the reasonableness of Nelly's suggestion moves me, the logic of what she's saying sinks in, and I agree, following her downstairs and out onto the rainy square: Nelly has helped me before.

'What's the fucking point?' I say, over a huge plate of Vienna schnitzel, chips and coleslaw – I can't eat all of this – 'If I find a nice guy – like you helped me to when I left bastard Daniel and got together with Reed, the nice guy's going to leave me anyway and go off with someone else because I can't stop drinking. Other than Reed they've all been like Tomas, so what's the point of leaving Tomas if I'm going to go straight out and find someone else just like him? The thing is,' I continue, managing to get a few mouthfuls down without choking – this schnitzel is actually pretty good – 'I sleep with a guy a couple of times and if I like the sex then that's it, I'm hooked, and I can't leave him, especially if he's a bit of a player, you know, if there're other people hanging around. That seems to be when I get really stuck.'

'But the fact that you met Reed and married him shows that there are other kinds of guys,' Nelly says, sipping from her mineral water. 'They're not all like Tomas and Daniel. If you really try, you can find someone who's different, right? But also, I would have thought you'd be better off single than being with someone like Tomas. I mean, Sarah was quite explicit: she said if you mess up New York you're through. She'll never be able to book you another show again. She managed to cover up the Copenhagen thing by saying you had food poisoning – remember? – but she won't be able to do that again. You've got one more chance, Cathy. This is it.'

'You're not listening to me,' I say, only halfway through the schnitzel and already full. 'There's nothing in the tank. I can't see the point of doing anything. Reed was the exception, Tomas is the norm.'

'In your experience –'

'Well, what other experience is there?' I say, pushing my plate away, badly needing a drink to wash it all down. 'What are my options? That seems to be who I am, these are the sorts of guys I meet. Other people meet different kinds of guys, but I just meet guys like this. After all this time, even after working with you, it's fucking happened again. It's the same old shit.'

'It's true,' Nelly says, 'you've gone out with a lot of what I would call narcissistic personality types – we talked about this, remember, you're playing out your mother stuff with them because it's familiar. Your mother's a narcissist, right? It's the compulsion to repeat, part of your post-traumatic stress disorder.'

'Well, now that I've been cheated on by yet another fucking narcissist, if that's what Tomas is, all I want to do is kill myself.' I snatch up my handbag ready to leave.

'You plan to drink yourself to death?'

'Just for once I want the fucking narcissist to bloody change – I want Tomas to stop being a narcissist.'

Nelly shakes her head.

'Never going to happen, right? It doesn't matter what you say – you and I both know that as soon as I can get away from you I'll be straight out drinking again, and once I'm drunk all

I'll want to do is fuck some loser bastard. Meditation can't fix it, listening to you can't fix it, nothing can once I get like this. It's happened again – I'm fucked! No matter what I do, I can't seem to protect myself from these guys –'

'That's your Stockholm syndrome thing.'

'Fuck my Stockholm syndrome thing,' I snap. This whole conversation is stressing me out and I'm so desperate for alcohol that I'm actually sculling the mineral water.

'But you stopped before, didn't you? You left Daniel and you married Reed and you cut down your drinking, right? And yes, you slipped a few times – you messed up pretty badly in Copenhagen, actually – but overall you've been pretty steady now for, how long, one or two years?'

'But I had Reed's arms to run to. Now all I can see is an endless string of Tomases, just like the bad old good old days when I was still drinking all the time.'

'So what do you want to do, Cathy?' Nelly says and pauses. 'Do you really want to throw away your career because things started to get a little rough?' she continues in her quiet voice. 'Your husband demanded you go to rehab – but you and I both know he has a point, right? – and you slept with the wrong guy. Do you really want to throw your life away because of some dickhead?'

'You know, Nelly,' I say – Nelly's picking at my chips and watching her I start to eat them too – 'it's not even the guy thing: it's Deutsche Grammophon, it's the Rudolfinum, it's my mother –'

'But I'm here to help with your mother –'

'– It's Sarah and Reed – and – God, I lost Mouse, just completely forgot about her, left her somewhere at the castle …'

'Mouse? Well, let's call up and find her, OK?'

'You've got to help me, help me with Mouse. Whatever I do to myself, I just can't abide cruelty to animals …'

'Don't worry, consider it sorted.'

'Can't you see? I'm just broken.'

'Sometimes life does that to a person –'

'And there's something else – something else happened at the castle …'

'Something else – like what?'

But here my mind jams, stalls, shuts down.

'Cathy?'

After a few beats I look up and then suddenly I'm talking again. 'I'm not even sure how it happened – all I know is that life has done it to me. Maybe I'm weak, immature – you once told me I was spoiled, maybe you were right? It's just, I am what I am – nothing. I just can't … I don't …' Unable to stop the tears – why do I always fucking crack at this point? – I just let them stream silently down my face. After a while, Nelly hands me a tissue and I wipe them roughly away.

'If you keep telling yourself that, you'll talk yourself into believing it.'

To this pearl of wisdom I have nothing to add, and for once my mind is just completely blank.

After a while Nelly asks, 'So what's the solution, Cathy? You ready to try again?'

I shrug. Nelly's been right before. 'Just tell me what to do and I'll try to do it. No promises,' I say, snatching another handful of chips. 'You know what I'm like.'

'OK.'

'OK.' I loosen my grip on my bag.

'Well, first things first: a walk, some fresh air, and a decent night's sleep. Maybe a bath. How does that sound?'

'Fucking awful. Horrible.'

'OK. I'll get the cheque.'

And while Nelly's chasing up the waiter, the thought *A shot of vodka would fix this* hits me with a force that's almost tidal. Just then Nelly glances over, catching the look on my face. She's been good for me, I remind myself, helped me in the past ...

There'll be a ball later this evening and we're all dressed in formal attire, the men in black tie, the women in long gowns. The drawing room is decorated throughout in pink and green, everything's incredibly luxurious if slightly worn. Approximately fifty people are gathered around the piano, waiting for the 'impromptu' concert to begin. Giving me a nod to get ready, George, my student from the Royal Academy and the youngest son of Lord Bradford, noisily clears his throat. It was George's idea for me to come tonight.

Standing at the back of the room, I glance nervously about. The drive down from London was long and wet, the room Lady Bradford has placed me in has no fire and I found it impossible to nap. I hold my hands out in front of me and watch them tremble, then look up quickly and catch the eye of George's handsome older brother, William, who's standing close by.

'Ever tried this?' he says, sneaking me his pewter flask which is full, I discover, of fine brandy. 'Always works for me.'

I take a few swigs, hopeful no-one will notice me scoffing grog here at the back of the room, and hold my hands out again. Steady as. I look up at William, who winks slowly and says, 'Break a leg.'

'Ladies and gentlemen,' George is saying, 'It is my great pleasure

to present the dazzling Catherine Bell, the toast of London, and the most exciting new performer of her generation according to this weekend's edition of The Times.'

Suddenly all eyes turn with George's and I freeze. But a gentle nudge from William brings me round and I'm soon picking my way across the crowded room towards the piano on automatic pilot. Christ! I remind myself that being nervous is a good sign because it means I'll be more alert and will probably give a better performance as a result and that the time to worry is when I'm not nervous ... Right.

Seated at the piano, I'm just about to begin when I make the great mistake of looking up – which I never ordinarily do – but something about this woman's gaze snags my attention. Thankfully, the unplanned deviation from my routine sends a wave of absolute terror sweeping through me, a feeling which is only exacerbated when I catch William's flirty look and smile, and I'm soon bullying myself back to the keyboard where I wrestle myself to the beginning: Chopin!

Anxiety overruled by discipline, I hold on tight as the enmeshed left and right hands go cascading up and down the keys at a frantic pace. Each note must be struck absolutely cleanly, precisely. Hitting the key harder does not give the playing more force, and I remind myself of this now as I have a tendency to hit hard when I'm nervous. There, I have it! As the 'Fantasie' reaches its climax, I realise I've nailed it. Now, easy does it, tiptoe right through the ending, and then out the other side!

I've barely stopped – am still seated, in fact, and panting slightly – when the applause crashes in on me, so loud it dwarfs the surrounding grandeur, making the generously proportioned Georgian room seem small. I haul myself upwards, giddy with *relief, pleased but already making mental adjustments for next time. Suddenly George is kissing me 'Bravo' on each cheek, so public a declaration, I'm completely taken aback – this shy, quiet man is full of surprises…*

Later, George has just introduced me to the program director of Carnegie Hall, who has invited me to New York to play – wow! – when he turns to the woman with the intense gaze. 'Nelly is a very dear family friend.'

But no sooner are the words are out of his mouth than he's snatched away, leaving Nelly and me smiling at each other. Noticing there's something lovely about her eyes, I let myself relax. The ball will start in just a few minutes.

'So have you always played piano?' she wants to know, speaking in a European accent I find difficult to place.

It's not the usual question and I have to think about it; 'How long have you been playing?' is more common. 'No,' I say. A tight smile.

'I used to be a doctor,' she says, her teeth lovely and white, her skin tanned. 'I'd always wanted to be a doctor, even as a child. But after a while I became bored – I realised I'd changed.'

'What do you do now?'

'I'm sort of a life coach, though some people call me a guru. Bit embarrassing, really.'

'A guru? How interesting.'

Later, the ball over, the serious drinkers head for the sofas in front of the fire. Excusing herself, Nelly hands me her card. 'This man you're with,' she whispers, leaning in close, 'he's no good for you. No good at all.'

While I'm trying to puzzle out how she knows about my private life, the man sitting on my other side, tall, thin but with lovely soft hazel eyes, looks around and asks, 'So who's your favourite composer — not to play, but to listen to?'

'That's easy,' I tell him, without needing to think about it. 'Mahler.'

'How funny,' he says, 'he's mine too.' He introduces himself as Reed, and hands me a plate of chocolate truffles. 'You gave a wonderful performance tonight, by the way,' he continues.

'Thank you. It felt quite good, once I got started, though I was a little wobbly at first.'

'You hid it well,' he says. We smile.

'You know, just last week I was talking to a woman who was writing a book about Jane Stirling, one of Chopin's greatest admirers, as well as being his patron. She died of an ovarian cyst but I always suspected that it might have been unrequited love that killed her. What do you think about that? Is it possible to die of unrequited love?'

I later replay the conversation, awake and unable to sleep in my room, wondering why he wanted to know. Then, unable to decide who I like more, William, George or Reed, I reach for that guru's card. Our conversation felt unfinished somehow and I realise I want it to continue.

One week later and, having been arrested during a blackout — a policeman had enquired what I was doing crawling around on my hands and knees between parked cars at 2.15 a.m. on a Saturday night and my answer began with the f-word — I decide to call George and ask him for Nelly's number. I've lost her card, of course. The arrest was impossible to keep out of the gossip magazines, and I'm starting to feel it might be time I sought professional help.

George picks up after two rings, and after congratulating me on my performance again, says of Nelly: 'She's supposed to be an absolute whiz at that sort of thing. Changes your life and all that.'

'And her accent?'

'From Sarajevo,' George informs me. 'Some kind of refugee. Has a small daughter and a very powerful mentor, one of the top psychotherapists in the game, apparently. In the middle of some complicated residency application …'

'I see.'

I call Nelly the next day and am surprised when, a few days later, my first session takes place at a private residence in Earl's Court. Nelly, first hugging her daughter and then ushering her into her bedroom, invites me into the master bedroom. She indicates that I should sit in a fold-up chair in the corner and then climbs up onto the bed.

But any misgivings about Nelly's unorthodox methods or training – she's an expert in a number of alternative methods – are soon dispelled. She lets me whine on about the Hello article, my failing career and my disastrous relationship with Daniel for about ten minutes before interrupting.

'I'm a little bit psychic,' she says, 'but I get the idea that this Daniel, he's no good for you. I can't see him in your future. You need a man who will support you, who believes in you and what you do – not someone who is always working against you, who abuses you.'

'How did you know,' I say, 'about the abuse?' I'd said nothing about it.

'I just sensed it,' she says, and shrugs. 'In fact, tell me if I'm wrong – he's actually a bit of a monster, right?'

I nod. This really is quite odd.

'But I see another man around you,' she continues, 'a good

man, a kind man. You think Daniel's the only guy for you right now, but you're wrong. You're surrounded by men, some good, some bad. You just don't see them.'

While there's no way George could have told her any of this – George just doesn't know – what she says rings true. From that moment on I decide to, tentatively, put my life in Nelly's hands.

I listen: not a sound. I'm stretched out in the bath with one of the worst headaches I've ever had and Nelly – who managed to get hold of Libuše, who said Mouse is safely housed in one of Franz's aquariums (!?) – is out trying to find me some Panadol. There's no alcohol at all left in the suite; I've promised Nelly I wouldn't have any anyway, but my mind can't help thinking about the cafe downstairs and how I probably have just enough time to down a couple of neat vodkas before Nelly comes back.

Fuck, that sounds good.

Just then my phone beeps as a text comes through: Libuše, inviting me out to supper and to see some more of the sites of Prague. There's a moment's hesitation while I'm struggling into my shoes when I think about New York – stupid bloody … why won't they go on! – but then I'm over it and just stomp my way into my shoes. A couple of vodkas will just take the edge off, then after New York I can go cold turkey and start again. I just need to wean myself off slowly, there's no point in putting myself through any unnecessary stress in the build-up to New York, and if this agony – Franz! – can possibly be avoided then it makes sense to –

As I turn from the door to check whether I've left anything behind, my eyes snag on the roses, propped against the wall and standing up in a too-small glass. The perfect buds have just started to open, releasing a heavy, old-fashioned scent. I slam the door, not bothering to lock it.

The cafe is pretty deserted at this time; it looks like it's about to close. I approach the bar to be told there's only table service, little prick, and then I'm sitting down at a table away from the windows in case Nelly happens to look in, thinking, *Hurry up, hurry the fuck up,* when I realise I haven't got any cash and they don't accept cards. None here in my handbag and none up in the room; Nelly made sure of that. I'll just have to sign the booze to our tab but then Nelly will know … But that won't be until tomorrow and by then it won't matter – because we'll be on our way to New York and –

Rescuing my suitcase from the cranky porter, I buy a ticket at a *tabak* with some loose coins and jump on the number 7 tram to Žižkov. While it's true that Nelly's been an absolute rock for such a long time, it's starting to feel like her advice is a little counterproductive, not to mention downright restrictive. What I need is to go out with a few friends and relax and forget about things for a while. Have a couple of glasses of wine and …

Ducking out of the interminable bloody rain, I find an internet cafe that takes credit cards just off Náměstí Jeřího z Poděbrad and decide to down a couple of drinks while I check my emails, but a link sent in a message titled 'FYI' from an old schoolfriend soon has me so angry that I'm actually physically hitting the computer with my fingers: bastards! First I thump out an email to Reed, copying it to Sarah, then I start thumping a second email to Sarah. Finally, I click back to the 'FYI' article in the *Daily Mail* wherein Sarah publicly declares her relationship with Reed, no doubt as a promotion for some new performer she's launching. The article quotes Reed blaming my drinking problems for the demise of our marriage.

I've just topped up my account, so I try Sarah's mobile but my battery needs charging and the call cuts out mid-ring. Then, when I reach for my vodka to calm down, I end up spilling it. Accidentally knocking the chair over backwards as I stand up too fast, I sign the receipt without looking. Guzzling the rest of the vodka — I need a phone desperately — I rush out, only remembering my handbag when I reach the first corner of the square. I start to go back for it, change my mind, and then run towards Tomas's and his phone. I get halfway there before I turn around and go back for my handbag. Thankfully it's still there on the back of the upturned chair where I left it. I grab it, right the chair and run back to Tomas's flat. I'm so angry about the *Daily Mail* article that homicide seems reasonable. I've got to get back to London as soon as possible.

Tomas's spare key is blue-tacked to the inside of the lid of his petrol tank (he'd said something about having one hidden in an obvious place when I first came here). It's a difficult fit and I struggle for a while with the ugly security door. The key looks new and the cut obviously isn't that good, but finally the lock gives way.

Inside, Tomas's flat looks dingier than I remember it, and when I enter, a cloud of Tomas obsession descends, threatening to take over. Pushing all thoughts of Tomas from my mind, I go into the kitchen to make myself a drink and plug my phone and charger into the wall. It's a makeshift kitchen, although surprisingly clean, consisting of a sink, a fridge, a cupboard, bookshelves and a small rectangular table with an electric stove on top. I find a bottle of scotch and pour myself a glass. I haul my bag into the bedroom and lie down on the bed, trying not to smell the sheets. I'm so exhausted the scotch actually sends me to sleep. When I jolt awake just a few minutes later, I gaze out the window onto the street below. While the rain has eased somewhat, it's still coming down in even sheets. Protruding above the apartments across the road is the Prague Television Tower. The giant brass babies climbing up its white trunk seem hideous or funny, I can't decide.

OK. Time to make a move. Retrieving my phone from the kitchen, I see there's a text from Hedley, inviting me to lunch – hmm, Hedley is actually quite good-looking, from memory, if a little overweight – and a missed call from Nelly. I consider Hedley's text: maybe I should meet him for lunch tomorrow before my flight. Maybe a little fling with a groupie is just what the doctor ordered?

What's the time? Nine-thirty. A bit late but worth a try. I call my travel agent – who tells me that it will cost £350 to fly back to London tomorrow! My professional relationship with Sarah is now an absolute priority – and then reschedule my itinerary so that I can continue on to New York straight from London for my performance at the Lincoln Center, which I'm now determined to do.

First things first. I change into an ecru T-shirt, a matching silk sarong and orange mules, and throw on my good old faithful Burberry raincoat. Disliking this outfit, I decide to go shopping first thing tomorrow. I'm just about to try Sarah again when my mobile rings and it's Libuše.

'Cathy, hi,' Libuše says. 'I just wanted to check that you're OK.'

'Yes, fine. Where are you?'

'Well, we're just heading out now,' Libuše continues over the background noise of voices and laughter. 'Why don't you come and see some more of wonderful Prague tonight? We'll be in Žižkov. I can text you the address.'

'Great, thanks.'

'By the way, it looks like the rain is going to continue. Prague is turning into a bit of a zoo with the flood coming.'

A flood? Great, that's all I need. 'Thanks, Libuše,' I croak. 'If I get lost I'll call you.'

When I get Sarah's voicemail again I leave a message to call me urgently, call Reed without leaving a message, pick up my mobile, ignore the missed call and two texts from Nelly and rush out the door.

2

I text Hedley the address of the restaurant and head straight to the women's toilets. I wash and dry my face, add some red lipstick, fluff my hair and smile at myself in the mirror. That's more like it.

I join the table of people I don't know and quickly down a glass of white wine, unable to decide where to sit. Libuše sits in the middle and pats the seat beside her for me to sit down. Across from me sit two Englishmen, friends of the Czech Canadian woman on the other side of Libuše who is visiting from London. On my other side is Bret, Libuše's American boyfriend. The rest of the people are Czech except for an Australian woman right down the far end of the table whose name I instantly forget.

Libuše is talking loudly in Czech. 'She's been talking about the apartment all night,' Bret explains for my benefit.

It seems Bret is moving to Prague from New York next month and they need to come to some kind of decision about Libuše's flat. The question is: should Bret move in to Libuše's tiny rent-controlled studio, or should they look for a bigger rent-controlled apartment? Then again, perhaps they should try to find a friendly bank manager who will lend them money on the strength of Bret's freelance journalism and buy somewhere out in the suburbs?

'Have you been following the news about the flood?' Bret wants to know.

I shrug. 'Not exactly.'

'People are leaving the city in droves, whole suburbs are being evacuated.'

I nod, I guzzle a second glass of wine and pick at the finger food – vine leaves, hummus and flatbread. I check my mobile. Still no reply from Sarah or Reed.

Hedley, who has just arrived and who has actually lost quite a bit of weight since I last saw him – not bad – asks, 'How are you liking Prague so far?' He pulls up two chairs and introduces me to his friend, another musician, I don't quite catch his name. 'Are you here long?' Hedley adds.

'I'm not quite sure,' I say, as our hands brush reaching for the wine. Smiling, flirty, I pull my hand away and let Hedley do the honours. 'Prague's been a bit of a mixed bag, actually.'

'You must allow me to introduce you to the gang before you leave,' Hedley says, refilling my glass. 'Expats, local talent – the most brilliant people.'

Meanwhile, the young Australian woman is telling a story about a shark and the table collectively grows silent. We all turn to listen.

'There was this guy,' she says in her nasal drawl, 'and he'd been out drinking with his mates one night, they were all at this bar right on the water somewhere just out of Perth. Anyway, he ended up swimming out to a buoy on a bit of a dare, but when he got out of the water his mates were like, "Jesus bloody wept." He looked down and there was all this blood gushing from a huge shark bite in his thigh.'

The Czechs gasp and talk loudly among themselves. Hedley and I exchange smiles.

'The guy was so drunk he didn't feel a thing!' she continues. 'The shark obviously hadn't thought he was very good to eat, maybe put off by all the alcohol – anyway, it had clearly just stopped to take a bite of him and then swum off. In the meantime the guy lost one of his balls and the rest of him was in pretty bad shape too.'

The table completely erupts at this: Czechs verifying the details, general laughter and Hedley's friend saying loudly, 'Sounds like a bit of a tall story, if you ask me,' and winking at me.

'No, no,' the Australian says, overhearing. 'I'm from Australia. This sort of thing happens all the time.'

'It was shark?' a Czech woman says, finally cottoning on.

Just then Tomas arrives, not looking me in the eye and kissing Libuše warmly on both cheeks. 'What shark?' he says, his eyes locking on to mine.

I'm a little drunk and Tomas is flirting with the Australian. Given there's still no word from Sarah – or from Reed! – I've decided not to care about anything and to concentrate on my drinking instead. Meanwhile Hedley entertains me with a story about a shooting party he attended recently back in Shropshire that got a little out of hand.

After dinner we walk to a nearby nightclub, The Black Cat disco, situated in a narrow cobblestoned lane. The entrance to the club is subterranean to the street and the windows are painted black with white cat shapes left clear in the glass. Great

— a nightclub should serve real alcohol; there was only wine at the restaurant.

We stand in the heavy rain trying to decide whether to go in or not. One half of the group wants to go to a pub and drink, but the other half, led by the Australian, wants to go dancing. The entrance fee is forty crowns which is less than a pound and cheap from my point of view but expensive for the Czechs. While I don't really feel like dancing, the promise of vodka is irresistible. I side with the nightclub group. Tomas is noncommittal.

'This is ridiculous,' I say. 'It's raining cats and dogs out here.'

Hedley jokes, 'Black cats?' and meanwhile the men who lead the pub contingent all speak rapidly in Czech.

'Well, I'm going in,' the Australian says. 'Send me a text if you go to a pub and I'll come and find you when I've had my dance.' With that she disappears into the club, followed by Libuše and the Canadian woman. Hedley and I soon join them.

Inside is an L-shaped bar which surrounds a split-level dance floor featuring two shiny poles where a few young women dance alone while men watch from the bar and slurp glass mugs of beer. We find a quiet table and make a pile out of our coats and bags. Hedley goes to the bar for drinks and the Australian and the Canadian hit the dance floor.

'You didn't say Tomas would be at the restaurant,' I whisper into Libuše's ear, looking over at Hedley, who's looking back at me and smiling.

'I didn't know,' Libuše says. 'Are you OK?'

I turn to look at her and shrug.

'Let me know if there's anything I can do.'

Just then Hedley returns with our drinks and Libuše joins the others. We toast, clink glasses. Watching the dancers, Hedley says, 'Shall we?' and I nod, OK, even though the music is techno and I'm not drunk enough not to care.

'This is a terrible song,' Hedley says, moving around half-heartedly.

I nod, and suck hard at my vodka. Musicians usually make rather odd dancers but Hedley moves quite well and I find myself admiring his swivelling hips and long legs. Eventually we abandon the idea of dancing, the music really is too awful, and Hedley goes to buy another round of drinks. I rejoin our group, which now includes Tomas and the Czech pub contingent and is spread out over three or four tables in the next room. Tomas smiles at me when I sit down but I look away.

Hedley has just arrived with fresh drinks and Libuše is resuming her deliberations about the apartment when the Australian suddenly appears and says, 'I can't believe it – I just had a free lesson in pole dancing!'

The entire table turns to stare and then erupts into raucous laughter.

'I read about pole dancing in last month's *Tatler*,' Hedley says, his lips brushing against my ear. 'It's all the rage in London, apparently. People are giving up Pilates and yoga and learning how to pole dance instead. Apparently it's the best work-out for your abdominals money can buy.'

'I asked this woman to dance,' the Australian continues breathlessly, but she's soon interrupted by Hedley's friend, who appears beside her, his T-shirt drenched with sweat. 'It was amazing,' he pants. 'You had all our hearts beating.'

'She was probably a professional,' Bret says. 'You know, they have lap-dancing rooms out the back.'

'Really?' Hedley says, blushing.

'They had every guy in the place watching them!' Hedley's friend says. 'It was so great.'

'I might go and ask her if she'll come to London,' the Australian continues. 'I'm having a birthday party there later this month and I'd love her to come and dance with me.'

'If her name was Samantha,' Hedley's friend mutters, 'I would take her home with me.'

'Let's go and dance with her again,' the Australian says, and she and Hedley's friend disappear back onto the dance floor.

Hedley is touching my arm and leaning in to whisper in my ear when I glance around the table: Tomas has gone. I empty my drink, tell Hedley I'll get the next round, and head for the bar, where I discover Tomas and Anna deep in conversation. Anna is wearing a strawberry blonde wig and not much else. My stomach clenches but I just nod hello and head over to the toilets instead, where I give myself a stern talking to in the mirror.

Somehow Anna sneaks us all in to the VIP section of the club, where we mill awkwardly around a sunken bar with brown suede couches. I don't know where to look and Hedley, completely embarrassed, has disappeared. Beside me is a tall brunette wearing black lace suspenders, stockings and a matching bra and G-string. I watch as she starts caressing Tomas, who's standing on my other side.

'Maybe you'll come and dance for me and my girlfriend?' Tomas tells the girl and smiles at me. What – girlfriend? He's got some nerve ... But when Tomas moves closer and puts his arm around my waist I shudder at the electricity. The lap dancer backs off and then leaves. I give Tomas a look and he raises his eyebrows and taking me by the arm he leads me to a small table in front of the darkened stage. He sits and waits for me to sit down.

'Are you OK?' he begins, gulping at his white wine. 'You left so suddenly, I –'

I shake my head. This is ridiculous. Mustering my patience, I take a deep breath. 'What do you want?'

He stares at me without speaking, his eyes sad and dark. 'Listen,' he says finally, taking hold of my hand. 'I'm sorry I messed up and I'd like to make it up to you.'

'Make it up to me?' I stare at his silhouetted face as the lights come up on the stage while my heart hardens. My glass is empty as usual, and looking around I see Hedley with our drinks hesitating over near the bar, looking but not looking at me sitting here with Tomas. The room starts to swim.

'I could come with you to New York, see your show, then take you away somewhere for a few days ...'

An awkward silence descends as I stare at Tomas. Behind us a man in a black suit is being lap-danced by a skinny blonde in leopard-print lingerie. A brunette in gold lamé walks onto the stage and inspects the pole. I catch Tomas looking at her and roll my eyes. Make it up to me – sure. When the dancer sees him she smiles and approaches our table. She smiles at me when she sits down. I don't smile back.

'Hi, my name's Candace,' she says to Tomas, who takes her hand and introduces himself.

'Hi,' I say. 'I'm Tereza.'

'Oh really? That's amazing because Candace is just my stage name, my real name is Tereza too.'

'What a coincidence,' Tomas says.

'Were you named after the Tereza in the Kundera novel too?' the other Tereza asks me.

'I don't know.'

'Not forgetting Zola's Thérèse – you could have been named after her.'

'She had such a terrible time,' Tomas observes.

'So does Kundera's Tereza,' the other Tereza says. 'What do you think of him, by the way? Kundera?' she asks me.

'Well, I don't know – I haven't read much of his work, to tell you the truth.'

'Oh, but you've got to read our namesake, *The Unbearable Lightness of Being*.'

'I met him in Paris once,' Tomas says.

'I can't believe you haven't read it,' the other Tereza says. 'But you've seen the film?'

I shrug. 'I've seen the film.'

'Well, I re-read *The Unbearable Lightness of Being* recently,' Tomas tells her.

'And?'

'I didn't really like any of the characters. I was especially annoyed by the Tereza character, I found her weak and kind of pathetic. No offence,' he says, looking at me first but also at the other Tereza.

'That's funny, you being Tomas too! Kundera's Tereza is very dependent on Tomas.'

'Is she the one who marries Tomas?' I say.

'Interesting,' Tomas says, ignoring my question.

But the other Tereza answers it for him. 'She's Tomas's girlfriend, then his wife, and Sabina is his –'

But Tomas cuts her off. 'So what do you do when you're not working in a place like this?'

'Well, I'm an actress – or should I say I'm at drama school but I want to be an actress.'

'Is there anything showing where we can come and see you play?'

'Not right now, but there will be.'

'OK, great. Well, why don't you take my card and call me when you've got something on?' Tomas says.

'I will,' she says, and adds, 'I better go make some money.'

'How much do you charge?' Tomas wants to know.

'What for?'

'For a private dance.'

'Fifteen hundred crowns.'

'I'll have to come back when I've robbed a bank,' he says.

She laughs.

'It's been great to meet you,' Tomas says.

'See you soon.' She waves to me.

'Do you want another drink?' Tomas asks.

I nod, looking around for Hedley, who is nowhere to be seen. Damn.

'What a coincidence,' he repeats. 'Another Tereza.'

'Incredible, really.' Watching Tomas walk to the bar, I feel tired and not nearly drunk enough. I sigh. But when Anna joins Tomas – she's still in the blonde wig but has changed into a silver sequined bikini with a matching tiara – my heart starts pounding hard. Here comes trouble.

At first I don't feel anything much at all. Anna is giving Tomas a free lap dance and Libuše, who's sitting beside me, has just asked me how I'm going with Tomas. I tell her he wants to make it up to me.

She nods and sighs. 'He was quite worried after you left,' she says. 'He didn't mean to upset you.'

'Well, he has a funny way of showing it.'

Libuše nods. I look away, clenching my jaw. When I look back, an untidy length of dark brown hair has flopped down across Tomas's forehead and his eyes have turned black with excitement. When Anna straddles his lap, he glances over my way. He's still looking at me, our eyes locked, when Anna removes her sequined bikini top.

Gulping the remains of my vodka I get up and head for the bathroom. Inside, I splash my face with cold water, breathing hard, and pat my face dry with paper towel. Fuck him – and now I've messed things up with Hedley. Shit. I apply fresh lipstick. Drunk, I fail to keep inside the lines and have to wipe my lips clean and start again. Calmer now, I emerge from the bathroom and practically walk into Hedley, who's waiting outside.

'Time to make a move,' he says.

'You're leaving?'

'Yes, we're off,' he says. 'Back to the hotel. Why not join us for a nightcap?'

'That's really sweet of you,' I say and then freeze: my bags, at Tomas's …

He watches me, then nods his head. 'We're at the Hilton, down near the river. Surname's Lynton. We'll be up quite late, I imagine.'

I nod and kiss his proffered cheek. Looking up I see Tomas standing nearby, glowering at me. Over his shoulder I notice the Australian standing in her underwear and arguing with what looks like a bouncer. I guess guests aren't allowed to take their clothing off in a lap-dancing club. Catching up with Hedley outside, I realise he reminds me a bit of Reed now he's lost the extra weight.

Hedley goes to fetch our drinks. His friend from the lap-dancing club is here, as well as a blonde American woman called Marilyn and three of her Californian friends: Robert, Keanu and Michael. I'm not listening to their conversation, I'm miles away, a vodka martini my only link to planet earth. In my head Tomas is busy seducing the other Tereza and I can't stop it. My mobile is switched off, which means neither Nelly nor Sarah, Reed nor the Lincoln Center can reach me – assuming they can actually get through – but it also means that Tomas can't call should he want to either.

The television in the corner suddenly blares to life with a newsflash about the flood, dragging me out of my thoughts and into the present. Everyone in the bar stops talking and drinking and stares at the screen.

'Thousands of people today left Prague in an attempt to escape the worst floods to hit Central Europe in one hundred and fifty years,' the BBC reporter says. 'There are already signs of mass devastation in Germany due to the flooding of the River Moldau, and meanwhile Prague prepares for what's being called the One Metre Wall of Water with sandbags and mass evacuations.'

I watch, spellbound, while the camera feeds us shots of

the Karlus Most, of the empty streets in the city centre, and of ducks swimming near the banks of the rising river. Eventually another news item comes on and the barman mutes the volume.

The room buzzes with conversation. Sculling the rest of the vodka martini, I'm about to ask the hotel reception if I can use their computer to email New York when Hedley says, 'Would you like to come to a party?'

'What party?'

'Robert and Michael are having a Survive the Flood Party at their apartment on Wenceslas Square.'

'Sure.' I shrug. Maybe they'll have a computer I can use to email there?

To get to Michael and Robert's apartment we have to enter via the Lumiere, an Art Deco building which is also a theatre and a shopping arcade. The apartment, which overlooks the square, is the nicest I've seen in the Czech Republic so far: parquet floor, high ceilings, brightly lit chandeliers, enormous Persian rugs, elegant antique furniture. Hedley and I help ourselves to flutes of champagne from a table just near the door and move across the mostly empty room towards the French doors, which lead outside onto the balcony. The Grand Hotel Evropa is across the square and a bit further along.

'Cathy is a famous pianist on tour from London,' Hedley says. 'She's just done a show at the Rudolfinum and is on her way to the Lincoln Center in New York.'

'Wow – great to meet you,' Marilyn says as Michael, a film director, wraps his arm around her waist. 'I'm so drunk, Michael has to hold me up. I was in a car accident yesterday and I've buggered my neck. The combination of the painkillers and booze is a complete knockout.'

'Have you had anything to eat?' Hedley asks.

'No, I must get some food,' Marilyn says, gesturing at me. 'I'm feeling very Buster Keaton, you know. I could fall forward and tear your clothes off any second.'

'Feel free,' I say.

'I'm feeling very wild,' she says, 'very *naughty*.'

'We're all in the wars,' I say, thinking of poor Prague below us, of myself, of my mother. 'Does anyone have a computer I can use? I need to email New York.'

'I tried calling the Lincoln Center again but the lines are still choked with calls,' Hedley says.

'You're stuck here with us,' Marilyn says, and everybody laughs.

It seems no-one's computer has internet access and the nearest internet cafe is closed due to the flood. 'Maybe this is a good time for me to tell you my Nine Miles High story?' Robert says, batting his long-lashed eyes at me. Noticing him for the first time, I slug down my drink and bat my eyes right back.

'Oh great,' Marilyn says. 'I love this story.'

Somehow in his crushed cream linen Robert reminds me a bit of Tomas. Stiffening, noting my interest, Hedley moves away to the other end of the balcony with Keanu.

'I was flying first class on this Lufthansa flight from New York to Berlin,' Robert says, emptying his flute.

I try to catch Hedley's eye but he has his back to me. I turn back to Robert.

'I was scoffing lots of lovely champagne and flirting with

the cute stewardess when suddenly she said, "You must try zome of our special brandy, ve only giff it to zee very special first class customers," and she's cute, you know, she looks a bit like Kylie Minogue in her tight little stewardess uniform.'

Robert smiles a big smile in my direction and I smile right back. I look at Hedley, who has his back to me, and see safety. But then I look back at Robert and say, 'So what happened next?' I'm totally fucking screwed, I might as well enjoy myself – right?

We're all crammed onto Michael's king-size bed and drinking absinthe the Prague way, i.e. flamed, when Marilyn says, 'Will you play something for us, Robert?'

With a quick smile at me, Robert reaches into his coat and pulls out a set of worn-looking silver spoons and starts to play them against his legs.

'Robert's a genius,' Marilyn tells us as Keanu turns down the volume of the CD.

'Can you play Tchaikovsky's Piano Concerto?' I say, and everyone laughs.

Smiling, Robert tells Keanu to pause the CD and starts to play the Tchaikovsky gently against my thighs. I start to giggle while he continues to play me up and down my body. He plays me right until the end of the opening passage, and only then plays the other members of our group, passing quickly over them so everyone gets a turn. At the end of the first movement, we all clap and Keanu pours and flames us all another round of absinthe cocktails.

'This is the second time I've heard that played on the spoons!' I say, but no-one's listening.

One or two legless absinthes later, Neil Diamond's 'Play Me' blaring from the stereo, we all toast, laughing: 'To the flood!' Michael and Robert push back the furniture, roll up the rugs and start dancing around the bedroom.

Hedley starts dancing with me but Robert keeps looking over and smiling. I smile back and, catching me, Hedley moves away. Then Robert dances over and starts hamming it up, doing funny moves and making me laugh. I notice Hedley scowling at me from the armchair but I turn my back on him and sing the lyrics loudly at Robert. From here I can see Marilyn, who is now dry-humping Michael on the bed. We laugh, everybody laughs, even Hedley laughs.

Then Marilyn and Michael get up and start dancing. They group-hug Robert and Robert waves Keanu over and then I join in too. Hedley is the last to join in but finally he does and it's somehow so funny to hug and dance at the same time that we're all laughing like mad. Then someone starts pelvic-thrusting and pretty soon we all join in. Now I'm laughing so much I'm crying. Robert is on one side and Keanu on the other and Hedley is laughing from beside Marilyn and finally looks like he's having fun too.

We break apart and Robert grabs me and close-dances with me, body to body. His white linen shirt is wet against me and my heart starts to pound. Meanwhile Hedley stands alone on the outskirts of the group, staring morosely into his empty glass. Suddenly, Hedley is waving goodbye and leaving and something inside me tears. I run after him, kissing the others a hurried goodbye.

Robert follows me to the door and hands me his card. 'Call me,' he says.

I tell him I will, you can never have too many admirers, and hurry to join Hedley, who's waiting outside.

Hedley and I lie spooning between the crisp sheets in his hotel room, Mahler's First Symphony playing on his portable CD player.

'So which Mahler is …?' he wants to know.

'The First.'

'The First? Really?' he says, his breath warm on the back of my neck. 'People always say that's the least mature of his symphonies.'

'Exactly,' I sigh, turning around to kiss him again. 'That's what's so wonderful about it. Its freshness.'

'I once knew a fellow, big Mahler fan, you know, listened to everything he ever recorded – he kept going on about Mahler's piano rolls … Have you ever come across them?'

'Yes, of course. Wonderful: Mahler playing Mahler …'

'I love the interviews at the end. I mean, he was obviously an incredible perfectionist, though I wouldn't have wanted to have been on the receiving end of one of his … fits of perfectionism.'

'I just love all those great accents: German, Czech, Viennese.'

'"Good musicians don't need a conductor. A conductor is only a necessary evil," Mahler is supposed to have said. "Don't worry what I do, just play your music."'

'The best Mahler conductors are those that conduct like the orchestra's playing in a London pub – the ones that set the instruments and the themes free like little birds …'

'The conductors that don't control.'

'Exactly. But the other thing I always think of when I think of Mahler is — I mean, I think it's interesting although I disagree, partly — he thought Tchaikovsky's symphonies weren't real symphonies, that they were too Italian, that the melodies were like Italian operas. I have to say, while that may be true, I love Tchaikovsky, and I love his big fat melodies …'

'That's because you're a hopeless romantic,' Hedley says, squeezing me tight. 'You're just a dear sweet darling, beneath all that dazzle and brilliance, and we haven't even started talking about Beethoven yet —'

'— who wrote the closest thing to perfect music —'

'— but I'm going to have to interrupt this wonderful conversation to ask: how do you like the sound of breakfast in bed for two?'

'With champagne, of course …'

'*Naturellement.*'

Then, sitting up, seeing me naked in the light for the first time, he says, 'Hey, gorgeous — what's with all the bruises?'

'Oh,' I say, and look away.

'You been up to a bit of rough? Who's the guy with the heavy hands?'

My mind blanking, stopping short, heart pounding. I just shrug and look away. 'I'm not sure how I got them …' I mumble. Then somehow I manage, 'So, this champagne …?'

It's raining quite hard and the wind is blowing the rain horizontally beneath the umbrella. The Karlus Most is choked with tourists taking pictures as the waters rise, though most of the statues have been removed from the bridge in preparation for the wall of water that will hit some time today or later tonight when the river is going to burst its banks.

I stand with Hedley staring into the dark churning waters and then we cross arm in arm to the other side where the water has covered the normally dry walkways below us.

'I should really start getting ready for New York,' I say. 'I'm playing at the Lincoln Center tomorrow.'

'I wouldn't worry too much about that now,' he says. 'You'll never get out, not with the flood.'

'What?'

'You're a star, they'll understand. Besides, this is history in the making. The biggest flood in over one hundred and fifty years and all that!'

'Still, I should call them and explain,' I say, as the umbrella snaps back on itself in the wind and I'm drenched again. 'Fifty crowns,' I say, looking at it. 'What can you expect?'

'Try them when you get back – though I suspect the lines might all be a bit jammed with the flood,' Hedley says as we pull the umbrella back into shape and continue along the bridge towards Malá Strana.

'Hey,' Hedley says, changing the subject, 'I heard about your gaffe at the Rudolfinum –'

'Don't –'

'You know that even the greatest pianists struggle with the Rach – many come unstuck –'

'Put a sock in it, Hedley. I mean it.'

Within moments the umbrella snaps back again. We both laugh while Hedley tries to fix it. Then, the wind whipping everywhere around us, our eyes lock and we fall into a stare. Just for now, standing together in the middle of the crowded bridge, the tumult all around us, we're somehow alone; the Lincoln Center, Tomas, all my problems, fade into the background with the thrill of this new affair. We kiss, a quick kiss, and then cross the bridge into the New Town. Walking close together, we ignore it when the umbrella is blown back again almost immediately and then throw the umbrella away.

Stepping from the bridge, we watch people filling hessian bags with sand and then piling the sandbags up in the entrances of buildings and across the front doors of houses, their labour dramatically lit by spotlights powered by noisy electric generators.

'I wonder how effective they'll be?' Hedley ponders.

'I want to help them. The poor people.'

'I want a drink,' he says, his eyes bright with mischief. 'Let's go back to my hotel. You can make your calls and I'll get us a couple of martinis.'

'I should really go and get my bags. My flight leaves at four-thirty and I don't want to be rushing around at the last minute.'

Heading back across the crowded bridge, I hear Albinoni's Adagio in G minor playing through one of the upstairs windows; it's got to be some of the saddest music ever written.

Unable to get through to New York, I hurry over to Tomas's – I still have the spare key from last night – and once inside I pour myself a generous double scotch. Another text from Nelly comes through, which I ignore ... I hate scotch, but I drink it straight down staring blankly ahead, not seeing or thinking anything coherent at all. But instead of easing my hangover, the scotch gives me an instant headache. I've just started packing up my things when I hear the key in the door. Tomas smiles sheepishly and tells me, 'Hi.'

'What are you doing here?'

'I live here, remember?' he says and disappears into the kitchen. 'Do you want something to eat? I'm positively starving.'

I don't answer but follow him into the kitchen, where he's hacking into a loaf of rye bread and arranging slices of Jarlsberg cheese, pickled gherkins, ham and salami on a plate.

'Do you want something to drink?' I ask, pushing past him to get to the scotch.

He pauses and looks at me hard. I ignore him, and, turning my back, pour him a drink.

'I'm sorry,' he says.

I turn around. We eye each other across the small kitchen.

'It didn't mean anything,' he adds. 'I was just having fun.'

I glare at him for an answer. Then spit, 'Did you fuck her? That night, in the castle?'

'No, of course not!' he says. 'Oh, shit …'

'You'll make it up to me – right?'

'Shit,' he says again. 'Look, a few years ago, we had this thing –'

'I don't want to know.' I turn away and screw the lid back on the bottle. Suddenly he grabs me from behind and pulls me against him, kissing the back of my neck and turning me around. I freeze in his arms. When he stops kissing me I slap his face, hard. He smiles. I want to laugh but I don't. There's a pause.

'Oh God,' he says. 'I've blown it, haven't I?'

'Hah!'

'It was just sex – it didn't mean anything …'

I don't respond.

'I really would have made it up to you,' he tells me, taking my hand. 'Can I still take you to New York?'

'I've already got my ticket.'

'Well, maybe I can come along?'

I shrug, nothing to say. But when he grabs me, his tongue sliding down my throat – 'Wait!' I try, in vain, 'I've got to think about New York' – the electricity takes over and I let him fuck me, hard and fast, against the kitchen cupboards, across the small rickety table and finally entangled together on the floor.

Afterwards, I push him away. I smooth down my clothes, go find my bag – which is where I left it in the bedroom yesterday – and swallow four Panadol with the dregs of the scotch.

Following me, watching from the doorway, Tomas says, 'God, I'm actually a little all over the place … What I meant to say is, if you don't like me carrying on with Anna, I won't – OK?'

3

I leave Tomas searching for flights and hurry outside. Deleting Nelly's texts – the last one says, *Just call me as soon as you can* – I feel light-headed, the Panadol barely taking the edge off my headache. I soon find myself in Zara on Na Příkopě killing time while I wait for Hedley to reply to my text. I'm stuck in a change room with too many clothes and I can't seem to leave. I want to buy everything I try on and have to remind myself that the only person I'll be punishing by pounding my credit card is me, now that Reed and I are no more.

I can't decide what to buy. When a voice-over blares from the PA, first in Czech, then in German, it only adds to my confusion. Not understanding, I peer out through the curtain hoping to find a sales assistant, but the only person I see is the woman in the next change room. When I ask her what's going on she says, 'Go. We must go out!'

Go out? What does she mean? Honestly, I don't think I can cope with any weird Czech stuff today …

The dance music loud in my head, I end up buying a black lace skirt, a red satin vest, red fishnet stockings, a low-cut black T-shirt and a tight-fitting black denim jacket. I don't have any shoes for this outfit but I decide my black Guccis will just have to do. I've no idea what I'm doing re New York. I still haven't heard back from Hedley about taking me to the airport this afternoon.

I'm in Tomas's bathroom in my underwear and while I'm waiting for New York to call and Hedley to text, I'm sipping from a bottle of Pilsner Urquell and sexy-dancing to eighties pop on the radio. Tomas, who repeated his apology as soon as I returned – adding, 'Let me make it up to you, let's give this a real try?' – is searching for airfares for us to go away together after New York, but soon he comes into the bathroom and just stares at me, slouched in the doorway. Hazy with tiredness, I remove my underwear and start running the shower. Outside, the rain continues to fall heavily.

The news comes on and the Vltava has already started to flood. Nelly texted me that Germany is in turmoil and that there's still no news about my mother. I haven't replied to Nelly or cancelled my earlier arrangements to go to London.

I get out of the shower, climb back into my knickers and without getting properly dressed start to pack my bags. I can't seem to find anything I need and my breath is fast and shallow. Despite what Tomas keeps saying, I'm still not convinced he's actually coming with me to America. 'How long will it take to get to the airport in a taxi?' I ask him.

'Ten minutes,' he says.

I frown and start throwing things into my bags. I check my mobile, just a text from Hedley saying he tried to call but couldn't get through and asking what time's my flight? I text him back, *Will get self to airport. C u in New York?* I find another beer, scull it down, wishing Tomas had some vodka. Tomas orders a taxi and carries our bags downstairs.

'Listen,' he says, as the cab speeds along a dual carriageway lined with glum two-storey apartment buildings in desperate need of repair, 'after your concert I want you to come meet my parents upstate and then I'll take you away for the weekend. We'll fly back to New York and see the sights and then fly to Prague the following evening.' He smiles and meets my eyes.

I watch him carefully, thinking about vodka: maybe I can get some at the airport on my card?

'My parents live out on this beautiful old farm,' he says, 'you'll love it, really.'

I shrug, 'OK.' He takes my hand and squeezes it.

We hit a bank of traffic. 'God, I could do with a drink,' I say.

'Everything's diverted because of the flood.' A police car drives past, lights flashing.

'I hope everything's OK with our flight.' I examine my reflection in the rear-view mirror. I like the new me. I'm wearing my new outfit with the Gucci shoes.

'By the way,' Tomas says, handing me a printed itinerary. 'Here's your e-ticket – we pick up our boarding passes at the airport.'

I look hard at the paper and then slowly up at Tomas. New York to Durham, and back to New York again. 'Thanks,' I say. 'You didn't need to pay for mine, but it was nice of you. How are you affording all this, anyway?'

'I spoke to my mother yesterday about having my plays translated, and she wired me through five thousand dollars.'

'Your mother? OK …'

'Better than a poke in the eye with a hot stick,' he says and we both laugh. 'You know they were in London during the war, my parents, but deeply involved with the Czech resistance from there.'

He reaches for my hand and he's just started kissing me when my mobile phone starts to ring and Nelly's name comes up on the screen.

'Sorry,' I tell Tomas, realising that I can't keep avoiding her calls.

'Where are you?' Nelly wants to know. 'Are you all right?'

'I'm fine,' I say. 'I'm in a taxi in Prague on the way to the airport. I tried calling you,' I lie. 'Did you get my messages …?'

'The airport? What? I didn't get any messages from you.'

'New York, I'm going to New York.'

'Cathy, this is important, I need you to listen to me. I've been to the police about your mother – can you think of anywhere she might be?'

'I can't deal with this now – I've got the show in New York.' I don't know what else to say.

'But I had an email from Sarah saying she couldn't get hold of you and that she cancelled the Lincoln Center.'

'She what? I emailed them just now from the hotel to confirm,' I tell her, a little desperate. 'As far as I know, they're still counting on me to perform.'

'OK, I'll try to sort things out with New York. Now, what about your mother? Any ideas?'

'Look, we're nearly at the airport. I've got to go.'

'Who's we?' Nelly says, irritation creeping into her voice. 'You're not with that guy, are you?'

'I've got to go,' I say. 'I'll call you back when I get to the terminal.' I hang up. Nelly never becomes irate.

My mother? I wonder … I turn back to Tomas as soon as I finish the call but he's busy rummaging in his bag, the unanswered question about my mother hanging between us. The traffic moving again, we pass the tram terminal on our right and soon after the modern airport comes into view. Tomas reaches for my hand. Letting him hold it, I take a deep breath – if only there were some alcohol – and finally, determined, I say, 'Did you ever meet my mother back in your dancing days? Her name is Odette.'

'Odette?' he says too quickly, looking out across the window and shaking his head. 'I don't remember an Odette, but there were so many girls in the chorus, you understand.'

'She wasn't in the chorus. She was a principal, the principal.'

'With the Czech National Ballet?'

'I think so.'

'Odette doesn't ring a bell.'

Relieved, watching the rain come pouring down in heavy sheets, I decide I have a good feeling about this trip. I look at myself in the mirror once more and smile at my reflection; the Largo from Dvořák's New World Symphony starts playing in my head and I grasp fervently at its sense of hope and promise. Surveying Tomas in his frayed jeans and ratty tweed, I imagine us speeding happily around Barneys, shopping bags bulging as we transform ourselves, making ourselves new. A second text comes through from Hedley asking me what flight I'm on, which I ignore.

Prague-Ruzyně is in chaos. The floor is slippery with water from the rain, the lounges and counters littered with people desperate to get on flights out of the city to escape the flood.

Joining the end of the line in front of the United Airlines counter, I realise I don't have my guitar with me. 'Where's my guitar?'

'Your guitar?' Tomas says. 'I don't know – you must have left it in the cab.'

'Shit. I mean, it's not the money, I mean, OK, it's a Strat, so it's … But it's more of a mascot.' When my mobile phone starts to ring, I hand my passport and ticket to Tomas and rummage in my bag. When I finally find my phone, I don't recognise the number. Shit. I turn away from Tomas and say 'Hello' too loudly. 'Who is it?'

'Hedley,' comes booming down the line.

'Oh, Hedley,' I say, turning back to Tomas and signalling with my finger for him to wait a moment, 'Look, Hedley, I'm in the middle of something, I'm going to have to call you back, OK?' Not waiting for a reply, I snap the phone closed.

'OK,' Tomas says, frowning, and looks outside at the rain. 'I might be able to catch the cab driver before he picks up his next fare. I'll be right back.' With that he runs off into the gloom.

I wait with our bags for Tomas to return but too soon it's my turn up at the counter. Mumbling, I let the people behind me in the queue go next but there's still no sign of Tomas. Fuck. Without a passport I can't even board the flight! I try calling his mobile but there's no answer. I want to call him straight back but decide I need to keep my line free in case he's trying to call me. I wait a few minutes more and then, leaving our bags, I exit the queue, hurry through the revolving doors and into the pouring rain. I look back over my shoulder. Tomas is nowhere.

Back inside I tell the woman at the United Airlines counter, 'I've lost my boyfriend. Can you please look after our bags while I go look for him?' I place our bags at her feet and walk swiftly away, ignoring her 'Excuse me, ma'am?'

I continue to ignore her until she shouts, 'You can't leave these here,' at which point I look back over my shoulder and see her talking to a security guard. I start to run towards the doors, just as they announce the last call for my flight.

Fuck. What about my bloody show?!

'Tomas,' I call, twisting this way and that in the rain. 'Tomas!'

A cab drives straight towards me and I try to wave it down but it doesn't stop, only screeching to a halt at the last minute. The driver opens his window and shouts something unintelligible at me.

'Oh, fuck off,' I tell him.

'Bloody English!' he replies.

I slowly move off the road.

My mobile rings again – this time it's New York. What to do? I'll give it five more minutes to see if I can find Tomas and then call them back. I check the time, we've missed our flight, and try to hail a taxi to take me back to Prague but the queue is twenty people long. Chaos, chaos, if only this blasted rain would stop. Where has he *gone*, for chrissakes? He couldn't have gone back to the apartment. Did I leave my guitar at his flat? God, I'm so bloody tired and hungover I can't remember. A couple of vodkas would fix this.

I check my mobile phone. No missed calls. I dial Tomas's number but this time I get a recorded message in Czech I don't understand. I grip my mobile tightly in my hand. No chance now I'll miss it if Tomas rings.

I run back into the terminal and check the United Airlines counter again. Our bags are gone, as is the attendant I left them with. I look around the room in giant sweeps. He's just not there. I run back outside, heart pounding, and, sprinting, just manage to squeeze onto a crowded bus as it pulls away from the airport.

'Praha?' I say to the driver.

'Yo, yo,' he says, as the doors close behind me.

Maybe there'll be cabs along the way and I can jump out and get one at one of the bus stops? But the bus I'm on turns out to be an express. The first stop, a nearby passenger tells me, is the centre of Prague. At this my blood starts to boil. The bus slows and then halts in the heavy traffic and my thoughts shoot up a gear. My passport, New York, the show, Tomas … I don't even know if I can get into Tomas's flat.

Finally we clear the traffic and roadblocks and sandbags line our path as we approach the Wilson Bridge and the muddy river climbs steadily higher. The beautiful domed and pointed roofs of the Prague skyline make me feel like crying.

'Příští zastávka,' the automatic voice says and reminds me of the letters of the Czech alphabet from Bohumil's lesson at the castle – '*A-b-c-ch-d-e* …' – and I start to cry. Soft, silent, warm tears course down both sides of my face. I need to speak to New York. Now. But I can't get through.

Nobody answers when I press the buzzer at Tomas's flat and suddenly I can't cope. I don't have an umbrella and the rain is still coming down and I'm drenched through and desperately cold. On a whim I check inside the petrol cap of Tomas's car. Voila! The spare key is back in its place! But where the hell is Tomas? Maybe he's gone back to the airport? I don't know what to do. Unless I find him now, the chances of my getting to New York on time are zero. Unless I call the consulate?

The rain continues to pour heavily down as I approach the security door and try the key in the lock. It gets stuck halfway and refuses to budge. I hear Nelly trying to ring me again but I wish she'd just leave me alone. I try turning the key the other way, but the same thing happens. Tomas – where the fuck are you? I turn it and turn it and jiggle it and rattle the door, but still the door won't open.

Just then three policemen come into view on the other side of the street and they're heading my way. Remembering what Libuše said about Czech police, I beg the door, 'Please, please,' twisting the key again to no avail. *Open!* I try all the numbers on the intercom but, impossibly, no-one's home. Where has everybody gone? When I turn around to look again, the policemen are right behind me.

'Ahoj,' I say.

The big blond officer starts speaking to me rapidly in Czech.

'*Anglicky?*' I try.

They speak among themselves. It's clear none of them speaks English. Suddenly the blond one takes the key from me and violently tries the lock. He twists it and turns it so hard I feel sure either the key will break or he will break down the door. But nothing happens and the door remains closed. They speak again among themselves. Then the tall brunette has a turn. The same thing happens. Then the short one tries. He looks at me, and then speaks unintelligibly in Czech and turns the key, gently this time. But still the door doesn't open. The big blond tries again, getting rougher and rougher with the door.

Meanwhile, convinced he's seen the light of a television set in one of the apartments above, the brunette policeman buzzes on the intercom but no-one answers. He tries a few other apartments with the same result. I guess the intercom must be broken. He then goes to the gutter and picks up some small stones and throws them at the windows. Each time a stone clicks I worry he'll break the glass but the door still won't budge and the three Prague policemen won't go away. Given the stories I've heard about corruption, I consider offering them my credit card … But after the blond makes a particularly violent attack on the door, I call Libuše on my mobile, hoping she can help somehow.

Libuše answers straight away. Trying to keep the hysteria out of my voice, I explain the situation and then practically beg her, 'Please, just tell the police I'm OK, that I have friends.'

'OK, OK,' Libuše says. 'But why don't you come down to the Kampa Gallery and we can see if we can sort this out? Maybe we can get hold of someone at the consulate? I'm not sure if the Metro is still running but you should be able to get here in a cab.'

I tell her I will but deep down I just want to find Tomas, get my passport and then get on another flight to New York ASAP.

The blond officer's approach changes after talking to Libuše. He now twists the lock gently and stops hefting his weight against the door. Meanwhile the small officer appears close beside me pointing down at the ground. A hedgehog, no doubt a refugee from the nearby square, is trying to hide behind my feet. The officer picks it up and walks off with it into the rain.

'WD-40?' I say, as they wave at a passing police car, which slowly comes to a stop.

'*Kde?*' the blond policeman asks me.

I don't understand but I tell him 'Friends' hopefully. Then, not wanting to have to call Libuše again, add, 'Kampa Gallery? Friends?'

They talk among themselves in Czech and then the blond says, 'Kampa?'

I tell him, 'Yo,' guessing at the meaning.

The police escort me to the police car and usher me inside. I didn't really want to go but now I have no choice.

'Gallery?' I say nervously. 'Friends?'

'*Kamarádes*,' the blond says.

As the police car accelerates along the deserted street, I hope *kamarádes* is the Czech word for friends.

I start to call New York again but then change my mind and try information for the consulate instead but can't work the prompts, which are all in Czech. I push my way onto a crowded tram which is heading down towards the Charles Bridge – the police couldn't get any further than Wenceslas Square with all the roadblocks – trying to remember the directions to the Kampa Gallery.

'That will be the last Metro to run,' I overhear a fat American tourist tell his wife. 'They're closing the Metro C line, the one that goes under the river, because it may not be safe with the extra weight of the floodwater on top.' Piece by piece Prague is closing down.

I check my mobile but there's still nothing from Tomas. I search for and then find the number for Tomas's landline. I press enter and wait. It rings and rings and finally a woman's voice answers in Czech. I hang up, heart pounding so fast I can barely breathe.

Obviously I didn't dial the correct number. I search again, enter again, hold the phone to my ear – I can't *believe* this! The phone rings, and rings, and rings … And finally the answering machine comes on, Tomas's voice, the words in Czech.

I'm the first passenger off the tram – the rain now teaming down – though I've no idea where I'm going. I recognise the river, which means I must be near Hedley's hotel. What? I must have caught the wrong tram. I follow the milling crowd, not knowing where I'm heading.

I'm just about to try Tomas's number again when my phone rings. *Nelly.* Thank God – I pick up –

'Cathy, is that you?'

'Yes.'

'Are you OK? Where are you?'

'It's Tomas,' I say, irrationally turning in circles now in the Old Town Square, hoping he'll suddenly appear among the crowd, the rain drenching me through. 'He was coming to New York with me. Then I left my guitar in the taxi and he went to get it and never came back. But Nelly – he's got my fucking passport!'

At this I start to cry and, losing it, I sit down on one of the sopping wet benches.

'Wait, Cathy,' she soothes. 'Slow down. All your words are running together. So where are you now? Where is this guy – Tomas, is it?'

'I just tried his landline,' I moan, struggling to keep it together. 'And some other woman picked up the phone.'

'OK, Cathy, I hear you're really upset. But calm down, deep breaths, OK? We can work this out – it's probably not as bad as you think, but you've got to help me, all right? Take five deep breaths, that's a girl.'

I take a deep breath but I can't help it. 'Who is she?' I cry. 'He left me at the airport to go running home to meet her. He didn't even care about my passport or his bag, he just dumped it with me.'

'You're shouting at me, Cathy. I can't help you if you're shouting.'

But I don't stop. 'It's Anna, it must be her, who else could it be? And now I've messed up New York, it's all just a complete mess …'

Moisture dribbles from the end of my nose and I wipe it away with my fingers. I look up and see a ring of concerned Praguers gathered around me, their umbrellas steady in their pale hands. An old lady with a purple rinse offers me a tissue from her handbag.

'Cathy? Cathy, are you there?'

Nelly's voice is distant now. The tissue is soon drenched and one by one the Praguers shake their heads and walk away.

'I can't do this anymore.'

'What?' I hear. Then, 'Cathy, that's not a solution.'

I hear myself shouting between sobs, 'I can't keep doing this … And it's always like this … I've tried and tried. You helped me, you really did … But there's just no point – *it always turns out the same …*'

And then I'm blubbering, blubbering like a small child,

and I drop the phone. I reach for it blindly, press it to my ear.

'Cathy? Where are you? Tell me where you are and I'll come and get you. You've got to hang on. This is old stuff, the betrayal, the trauma. Remember, we've talked about this?' I hear Nelly say in a loud voice.

I sob, trying to digest her words, but they don't help this time.

'Can you find your way back to the Grand Hotel Evropa? Go there and order yourself a cup of tea and I'm on my way,' she says, softer now. 'Do anything, just do something for yourself. And don't forget to breathe. Cathy, Cathy, are you – ?'

But I hang up the phone and heave myself giddy to my feet: what did Nelly just say? Do something for myself …

… Hedley?

Somehow I retrace my steps and soon I'm at the Hilton, where I wash my face in the bathroom. I still look awful in the mirror but the tears are subsiding. There's no sign of Hedley, in his room or at the bar, and when I try calling him I can't get through. As I hurry outside, I discover I'm much closer to the Kampa Gallery than the Evropa, so it makes sense to head there. I realise Hedley is probably looking for me at the airport …

4

The second movement of 'Má Vlast' is blasting fortissimo inside my head when it hits me: the woman who answered Tomas's phone wasn't Anna, it was the other Tereza – Candace, from the lap-dancing club. Swigging from the bottle of wine I stole from Hedley's minibar, I can't find anyone who knows how to get to the Kampa Gallery, no matter who I talk to.

I'm crying and I wish I could stop. I emailed New York again from the Hilton reception but there's no way of being sure it went through. I swig at the wine but it doesn't help. I've been in Prague, my mother's hometown, for barely a week and that's all it's taken for things to go completely wrong. I cross the river and turn right into a narrow street so I'm heading towards Malá Strana but end up mistiming my crossing and am nearly run over by a police car. In the back seat, I notice as the car passes slowly by, is a policeman with a megaphone: '*Prosím Pozor!*' he announces. '*Ušeobecná evakuace. Povodňová pohotovost. Prosím, opusťte unychleně toto území.*'

I wipe my cheeks dry and swig at the wine. To my left a man stands in a domed archway, watching the rain. He has grey hair, brown eyes and a hooked nose, and is wearing shorts and a white shirt. He looks vaguely familiar, though I can't place him.

'Do you know how to find the Kampa Gallery?' I try.

'You shouldn't let yourself get so distressed,' he says, stepping forward.

'Have we met before? You're a violinist – yes? You were playing violin in a steakhouse in Budapest …?'

He reaches for my hand. 'May I?'

I shrug, mystified, as his warm hands clasp my right hand, turn it palm up and hold it out to the light. Is he reading my palm?

'Hmmm,' he mumbles. Then bursts out with, 'This is a very good line, career brilliance and success, yes?' He turns my palm so I can see and points to a line running straight up the centre of my palm.

I nod, 'I guess so,' not wanting to think about the Lincoln Center or anything else to do with my work.

There's a long pause. 'This man,' he says finally, 'he doesn't want to let you go. But you must be strong.'

He looks up from my palm and our eyes meet. Uncomfortable, I pull my hand away.

'You must go home,' he tells me. 'You must leave this man. There's a threat to your life while you remain here. You must leave. Now.'

I grip the wine bottle, wanting to lift it to my lips. The man follows my thoughts with his eyes. I look away.

'Call me,' he says, handing me his card. 'Any time.'

I pocket the card and when I look up he's melted back into the shadows of the building. I hold the wine to my lips. There's no-one else to ask.

Continuing down the narrow street, I wonder about the man's words before dismissing them as groundless nonsense.

In actual fact, I should be on the plane to New York right now; then again, even if the email does get through, given what Sarah said, I'm clearly finished. My mobile phone starts to ring – I don't recognise the number – and I pick up. 'Hello?'

'Cathy,' booms an accented voice I can't quite place. 'I am coming with Mouse, I am in Prague. Where are you? I will bring her …'

Oh God, Franz. I completely forgot he had Mouse. 'Franz, look, I'm down near the river somewhere, but could you give her to a friend of mine –' but just then my phone cuts out. I try to call him back but I can't get through. Shit. Mouse, please let her be OK …

I keep going along the narrow lane, which is lined on both sides with grey-brown apartment buildings that would have been elegant once but which look a bit shabby now, past piles of sandbags and temporary barriers, and try to get as close to the river as possible. The steps, however, are completely underwater, it's all flooded here, and I can't get any closer to the water because there are too many sandbags and barriers and crowds of people.

'The biggest flood in over a hundred years and more rain coming!' I hear an American woman tell her friend.

I swig at the bottle again and hurry away, following the riverbank in what I hope is the direction of the Kampa Gallery. I stop in a phone box to shelter from the rain and try calling Tomas's landline from my mobile – maybe he can help with Mouse – but there's no answer, his answer machine must be switched off? I try his mobile which rings and rings but he doesn't pick up. Then, as soon as I snap the phone closed, it rings straight back and miraculously, it's Tomas.

'Hello?' I say. 'Tomas?'

'Cathy,' he says, and then there's a long pause, the rain noisy on the roof. 'Cathy, I'm sorry,' comes his voice again. 'I just couldn't ... You see, there was a message on my phone after I left you, a message about your mother.'

'My mother?'

'An old friend from our dancing days –'

'What?'

'I'm sorry,' he says, as the line goes dead.

'Tomas!' It's not possible. I dial the number again immediately but Tomas's mobile rings out unanswered. When I look at my phone again there's a text from Hedley from the airport. I clench my jaw and sweep my tears away from my face. I just can't deal with this. Everything's gone wrong and I can't stand it ...

... this is your primary trauma, Cathy ...

... I find myself in a park. Further ahead the river has broken its banks and the grass is partly underwater. A willow tree with a bent trunk grows out of the swirling muddy water. I stare into the roaring river, thinking about my mother and watching the flotsam churn. My mother ... I'm very distressed, I –

The water's cold when I step in but it's only knee-deep. Even so, the current is strong. When I reach the bent willow tree I climb it and sit on its right-angled trunk. I take out the wine and finish it. I look down into the water. New York. Tomas. My mother ... The last bloody straw.

It's still pouring with rain and I'm completely soaked through. I'm freezing cold too, even though it's summer. A bottle of vodka would fix this, but there's no vodka here; the wine will have to do. Czechs at the other end of the park rearrange the sandbags because already the river's getting in, creeping under and around the bags.

Climbing down from my perch on the bent willow I walk towards the original river's edge, which is now submerged and some distance away. There are more willow trees and I see some ducks trying to find shelter. Up ahead all sorts of things are floating down the river — bits of houses and clothing and broken tree limbs and the water is all muddy with dirt and not the usual magical blue-brown colour I'm used to. Soon it's dark and the street lamps don't come on. I look around but the men doing the sandbags have all gone. I hear someone behind me, feet squeaky on the drenched grass, and I turn to see a couple under a large black umbrella walking my way. With a stab I recognise Tomas and Anna and look quickly away, but then, turning back, I notice the woman isn't tall enough, even in this light I can tell that. I turn away, cut to the quick by the way he pulls her to him with his arm around her shoulder.

I watch the swirling river some more and when I turn around the couple are gone. At least, the woman has gone and the man — at least, I think it's the same man — is standing not far away, still holding the black umbrella, though it's closed now. When he sees me looking at him he starts walking towards me. I freeze, not knowing whether to run. Is it Tomas? I can't tell, it's too dark. Should I call out hello? I'll be able to tell by his voice and if it isn't Tomas perhaps I ought to start running away?

I turn back towards the river. While I've been standing here the water has been steadily rising and it's now over the tops of my knees.

I turn back to see the man approaching and recognise Hedley, not Tomas – but how did he get here so quickly – how did he find me? Hedley is in the water now too, maybe a hundred metres away – no, it's not Hedley, Hedley is thinner – this man is too bulky, 'Hello – who is it?' I ask, and when there's no answer – the rain deadens my words – I turn and run away (wading through the muddy water), throwing the empty bottle into the muck.

I reach firmer ground. The man follows at a distance. I climb out of the water and up onto the back of a park bench which I find poking out of the water. It's like being a child again, sitting on the bench like this with the flooded river all around. The man comes closer again – Franz? – the rain is still pouring heavily down. My mobile phone rings and I pick it up.

'Hello? Cathy?' Nelly's voice says, 'I've been trying and trying to reach you but all the lines are jammed. I'm at the Grand Hotel Evropa. Where are you? Cathy, are you there?'

I want to tell her about my mother and Tomas but I can't, so I throw the phone into the water. Useless thing. Now I want vodka, now I want to die.

I'm crying again and thinking about Tomas and my mother and the Lincoln Center and tugging at my hair – tearing at it in lank clumps – why does this keep happening? The pain rises up huge now and swallows me in a giant wave. I'm completely fucked, just broken; I never get what I want (I can't stop my thoughts, round and round they go in circles inside my head, *Jump in, jump in*, they say, I'm a prisoner of them, please, someone take them away!) and then I feel a blow to the back of my head and I'm falling – and suddenly – *shit!* – I'm in the water – idiot! – and I'm just like Vanda, the unhappy heroine of Dvořák's opera, or Libuše, the heroine of Smetana's (all those Czech heroines seem to end up here in the Vltava, one way or another). Then – thank God! – my feet find uneven steps below, though the fence is gone too quickly from my grasp, and the current is strong, much stronger than it was in the shallower water before. And then in a whoosh there's nothing beneath my shoes, just the water – COLD! – and panicking, I thrash about, swallowing it in huge shaking gulps, choking – coughing it out ('WHY DOES THIS KEEP HAPPENING?' I scream), my eyes sting, I force myself to calm down: I kick off my shoes / somewhere above me there's a bridge / that man on the bridge in silhouette / and I'm moving swiftly towards it / everything's happening in some kind of crazy waltz time. There's something sticking out of the water, if only I could catch it / the man on the bridge is waving: SWIM! Like in swimming classes, head out of the water and then – *aargh!* – I'm swept against it, whatever it is, the roof of a house? *Shit! My head! my back!* – incredible pain – *and then it's dark and cold and I'm very tired and numb …*

… and the numbness swallows me up until I'm –

… so cold …

… can't keep fighting it!

'This is your primary trauma, Cathy …'

'When did you know about my mother?'

5

This is what I want to do with my life. I've practised every day – my piano teacher gave me the key to the music room so I can come and go as I please – before and after school, during free periods, and for hours and hours on weekends. My maths teacher says he doesn't approve of what he calls my 'unhealthy obsession' with the piano but my therapist says it's helping. I love what I'm doing and I feel really good about doing it so how can it be wrong?

I've been waiting now for nearly half an hour, all the other pianists being examined have come and gone. That means I'm next, and yet the short wiry lady still doesn't come to call my name. Time drags and drags. And then, when I can stand it no longer, it's suddenly my turn. And not seeing a single face, nor hearing a single word of what the examining panellists say, my heart jumping up through my throat, suddenly I'm at the piano and my piano teacher's words are there waiting for me inside my head – lean into the opening, push through the semiquavers in the left hand, don't linger on the descending crochets in the right hand – and I'm seated at the piano. And, illuminated from within by my own private pool of radiant sunshine, I close my eyes, and begin.

BOHEMIA BEACH

1

I'm at Rossbach again and Tomas, Libuše and Anna are all there partying and having fun with Ray Kroc and President Clinton, but all the time there's something dark lurking in the shadows. Then Nelly arrives and says, 'You're dying here,' and that's when a wall of water hits, a tidal wave comes crashing through the castle and sweeps us all away – at which point I wake up. I shiver and reach for my coat. The car is swishing down a winding country lane. I rub my eyes open. I must have dozed off during the long drive from London to Surrey, and now that I'm awake memories of Prague flood my mind, mixed with fragments of the dream. The rain is darting, and on the other side of the meadows and trees, more heavy storm clouds are moving rapidly towards us.

Edgar turns into a hedge-lined gravel drive and pulls up in front of a medieval chapel and its adjacent priory. Overgrown with ivy and moss, the priory is shaped like a square horseshoe: the longer wing fronts onto the drive and two shorter wings extend backwards.

Checking his watch, Edgar says, 'Isabella is going to meet us at reception at five. It's only four now – why don't you join me for a cup of tea and then I can take you around?'

'You live at the priory?' I say, forcing myself away from the dream, to come back to Edgar fully.

'I run a small private practice from the priory, but yes, I live here too sometimes, though I tend to be up and down to London quite a bit.'

We enter through a low door which leads into a narrow hallway, where Edgar is pawed by a heavily built chocolate labrador named George with whom, after one wet nose into my open palm, I fall instantly in love. Edgar deposits my bags in the hallway and we continue along a corridor painted white and crossed overhead by heavy wooden beams, his dog loping beside us. The floor is made of worn grey stone and littered with silk rugs in burgundy and earthen tones. I remark on the lowness of the doorframes and beams and Edgar, who has to significantly duck his head each time he passes through, says, 'People were shorter then. The ceiling is higher here in the corridor and in the adjoining rooms because we took out the original medieval ceiling and raised the floor. We made one storey out of what was originally two.'

I nod mutely, feeling as if I'm still trapped in the dream somehow. We go gliding past a large, formal lounge room on our left which is bursting with oddly assorted antique sofas, mismatched lamps and tables, and a mahogany dining table with matching chairs. The next door on the left is closed but the windows to the right look out onto a fiercely clipped lawn fringed with tall trees. Then we turn a right-angled corner to the right, pass along a shorter corridor with two more closed doors on the left and finally emerge into a large, low-ceilinged kitchen with a blue Aga stove. A kettle steams on one of the hotplates and Miss Fairfax, Edgar's housekeeper, petite and smiling, greets us with two fresh cups of tea. As I take in the steaming warmth, I feel my memories of Prague begin to slide fading from my mind.

At 4.45 Isabella calls to say her car's broken down in the rain and she's not going to make it back in time to process my admission; I'm going to have to wait until first thing tomorrow morning.

'Would you like to stay here?' Edgar asks as he hangs up the phone. 'Or I can see if I can get hold of Nelly or your father, if you like?'

'No,' I say, 'here will be fine, thank you.' George, lying at my feet, gazes up with wet brown eyes that seem to plead with me to stay, and the idea of spending more time alone with Edgar is not unappealing. I find myself wondering whether the feeling is mutual.

'You know, I'm quite curious,' Edgar says, as I follow him up the stairs to the upper level of the priory. 'What happened on the beach?' Sadly, George isn't allowed upstairs.

'It was all very confusing,' I say, pausing on the stairs to study the dozen or so dark portraits lining the way. 'Are these all your relations?'

'The faces of my forebears.' Indicating a slightly less sinister portrait in dark greens and browns, he says, 'This one here is of my paternal grandfather.' While Edgar's grandfather isn't exactly smiling, the eyes have something of Edgar's warmth about them.

We continue, but the next few portraits make me shiver, and it's all so Gothic I start thinking about women imprisoned in attics by cruel husbands. Finally, we emerge into a large informal living area filled with more antique furniture, a TV and a stereo. Tapestries hang from the walls and at the far end stand two suits of armour, one holding a staff with a crested flag. I've always found suits of armour to be incredibly creepy. There's a closed door on the right, perhaps leading to a bedroom? I follow Edgar around a right-angled corner and down another corridor and then he stops at the first door on our right.

'Perhaps the beach was just a dream,' I say as he opens the door, 'just the morphine?'

'No doubt the morphine played a part,' Edgar says, 'but the content of dreams is often highly significant.'

I shrug, evading his gaze, and peer into the L-shaped room. Directly opposite is a second door, and in the middle of the room, almost piercing the nearest of two single beds running up and down the length of the room, is a sturdy vertical wooden beam – how odd. I shiver again.

'I thought I'd pop you in here,' Edgar says. 'Miss Fairfax is just at the far end of this corridor and I'm not far away, just a few rooms in that direction.' He waves vaguely at the second door, back in the direction from which we've just come.

He places my bags on the floor and I cross to the second door. 'What a curious room,' I say, turning the handle and finding it locked. 'Where does this lead?'

'To a secret passageway,' Edgar says, raising his eyebrows, 'and then into the next bedroom where my nieces sometimes stay.'

'You have a brother?'

'A sister,' he says, and opens the window. 'There, that's better, not so stuffy. There's just my sister and I – my mother died when we were both very young,' he explains, adjusting the curtains. 'My father has remarried and lives abroad. My sister has two daughters, my nieces.' Then, giving me his sweetest smile, he says, 'You're not frightened of funny old houses, are you?'

I shake my head and walk away from the second door. 'Not at all.' So we've both lost our mothers ... Still, a secret passageway, a beautiful housekeeper, the mysterious death of his mother and an absent father ... His life is sounding more and more like the plot of a Gothic romance.

I stand in front of the large mahogany chest of drawers and study the books lined up against the wall. Some of my childhood favourites are here: James's *Ghost Stories*, Haggard's *She*, Brontë's *Wuthering Heights*. I pull out the last – my fictional namesake, how apt given the current circumstances – and absently flip through the pages.

'Some old books from school,' he says. Then, clearing his throat, he says, 'Tell me – you don't mind me asking you a few more questions, do you? Professional curiosity, I guess, but also I do want to help if I can.'

'No, that's fine.'

'This beach you've been dreaming about, is it in any way familiar to you? Does it remind you of anywhere you've been before? A beach you visited during your childhood, perhaps?'

'No,' I say, 'I've never been there before.' I close the book and place it back on the chest of drawers. I really don't want to talk about the beach or my childhood.

'I see,' he says and looks at me, but says no more.

'Is the beach terribly important?'

He shrugs. 'That's what I'm trying to find out. In the

meantime, make yourself at home. Dinner's in the kitchen downstairs at six-thirty.'

He leaves and I'm suddenly alone in the room. Outside, the wind begins to tear at the leaves in the trees and the sky grows darker still. A strong gust rattles the window and, cold, I close it and lock it tight. I turn up the central heating to full.

Edgar takes a sip of his water, impervious, but I jump when lightning flashes and the wind starts to howl in the trees as the storm hits with full force. He loads his fork with roast pheasant, baked potatoes and green bean and almond salad and says, 'What about your time in Prague? Do you remember anything about Prague itself?'

I look down at my plate and cut a potato into slow squares and meanwhile my heart starts to pound as memories of Prague and the flood bombard my mind. I imagine how a psychiatrist might see it: my marriage falling apart, the disaster at the Rudolfinum, the Deutsche Grammophon deal, my mother, Tomas and Anna, Reed and Sarah ... I reach down and ruffle George's ears as my mind flashes with its very own horror show: Anna and Tomas in the pub, Sarah and Reed, and Daniel and Jonsey ...

Suddenly Edgar's voice cuts into the flashbacks. 'Who's Tomas?'

I choke on my tea, spitting it across the table as thunder claps loudly above and George jolts upright – have I been thinking aloud? 'Tomas – Tomas who?' I instantly need vodka and I wonder where Edgar keeps his alcohol.

Edgar just looks at me steadily for an answer, his eyebrows slightly raised.

I close my eyes as last night's dream forces its way into my mind. I push it down but it's too strong. Finally I give in. I can't suppress it a moment longer.

I'm walking along a beach, the family retriever, Bronte, at my feet, when I discover a beautiful deserted pavilion. Sitting outside on the stone steps is my mother, a baby at her breast.
'Go home,' she says. 'It's not safe here.'
But I don't go home.
Then a man starts following me along the beach and away from the pavilion, an angry man. I run as fast as I can. He gives chase.
My mother follows in a small boat. She comes in close, right in to the beach, but then idles in the shallows, calling, 'I can't come any closer. You'll have to swim out. It's your sister, you see. She's sick and I can't leave her.'
But as soon as I step into the water, the man appears at my side. I start to swim out, and he swims beside me. Just then I realise who he is. When we reach the boat my mother won't let him on with me so she speeds away, calling out, 'Be careful, Cathy …'
I turn to the man and hold out my arms, but when I finally embrace him, he says, 'I love you,' and dissolves into thin air.

Tomas … I feel the tears go streaking down my face and watch them drip onto my plate: Tomas.

Edgar leans forwards, hands me a tissue and says, 'Here.'

I open my eyes, take the tissue and blow my nose. I shudder and soon my breathing grows more even. George's paw, pressing on my knee.

'Do you love him?' he says.

I struggle to speak but nothing comes out.

'Something like that once happened to me.'

'Like what?' I manage.

'Someone I loved let me down and hurt me.'

I start to cry again, this time more insistently. 'I'm sorry,' I say, when after some time I can't stop. 'Can we please not talk about it?'

'Of course, but you will need to talk about it, when you're ready. I don't think you'll make much progress until you do. By the way,' he adds, drinking from his water again, 'your case notes showed quite a bit of alcohol in your bloodstream when you were admitted to hospital. Do you have a drinking problem?'

I open and close my mouth but nothing comes out. My cheeks flush red.

'So no alcohol, not while you're my guest, OK?' he says.

I nod. 'You sound like Nelly, she's always telling me not to drink,' I say with a little laugh, trying to make a joke of it.

'Nelly has a point,' he says, not going along with the joke. 'Now,' he adds as he starts to clear our plates. 'What do you say to an early night?'

Edgar makes two mugs of chamomile tea and escorts me up to my room, leaving George moping at the foot of the stairs. 'You've made quite a friend there.'

'We used to have a retriever when I was growing up.'

'They're great dogs to have around children,' Edgar says. Reaching my door he smiles and says goodnight. 'Call me if you need me, I'm just down the hall.'

I tell him goodnight and enter the room, switching on the bedside light. I study the books on the chest of drawers, momentarily lit by a flash of lightning, and shudder as thunder claps right above the house.

I hurry into bed but can't get to sleep. Tossing miserably I find myself thinking about Edgar – does he like me too? – and then my mind jumps to the Rudolfinum and that funny pianola feeling, the sense of the piano getting away from me again. At this my heart starts to pound. Wide awake, I lie staring at the second door, worrying about it bursting open in the night, that there's someone waiting on the other side. Eventually I take *Wuthering Heights* from the chest of drawers and read myself to sleep.

No sooner do I drift off than I'm woken by a thunderclap which rattles the window. Sitting up in bed, I pull back the curtain and peer out into the wild wet gloom but there's nothing there.

I close the curtains, lie back in bed and watch the second door. I switch off the bedside light and attempt to go back to sleep but hearing another loud noise, this time from downstairs, I switch the light back on. I attempt to read myself to sleep again but Brontë's Gothic doom only magnifies my fear. Drifting in and out of sleep, I imagine Edgar's mother isn't really dead but trapped in a room somewhere off the secret passageway and that Edgar's father has imprisoned her there because she's crazy. I'm the only one capable of finding her, of persuading Edgar's father that she's not crazy after all, and then emerging a hero. I close my eyes and sleep fitfully, drifting in and out of strange dreams I can't remember.

2

Edgar's gone when I wake the next morning and the storm has blown itself out. My room, though a little odd with its two doors and the peculiar beam in the middle of it, seems harmless enough in the daylight. Downstairs, Edgar has left a note on the kitchen table explaining he's attending to his private patients but will finish at twelve and meet me for lunch. He adds that Miss Fairfax is in the library if I need anything. I check my mobile. There's a text from an old friend from the academy about catching up and another from someone wanting to book me for a concert next year, but it's all too much and I don't reply.

Breakfast is laid out in silver dishes on the table. One dish contains scrambled eggs, another sausages, and a third holds smoked haddock. There's also a saucepan of porridge, and a plate of sliced bread next to the toaster, beside which is a dish of butter and an assortment of jams and marmalades. I help myself to some eggs and sausages, make some toast and then eat my breakfast reading, though not absorbing, today's edition of *The Times*. Afterwards, George enjoys most of the sausage and eggs from my plate, I'm so tired I go to the lounge room. The nurses said to take it easy for a while, that it would take time to recover from the coma and the impact of the flood, so I lie down on one of the sofas there. I study the landscapes and seascapes hanging on the walls and notice the 1920s liquor trolley covered with crystal decanters and various bottles of gin, scotch and brandy, and as I register its proximity my heart leaps. Determined, however, to follow Edgar's advice, I wrap myself in a mohair throw and fall asleep over *Wuthering Heights*, George sprawled at my feet, my fingers in his thick fur.

At twelve Edgar wakes me and we have lunch in the library and sunlight streams in through two full-length glass doors. The furniture here is more formal: a pair of red velvet armchairs and a tattered chesterfield dot a large pale green Persian rug. Two walls are lined with floor-to-ceiling bookcases and at the far end of the room is an upright grand piano. I recognise it as a Steinway from one of the newish ranges, and am about to go for a closer look but I check myself. No thanks.

After lunch Edgar unearths a massage table which had been hidden beneath piles of folded towels. 'How's your back?' he wants to know.

'About the same as yesterday,' I say, 'a dull ache between my shoulder blades.'

'Do you want me to take at look at it for you? I might be able to help you.'

'You think a massage might help?'

'What I'm proposing is like a massage, only stronger.'

'OK,' I say, looking at his long fingers and smooth skin.

'Right,' he says, 'I need you to strip down to your underwear and lie down on your back.'

I do as he says, noting the way Edgar turns away as I do so and then, when he turns back, that he concentrates his attention on my face and avoids looking at my black underwear. Carefully lifting my torso, Edgar removes the bandage, covers me up with warm towels and begins to massage my right forearm. At first my stomach gurgles happily – I like the feel of his hands on my skin, I realise – but soon he's pressing down quite firmly with his thumb and stretching hard through the muscles. I draw a quick breath in sudden pain and my mind automatically reaches for the brandy in the other room. I pretend I didn't think that. Edgar waits until I'm breathing normally again and then presses deeply into my feet, one at a time. While this also feels uncomfortable, it isn't particularly painful, but he soon moves up to my other arm, which is painful, and, asking me to turn over, finally begins to massage my back. He digs his soft-skinned fingers in deep, manoeuvring up and down the sides of my spine and manipulating me vertebra by vertebra. I gasp. That really hurts – God, do I need a drink. He pauses and I tell myself to relax but it's no good. Then Edgar presses his fingers firmly into the sore tingling spot between my shoulder blades.

'Ouch!' I cry as tears prick the corners of my eyes. Vodka – I desperately need vodka, now.

He pauses again. 'That's definitely the spot.' Then he digs his fingers into it again and drags them right through the sore part and then away across my back while tears stream uncontrollably from my eyes. I moan, cry out in pain.

'Yes,' he says, pausing. 'That's got it.' He hands me a tissue and I blow my nose.

'God, I need a drink,' I say, and laugh.

'Believe me,' he says, 'that's the last thing you need.'

Gradually my breathing becomes even again and my sniffles fade. He picks up my left arm again but this time, as he gently turns and rubs my arm, my stomach gurgles contentedly. He places my arm back down. His fingers reach around for the spot between my shoulder blades and he feels around it gently. I take a deep breath, getting ready for more pain.

'Have you ever had an injury to your back? Something from your childhood, perhaps?' he wants to know.

My jaw clamps tight and I look away. There just isn't anything remarkable about my childhood; not that I can remember, anyway. 'No, I don't think –'

'Just there,' he says, pressing the spot hard again and bringing fresh tears to my eyes. 'I think you'll find that that's the cause of all your problems with your back.'

After a while I'm panting from the pain, and he steps away and looks kindly down into my face. 'What musical instrument did you say you played?'

'I didn't.'

'Piano, wasn't it?' he persists.

'Piano, mainly,' I sigh.

'How was your posture when you first played the piano?'

'My posture? Well, it was pretty good, I should think. I had excellent teachers …'

'Yes, I'm sure. But some of the greatest musicians get injuries of this kind from their work.'

'Injuries?'

'The injury you sustained to your back in Prague has mostly healed. See this here,' he says, indicating the discarded bandage, 'this is padding only, to help with the chronic pain. My guess is this recent injury has come on top of a childhood injury, compounded by your work as a musician. What you're feeling now is chronic pain.'

I look at him doubtfully: this pain, a series of injuries compounded by *playing the piano?* That seems far-fetched.

'Come on, sit up,' he says. 'Your back should be feeling quite a bit better now. If it's OK with you, I'd like you to step up to the piano so I can check your posture.' He indicates the piano at the far end of the room.

While my back does feel better, there's no way I'm going to play the piano. Music is completely off the agenda.

'From memory, you're pretty good,' he coaxes, smiling, 'Come on, I want to hear you play.'

I shake my head. 'I don't think I'll ever play again.'

'If you talk like that you may not play again,' he says. 'Come on, Cathy, don't let yourself down. You're a musician, it's what you do, I'm sure you'll play again.'

I stare back for an answer, my eyes hard, not even considering it.

'Anyway,' he says, 'whatever caused the immediate injury you sustained in Prague, I'm sure it's come on top of an old injury, that's often how these things work, you know.'

'But I never had any childhood injuries! I can't remember any.'

'Well, have a think about it – if anything pops up you can tell me about it next time. You were definitely injured during the flood. My hunch, however, tells me that what you're feeling now probably has more to do with your childhood.'

'You keep asking me about my childhood,' I say. 'But I don't understand – what does my childhood have to do with any of this?'

'Everything, I suspect.'

I frown and look away.

'That's all for today,' he says, stepping back from the table. 'You can get dressed again now.'

I climb back into my polo-neck jumper, cardigan and tracksuit bottoms and am struggling with a sock when he adds, 'Would you like me to teach you how to meditate?'

I drop the sock to the floor. Nelly is always going on at me about meditation – the whole mind/body/spirit thing.

'You've probably guessed by now that I prefer to work holistically in my private practice – that is, with the whole person. The reason I want to teach you how to meditate is so whenever you feel distressed or anxious you can make yourself relax. It may also help lessen your compulsion to drink.'

Sighing, I pick up the sock and sit down to put it back on. 'I just want to know what's wrong with me so I can fix it.' I tug my other sock on and slide into my slippers.

'As they say, Rome wasn't built in a day.' It's his turn to laugh a little laugh, but I don't have the energy to even smile.

'By the way,' Edgar adds, 'you'll need to talk to the police about the assault.'

'Sorry?' I look at him not understanding.

'You remember, you said someone attacked you when you were in Prague during the flood?'

I nod but turn my back on him as my body tightens.

'I know it must be painful for you, especially in your delicate health, to go back over the past, but when you're ready it will help you to heal.'

When I still don't speak – the police? you've got to be joking – he excuses himself and leaves. Alone again, my mind goes straight to the brandy in the other room, and then I remember Edgar's eyes avoiding my body. He doesn't seem to have a wife, unless she's up in London … I wonder. I look into the garden and watch as the blue sky fills with fluffy white clouds. I'm just checking my mobile phone when — what?! a missed call from Tomas … I drop the phone, pick it up again, delete the missed call, start to dial his number and stop again. I remember what Edgar said about not drinking, and feel Edgar's gentle touch at the beginning of the massage — and for once I don't return Tomas's call. Whatever else, calling Tomas probably means drinking and I promised Edgar.

I check the rear-view mirror and adjust the angle. I'm so tired I have to do it twice because I forget I've done it the first time. Edgar's car is a manual but I'm used to driving automatics and sitting in his car I can't help thinking about Edgar and the massage yesterday, but I instantly dismiss the thought.

I adjust the seat so it's a comfortable distance from the pedals and hunt for the key to the ignition. I can't find it in my bag so I rummage through the litter on the front seat. I must already have the key somehow, otherwise how could I have opened the door? Then I look again and there's the key, already in the ignition. Idiot. I blink my eyes a couple of times trying to wake up. I'm so tired I'm terrified my eyes will just close on me when I'm driving and I'll have an accident.

I start the car but I don't press the accelerator hard enough so the engine cuts out as soon as it starts. I try the ignition again and this time I press the accelerator harder, too hard, and the engine growls noisily as the car lurches forwards and I anxiously look around to see if anyone has seen me, a stupid idiot at the wheel, but there's no-one there. father, who's visiting today, went to explore the grounds and Miss Fairfax and Edgar are busy in the library. OK. Into the village, then a cappuccino, then home. I check in the side mirror but it isn't in the right place so I open the window and adjust it. I look in the rear-view mirror – I'm just *so tired* – and release the handbrake. I look at the side mirror and am just taking my foot off the brake, the clutch is down, when the car shudders and the engine dies. I must have taken my foot off the clutch too soon.

Damn. I can't do this today. I close my eyes. I'm fed up with being bloody sick and injured.

I lock the car and stand cold and umbrella-less in the grey drizzle in the middle of the driveway staring at the neatly trimmed hedges and the parkland that surrounds the priory. To my left, meadows and hilly farmland stretch as far as the eye can see. I can't see my father anywhere and I want to see him before he returns to London tomorrow.

I turn and hurry back to the house.

I can't sleep. I'm so tired and still I can't sleep; it's like I'm overtired or something. I want to stop reading *Wuthering Heights* but I seem to be addicted to it and can't put it down. It doesn't help that Edgar misses supper and still hasn't arrived home or that my father went back to London early. Meanwhile there seems to be something wrong with the central heating. It's so cold my hair is standing on end, but when I check the element it radiates warmth. Puzzled – isn't this what happens in movies just before the poltergeist arrives? – I climb back into bed and lie with my eyes open staring at the second door. I stare at it until my eyes ache. I'm about to go and see if I can get into the next room from the corridor when the round white china door handle turns of its own accord. I swallow and rub my eyes. It's late and I'm tired. I look again: now the door handle is still. I get out of bed and am pulling on my slippers when the handle turns again. This time my heart flips in my chest. I freeze and drop the second slipper to the floor. It can't be, I must be seeing things, and this damn book is putting ideas in my head. The next thing I'll be imagining Heathcliff climbing in through the window!

I close my eyes for a moment and sit down on the bed. Maybe I imagined the door handle? Or maybe I've taken the wrong pills for my back, thinking they were Nurofen? I check the foil beside the bed: no, I'm definitely taking Nurofen. Whatever, I'm clearly hallucinating. When I open my eyes again the door handle is still. So I *am* seeing things, unless …

My eye catches on the spine of James's *Ghost Stories*. I've never seen a ghost and I instantly dismiss the idea. I'm not sure I believe in ghosts. Obviously I've been influenced by that damn novel.

I watch the door handle for a while, daring it to move. I always thought ghosts, if they existed, haunted the living because they had something to say. My mind drifts back to the beach in my dream, the deserted pavilion, my mother, the stranger …

I lie down for a while watching the door handle in case it moves again. Finally, I take a deep breath and tell the ghost out loud: 'I'm going to sleep now. Please leave me alone.'

But as soon as I switch off the light, my breathing grows strained and I struggle with every breath. It's like my lungs are full of sawdust and I just can't get any air in there, there isn't any room, or like someone or something is sitting on my chest … Another panic attack? I try to go to sleep propped up on three pillows with the light on but it's no good. Each time I start to drift off my mind jolts back to the beach and I'm suddenly awake. Eventually I do fall asleep, only to dream of my mother. And when my mother says, 'Cathy, you've got to listen to me. It's important,' I wake up once more.

I get out of bed, wrap a blanket around my shoulders and run out the door, turning a right-angled left into the corridor that leads to Edgar's room. But when I reach the first door on the left, the door to the bedroom with the secret passage adjoining mine, I stop. I seize the handle, my back aching, and with one savage twist throw open the door. I reach inside for the light switch and blink in the brightness of the light. To my left an open door leads down a short low passageway to the door that adjoins my room. The corridor and the room are empty. A double bed fills most of the room and it and a small single bed are laid out with fresh soap and towels. I force my brain to work, to remember what Edgar said. That's right – I'm so tired – Nelly's visiting this weekend.

I hear footsteps approaching down the hallway and jump with fear.

'Is everything all right?' asks Miss Fairfax, dressed in a burgundy dressing gown and slippers.

'It's OK,' I say. 'I thought I heard something.'

'Probably just this funny old house creaking in the night, it does that sometimes. I always sleep better when Edgar's here.'

When Edgar's key turns in the door downstairs she blushes. At the creak of Edgar's shoes on the wooden stairs, I switch off the light, close the door and hurry on tiptoe back to bed; I'm definitely not reading any more of that novel. I wait for

Edgar to settle and find myself listening to Edgar and Miss Fairfax speaking together in low voices and then hear their voices fade as they head back downstairs. Why is it always the housekeeper in these sorts of situations? Sighing, I'm almost desperate enough to nip downstairs for some brandy but I fall asleep instead.

3

I'm waiting for Edgar to take me next door for my admission when I hear someone knocking on the front door and George starts barking loudly downstairs. I run my hands through my hair and wait to see if Edgar or Miss Fairfax will answer it. The knock comes again, louder this time. Three hard, precise knocks. Where is Edgar?

I trail downstairs to the front door and take hold of George by the collar. 'Who is it?'

'The police,' comes the muffled reply. 'We're looking for a Miss Bell?'

I open the door a crack to check that what the officer says is true. Spying the crisp uniforms of male and female officers, I let them in, George sniffs both of them and then quickly loses interest. I lead the police into the lounge room and offer them tea and a seat, both of which they decline, and then I stare at them blankly, unsure why they're here.

'Have we got you at a bad time?' the female officer says.

'No, now's OK,' I lie, forcing my face into a smile, when in fact my back is aching again this morning.

'We're here in response to your call about the assault,' the male officer says, jogging my memory. That's right. I called them yesterday at Edgar's suggestion.

'Can you tell us what happened?' the female officer asks.

'Well,' I begin, but stop, unable to arrange events into a coherent order. 'Sorry,' I say. 'On second thoughts, I'm not sure I'm up to this today.'

The police officers exchange glances. 'Perhaps this isn't such a good time?' offers the female officer, kindly.

'Actually,' I say, realising I do want them to come back another time. I *can't* talk about it now, what happened during the flood. 'I'm really not feeling very well. My back's giving me quite a bit of trouble today.'

'That's OK,' the female officer says.

'Just give us a call when you're feeling better,' the male officer says at the door, handing me his card.

I pocket it without looking, nodding quickly. 'I will. Thanks for that.'

And then they're gone. I breathe a long, low sigh of relief.

I lie down in my new hospital bed, I have my own room this time, and close my eyes. It vaguely registers that I'm in some kind of psychiatric hospital. I instantly dismiss the thought. I try to meditate but end up reaching for *Wuthering Heights*. When holding it up to the light makes my back ache, I try meditating again. I close my eyes, take five deep breaths, and concentrate on my breathing. In the meantime, my mind drifts all over the place: breakfast with Edgar, the receptionist's too bright smile, lunch with the other patients … Aha! I'm supposed to do something now; I force myself to focus again to remember. What was it Edgar said? That's right, five deep breaths, then focus on my scalp.

An image of a ragged pink ballet shoe pops unbidden into

my mind and is soon followed by the thought, *I'm just thinking about my mother,* she *was a ballet dancer.* But then I remember how Edgar said to just view everything I see as if it's happening in a movie. Soon I discover that the ballet shoe is connected to a beautiful female leg clad in pale pink ballet tights. Then the dancer appears in full: slim and exquisitely proportioned, she's spinning around and around and laughing and then a male dancer appears and lifts her up, high off the ground. He's handsome in a dark, brooding way and they're both laughing and staring into each other's eyes. He looks really familiar and I'm just wondering who he is when I think of Tomas and my heart thumps painfully in my chest.

Tomas and my mother – dancing together.

It can't be.

A tearful week passes while Isabella and I work through the likelihood of my mother and Tomas's affair. We try to reconcile the contradictions: Háta's account of the family history which suggests my mother didn't dance professionally in Prague; and what I've always been told by my family, that my mother was a principal of the Czech National Ballet, which seems to be supported by Tomas's reference during our last phone call in Prague to 'an old friend from our dancing days'; then there is Tomas's earlier assertion that he didn't know my mother. In the end, we decide that it's not possible for me to reach any definitive conclusions. Isabella suggests I learn to live with the ambiguity; that I forget about my mother and Tomas and get on with my own life. When not in therapy or group therapy, I do the homework Isabella assigns me in my room: I compile a list of all the traumatic incidents of my life. Isabella says I need to re-experience what's happened incident by incident in group therapy, that that's the way for me to heal, but God knows how I'm supposed to go through all that again without alcohol.

That afternoon there's a knock at the door and Nelly appears, all kisses and hugs and holding a parcel covered in stamps. I'm watching snow swirl in great swooping clouds outside the window when I notice that the stamps are from the Czech Republic. I don't recognise the handwriting and there's no sender. Nelly hands me the parcel and I hold it, my mind in overdrive. Who's it from?

'Aren't you going to open it?' Nelly says.

I look into Nelly's face, her lovely warm eyes. 'Will you stay with me while I do?'

Nelly sits down and I open the parcel, heart pounding in my chest. Inside there's a letter and a children's book. The letter's all in Czech, lines of hieroglyphs as far as I'm concerned, but the name Háta is clearly printed at the bottom of the page and my mother's name is handwritten at the beginning of the book. I let out a long sigh.

'That's nice of Háta to write,' Nelly says. 'You never did tell me about your visit. Such a pretty book. The Czechs are quite famous for their fairytales, though I don't recognise the title of this one, do you?'

I study the book and let it slide into my lap, then onto the floor. The parcel is from Háta …

Nelly picks it up and frowns. 'How's everything going? You've been here – what, three weeks now?'

'OK, I guess.'

'And how are things going with Edgar? Is he still visiting

you here? You know, he really is quite devoted to you, above and beyond anything he might be doing for me.'

Not sure how to respond, I say, 'He's been very kind. Thanks for recommending him.'

Nelly reaches for my hand and takes it in hers. 'I know it's a bit soon, but when you're ready again, someone like Edgar could give you everything you've ever wanted. I know he's different from the sort of men you're used to – that part of you that wants to rescue broken birds – but I really think someone like Edgar could make you happy.'

I frown at the book, now back in my lap, knowing she's right. During the last few weeks my distress has finally faded to a dull ache, aided no doubt by Edgar's kindness and attention. Edgar clearly doesn't have a wife in London; Nelly would know, though I wonder if Nelly would know about Miss Fairfax? I can't help a small smile.

'That's better,' Nelly says, removing her hand and handing me a flier. 'Your father really wants you to come, but only if you're feeling up to it.'

I hold the flier in my hand but stare blank-faced at the snow outside.

'Think about it,' Nelly says, wrapping her warm fingers snugly around my cold ones. 'No need to decide now. It's not till next week …'

I shrug, 'OK.' Outside the snow has turned to sleet.

The Czech literature seminar is held in a building on the north side of Russell Square; downstairs and around to the back of the building. When Nelly and I arrive we find my father and half a dozen or so staff members and students assembled around a hodgepodge of chairs and tables, smoking, gossiping and drinking red wine. The window is open, supposedly to let out the smoke, but this only results in the room being both cold and smoky. I switch my phone to silent. There's a text from my friend from the academy about meeting up later tonight but I don't reply. I'll get back to her after the seminar.

My father, who looks like he's already had a few, jumps up when he sees me and insists Nelly and I join his table. Sitting down, I soon lose track of the conversation and end up studying the faces of those present instead. I wonder if there are any Czech people in the room, and why they've come to London to study their own literature, albeit their own literature seen from a British perspective. I'm just studying the face of a pretty young woman when the room grows suddenly quiet as my father pauses to empty his glass before speaking.

'Setting the historico-political situation momentarily aside,' he says, '*The Unbearable Lightness of Being* is essentially about a love triangle. A beautiful, funny, but ultimately tragic love triangle involving the hopelessly amoral Tomas, the long-suffering Tereza and the femme fatale, Sabina …'

I watch father's face as he recounts the plot in a condensed form, and when he speaks of Tomas's betrayal of Tereza he pauses, unable to continue. He tops up his wine from the bottle on the table and, taking a gulp, clears his throat. Looking at me he says, 'We each love in our own special way, but Tomas's way of loving Tereza could only cause her pain.'

He then speaks in detail of the political situation in Prague at the time the novel was written, of Kundera's biography, and links the structure of the novel with the political circumstances of the Czechs as a nation, but I'm not really listening. Instead

I make little tears along the edges of the white napkin on the table in front of me. The meditation with the ballet shoe; my mother and the familiar-looking man dancing together –

I stand up and hurry from the room. Out on the street I hear Nelly calling me back but I don't stop. I hurry around the damp, ill-lit square towards nearby Russell Square tube station. I'm just about to enter a pub, thinking alcohol equals oblivion, when someone taps me on the shoulder.

'Cathy,' I hear and turn around. Magically, Edgar stands before me wearing a black suit and overcoat.

I try to walk past him but he catches hold of my sleeve. 'Are you all right?'

Swallowing hard, I tell him, 'Yes, I'm fine,' and push him away.

'It's funny I should run into you,' he says, letting me go but not standing aside. 'My shift at the hospital finished early today and I was just coming to meet you and Nelly at the seminar. Can I buy you a coffee?'

One look at his kind face and I dissolve into messy tears. I let Edgar wrap his arm around my shoulder and squeeze me hard. His warmth only makes me cry harder and I end up pushing him away. 'I'm sorry. I'm such a mess, I can't seem to stop –'

'No need to apologise,' Edgar says. Gradually I grow calmer and Edgar leads me slowly down the street, away from the pub and back towards the square. We pause in the lobby of a once fine but now slightly shabby hotel and then enter. Edgar settles me in one of the large velvet armchairs and then disappears to order some tea.

When he returns he gives me a half-smile but I don't smile

back. He fiddles with a black button on his coat and then stops. 'Listen, I was wondering,' he says, 'there's a Dvořák symphony coming up at Southbank and I was wondering – I know this is bad timing so feel free to say no – but I was wondering if you'd like to come and see it with me?'

I gaze down sadly into my lap. 'When do you want to go?' I say, and meanwhile my head is swirling with my father and Kundera and I'm unable to make it stop.

'I'll check *Time Out* when we get back to Surrey, but I think it's next week sometime.'

I sigh: it is bad timing. 'It's just …' I say, 'I'm not feeling very well at the moment.' When I look up his expectant face has crumpled.

'Oh, I'm sorry,' he says, quickly recovering his composure. 'Did something happen at the seminar?' But before I can answer our tea arrives and we watch the waiter unload the tray in silence. Then, pouring our tea, Edgar waits for me to speak, but when I don't he changes the subject, 'You know, it's a shame we're missing the seminar because I've often wondered how the Czechs feel about things now the Berlin Wall has come down. I was hoping to ask some Czechs tonight.'

'You mean since the Velvet Revolution?' I'm quick to correct him.

'Berlin Wall, Velvet Revolution – I thought they were the same thing?'

'The Velvet Revolution is what the Czech protest came to be called,' I say. 'But they're not the same.'

'OK, point taken. It's just, I've heard a lot of Czechs say they miss certain aspects of communism and I've heard East Germans say the same thing.'

At this, the blood rushes to my face. 'At the time of the Velvet Revolution, the Czechs were very naive about what it would mean to embrace the West,' I explain, repeating ideas gleaned during my recent trip. 'They thought everyone would be rich and they could have whatever they wanted. But the reality has been that the end of communism has been the beginning of destitution and poverty for many and wealth for very few.'

'I thought there'd been a huge injection of cash at the end of communism?'

'But the money didn't filter down to the ordinary people,' I say. 'My cousin Háta lives near Plzeň – do you know Plzeň? A large industrial town about an hour and a half south-west of Prague?'

'I've heard of it.'

'Plzeň is famous for its beer, Pilsner, and for its Skoda factory; up until recently it was a very important industrial town. During the Second World War the Germans made bombs at the Skoda factory, and under communism the Skoda factory made cars and trams. But the Skoda factory has recently closed down and the manufacturing has moved elsewhere. On top of this, Pilsner Urquell has been bought by a South African firm that buys its hops from the Japanese, which has had a dire effect on the local economy. Most of the fields surrounding Plzeň used to grow hops, but now they lie fallow. And the combination of Pilsner Urquell with Skoda makes things even more desperate for Plzeň and the region.'

'But would either of those factories have been able to compete in the global economy as they were in 1989?'

'Maybe not. All I'm saying is not enough was done to

develop the alternatives. I met a man who says he can't bear to walk around Prague anymore, a city he has loved through Hitler, the communists, all of his life, because all the wonderful Czech cafes and delicatessens have gone. He hates all the new shops and the fact they're just for the tourists, because there's absolutely no way the average Czech can afford to shop there. He believes capitalism has done more to eradicate Czech culture than Hitler or the communists combined.' I sigh down into my cup, adding more milk. Why's he doing this, arguing with me? The tea is still too hot to drink and I burn my lips slightly.

'But soon the Czechs will become part of the EU, so things will improve.'

'But why weren't they invited into the EU at the beginning – when they should have been?'

'The rest of Europe didn't want them, remember?' he says. 'The rest of Europe joined the EU to keep those Eastern European countries out.'

'The Czechs aren't Eastern Europeans, Russia is Eastern Europe. The Czech Republic is Central Europe.'

'Central Europe, Eastern Europe – the West didn't want them in.'

'The thing is,' I say, my jaw tightening, 'I don't think the Czech Republic *should* join the EU. I think they should form some kind of Central European Economic Union, get together with East Germany, Poland, Hungary, the former Yugoslavia. These countries have a lot in common given the economic devastation they've experienced.'

'But now the Czech Republic is rebuilding again. Britain's a big investor in the Czech Republic.'

'And we all know after Munich how much the Czechs can trust the English.'

'Wasn't it the Czech government that deserted its people and ran to England when the Nazis invaded?'

'But only after the English and the French reneged on Munich. And so the poor Czech people were doubly betrayed,' I go on, hands tightening into fists. 'But that doesn't mean it's what they wanted. I've heard the Czech people desperately wanted to fight the Nazis. Worse still, abandoning Munich made no real sense. Perhaps the Allies momentarily forgot that after the breakup of the Austro-Hungarian Empire, Czechoslovakia not only inherited the former empire's industrial might, but it was the tenth-richest nation in the world. Letting Hitler have Czechoslovakia was like some kind of wonderful, undeserved gift from the gods. Instead of giving Hitler Czechoslovakia, the West should have backed the Czechs to fight.'

'But surely Hitler is to blame,' Edgar says, his cheeks flushing faintly red, 'not the English or the French?'

'That's right!' I snap furiously, knocking my cup over in its saucer. 'Don't take any responsibility. Don't face facts.' And with that I stand up and grab my bag.

But Edgar stands up too and places his hands on my shoulders. 'Will you please sit down?'

I don't respond.

'OK,' Edgar says, reaching up to brush a stray hair from my face, but I pull angrily away. He drops his hand and frowns. 'I've got a better idea,' he says, 'Let's just get you home – I'm sorry if I've upset you.'

Softening after his apology – surely I can rely on Edgar to understand how difficult it still is for me to think, let alone argue, coherently? – I let him wrap me in his overcoat and escort me outside. I let Edgar guide me down the narrow streets and lanes through the commuter crowds. Once inside Edgar's car, the heating feels like a miracle on my feet and hands, which have gone numb with cold.

'I'll just let Nelly know I've found you,' he says and takes out his mobile phone, and I text my friend and cancel. The dark London streets blur as we go speeding south.

We stop at a traffic light, I have no idea where we are. Outside a light snow is falling, melting to nothing when it hits the ground. Turning my head to look past Edgar I notice an off-licence on the other side of the road – vodka – but Edgar follows my gaze. I push the thought of vodka away, hard. I want to pull away from Edgar's stare but I can't; such pretty green eyes … It's as if I'm seeing him for who he truly is for the first time: a good, kind man who really cares about me. There will be no more ghosts, I realise, no more thoughts of women locked up behind secret passageways. Whoever Edgar's parents are, however seemingly Gothic his situation, I now trust Edgar completely.

A car horn beeps from behind.

'All-bloody-right,' Edgar says and accelerates ahead.

I reach for his hand and his long fingers wrap mine safely inside. 'Are you sure I can't have a drink when we get home?'

He smiles. 'Absolutely not. There's something else, too,' Edgar continues. 'The police called today – they said the Czech authorities have arrested a man in relation to your assault, a Franz Myš.'

'Franz?!' I say, jerking my hand away.

'You know him?'

'The police think Franz pushed me in? Franz?' I say, twisting around in my seat and trying to find another off-licence. 'Honestly, Edgar, I'll die if I don't get a drink soon.'

'Relax, we're nearly there.'

I sigh, knowing he's bound to be right, and slump back in my seat. When I next glance across, he's staring at me closely but I can only briefly meet his eye before I look away again. Franz following me and pushing me into the river during the flood …? If it wasn't Edgar telling me, I'd find it impossible to believe. On the other hand, it makes a certain kind of monstrous sense. My mind reaches for alcohol again. 'I can't do this.'

'Wait,' he says, 'don't run with the feelings. Try five deep breaths instead.'

'To hell with five deep breaths,' I wail. 'It's going to take more than that to make me feel sane after this!'

'Look, this news about Franz has obviously come as a shock and it's setting off a bit of a chain reaction, but trust me, five deep breaths will do the trick,' he says, reaching over and taking my right hand in his and squeezing it. Unable to resist his velvet touch, I decide to give breathing a try. I close my eyes.

'In and out,' he says, the car slowing as we turn off the lane and into the driveway. We pull up and, magically calmer, I open my eyes to see Edgar gazing at me and frowning.

'Let me help you,' he says, getting out of the car and walking around to my side. He takes my hand and I let him lead me through the swirling snow. Once we're inside, it registers that the house contains none of its former dark mystery. It's just an old house, without my fear.

The hospital reception closed, Edgar leaves a message on the after-hours number — they should have been expecting me — and invites me into his part of the priory and out of the snow. I'm so tired after the evening's drama my eyes are almost closing as I stand and my back aches painfully. 'Where's George?'

'Can you stoke up the fire in the library?' Edgar tells Miss Fairfax, who meets us at the door. Taking me by the hand, he adds, 'And fetch a large bowl of hot salted water and a towel.'

'Very well,' Miss Fairfax says and hurries away.

Seeing me wince, Edgar guides me to the sofa and wraps me in blankets and I lean back into the bank of cushions. 'I imagine George is lying prone in front of the Aga in the kitchen,' he says. 'Now, can you try meditating?' he continues. 'Remember how I showed you? It can help with your back, too … That's it. Focus on your breathing.'

I close my eyes and hear the creak of a chair as Edgar sits down nearby. I take a deep breath and Bohemia Beach floats up before me, beautiful and serene. The long white curve of sand, the seagulls, I can even taste the fresh sea air…

'OK,' Edgar says, 'now let your thoughts drift.'

As my breathing gradually becomes calmer, I find myself drawn back to the empty pavilion from my dream, only this time it isn't empty; this time the white sand is dotted with holidaying families. Daddy is there, calling out to me over the sound of the lapping waves. 'Catherine, where are you?' What's going on?

I'm standing alone on the front steps of the pavilion looking down onto the road and the beach below. It's a sunny day though there are dark storm clouds on the horizon. I can see mummy sitting in the front seat of our car. She's wearing her nice denim shirt with her heavy gold charm bracelet and big sunglasses with the bug-like rounded panels of glass. We're on our summer holidays in Devon and staying nearby in a small cottage set back from the beach. As I watch, a man approaches the car and knocks on mummy's window.

'Catherine, where are you?' daddy's voice calls from somewhere inside the pavilion. He sounds angry, he's using my full name. I must be doing something wrong.

I'm just about to go inside when I hear mummy saying in a loud voice, 'No. No!'

The man has hold of mummy's arm and is trying to pull her out of the car. 'Come on!' he says, and with one huge tug he pulls mummy out of the car. 'Nothing can come between us.'

But mummy isn't happy. She's very pregnant and now she's shouting, 'No! I can't.'

'*Catherine?*' daddy calls, louder, but it's as if I don't hear him: *mummy; mummy!* My eyes glued to the scene, I find myself slowly walking towards mummy, down the stairs and across the pavement to the car.

'Come on, Odette – quickly, before he comes,' the man says. 'We were made for each other, darling, you know that. We can come back for Cathy later.'

But mummy doesn't like the man. She keeps hitting his arm where he is dragging her up the street. She screams, 'No, stop. I can't.' She doesn't want to go with him.

Just then mummy turns around and sees me following close behind her. The man sees me too and says, 'Cathy,' but mummy is telling me something, 'Go find your father, Cathy.

Go back inside.'

I'm staring at the ground, I don't want to go back inside, when the man snatches me up so I'm balanced on his hip. I give mummy a big smile – please don't go! – but she doesn't smile back.

'Put her down,' she says.

'But we could leave now, make a fresh start.'

'*Put her down.*' Mummy is very angry and she reaches for me but I start to cry. 'This has nothing to do with her.'

Then mummy starts hitting the man, but he just laughs and says, 'Come on, this is everything you want, everything we talked about. Let's go,' fending off her blows.

But then mummy's arms are around me, digging in and she's hurting me. I scream, and the man pushes her away, saying, 'You're hurting her,' but it's too late, and mummy slaps him across the face. He stares at her, saying nothing, but when she comes at him again he pushes her away, harder, and this time she trips on the uneven ground and falls down. I wail, I want to go to mummy now, but the man holds on.

'Catherine –' I hear daddy call again. But his 'Odette' is in a different voice and it frightens me and I start to howl as the man drops me suddenly and I fall to the ground, landing on my back, the breath knocked out of me; my mummy, small and round and groaning on the pavement holding her swollen abdomen, the man at her side.

Suddenly someone – *daddy*! – tears me up, throws me inside the car and slams the door. I come crashing down on the seat, this time my back hits the seatbelt and I lose my breath; it feels like my back is broken. I cry and cry, I scream as loudly as I can but no-one comes, daddy doesn't hear me, doesn't care, doesn't come. I throw myself at the window, fists and head, and scream as if I'm dying. I see through my screams that daddy is shouting at the man and that he punches him and then they're fighting, and mummy is still on the ground. Suddenly the man sends daddy crashing down with a mighty shove, grabs mummy by the arm and they go running together up the street. Daddy, who is back on his feet but not walking properly at first, soon starts chasing after them. I see them all turn a corner and disappear.

I press my face harder against the glass but they don't come back. I wait till my legs get tired and then I slump down into the seat. They're not coming back. This time the tears are slower, warmer, and I turn my head away from the window, as if not looking might bring them back.

I lie down on the seat. It grows cold, then dark outside. Occasionally someone walks past the car and looks in but I stare down at my pants where I've wet myself. One old lady passes, then on her way back knocks on the glass.

'It's a bit late for you, sweetie, isn't it?'

I look up at her but there's nothing I can say. She tries to open the door.

'Where's your mum, love?'

I look down at my lap. The woman walks away, muttering.

Then, suddenly, a dark form appears at the window and I see daddy's face looking down, but it's too late now, and part of me doesn't know who he is. Even when he snatches me up in his arms I don't respond, a limp doll.

'I'm sorry, darling, I'm so sorry,' he says, kissing me on my forehead, hugging me and then rubbing my back. I can't speak, or move. 'Now, let's get you something to eat and –

pooh! – a nappy change and then we need to get straight to the hospital …'

The hospital – Mummy?

Daddy's driving very fast. The car is white and has red vinyl seats that smell good when they get hot in the sun. I'm in the back seat. I lean forwards, looking at the road in front, watching to make sure the other cars get out of the way. It takes a while for my sobs to slowly subside and for the fresh tears to dry scratchy on my face.

At the hospital mummy lies sleeping in bed though she opens her eyes when daddy kisses her cheek. 'Is Cathy OK?' mummy asks.

But daddy doesn't answer.

'Is she all right?!'

'I think she's OK,' he says and then I see tears start to run silently down his cheeks as mummy's eyes slide closed again.

I've done something wrong, I can feel it. I shouldn't have been there with mummy and that man. I sit on the floor near the bed and press my sad, naughty face against the wall. Mummy is sick with the baby and it's all my fault. There's something wrong with me, I shouldn't have been there, and now there's something wrong with the baby and daddy's crying. I don't understand. What have I done?

'Meditate, good for me!' I say, opening my eyes and jumping up. 'He tried to abduct my mother and killed my sister!'

'Who did?'

'When I was a child, just two years old,' I say, 'I saw a man try to abduct my mother when she was six months pregnant with my sister, I never knew his name. He was fighting her because she wouldn't come with him and she was screaming and trying to push him away. She hit him, he pushed her and then she fell. I was supposed to be with my father in the pavilion while my mother waited in the car, but somehow I strayed out and saw the whole thing. At one point the man picked me up and tried to take me too, and then he dropped me during the fight and I landed on my back. And when my father found me with them, he picked me up and threw me like a football into the car and then slammed the door on me. I was shut inside on my own! It was like I was dying. Anyway, in the car I landed on something, the seatbelt buckle perhaps, and it hit the same place on my back as when I was dropped, and that's the injury – that's the spot on my back.' I twist around, pointing to the painful spot between my shoulder blades.

'Yes, I'm sure that's it – and that this abduction attempt must be your original trauma,' Edgar says. 'I'm certain what you've just described was incredibly traumatic for you. When we're very young, we haven't separated from our mothers yet,' he explains, 'so it's as if adult things, things we don't understand, are also happening to us. We become overwhelmed, terrified, but we can't process such enormous emotions. But tell me – your mother knew this man?'

'He must have been someone she knew before she was married – I never saw him again and she never spoke about him to me. But I'm pretty sure it was Tomas.'

'Your Tomas?' Edgar says, his eyebrows shooting up.

I nod. 'My father chased after them and then came back to get me and take me to the hospital. And at the hospital my mother kept asking my father if I was OK, and my father tried not to answer but my mother wouldn't give up so then he lied, he said I hadn't been hurt, but I had. I was dropped on the ground and then abandoned in the car. They were fighting over me, both pulling at me. And then I was dumped in the car. Anyway, because of my father's lie, I thought I'd done something wrong and blamed myself, but it wasn't my fault. I was just a child in the wrong place at the wrong time.'

'And the baby?'

'My mother lost the baby, my baby sister, that night in hospital, but no-one explained anything to me. All I knew was that my sister died and it was all my fault. I was there, but I shouldn't have been. And then she died. I should have come inside when my father called – I blamed myself for her death.' I start to cry again, angry tears, but he stops me.

'Wait,' he says, 'try not to go into the anger. My hunch says you should try again. Go back into the meditation. Take a few more deep breaths and look again.'

'*Go back?*'

For an answer, Edgar holds my gaze. Eventually I look away.

'Freud called it the compulsion to repeat, and many therapists today believe that we deliberately find situations that remind us of our original traumas so we can re-enact them and hopefully change the outcome. Unfortunately, though, without help we often just repeat the cycle, and sometimes things can even get worse. The best way to stop repeating the cycle is to heal the original trauma. What we're doing now is the first step towards healing.'

I close my eyes, wiping my tears on the backs of my hands, and try to understand what Edgar is saying. At first it makes no sense, but then I remember what Isabella keeps saying and, almost against my will, I find myself changing my mind. When he hands me a tissue I thank him and, sitting back down, take a deep breath. And then I take another, and another and another and soon I'm back there, back on the beach, standing on the steps of the pavilion. Heart racing, eyes darting around beneath my closed lids, I watch the scene play out again.

… I hear daddy calling my name while I stand on the pavement watching mummy arguing with the other man. But this time instead of walking towards mummy I grow wings, two huge golden wings, and turn into an angel. Then I fly down to the esplanade and scoop mummy and my baby sister up in my arms and carry them away from the man to a safe place further down the beach.

'Thank you, darling,' mummy says and smiles, kissing me softly on my forehead. 'My little angel …'

… When I come out of the meditation the second time, I'm elated. In a rush I recount everything to Edgar.

'An angel,' he says, a smile lighting up his face. 'I'm very glad about that – that's a very good sign.'

I smile back. It makes perfect sense: I'd wanted to make everything better, partly to ease my guilt – if it was all my fault then it makes sense that I had wanted to make it better – and partly to save my mother and sister from Tomas. 'But why haven't I known this before?'

'Did your family talk about it much?'

'Never. I mean, I knew my sister had died, though I didn't know in what circumstances. That my mother had a colourful past and that she'd been depressed.'

'So it was a family secret?'

'Yes,' I say. I guess it was.

'Because secrets can do the most damage of all.'

It's close to midnight when the hospital finally rings back. Snapping my eyes open I find myself stretched out on the sofa and Edgar slumped in the armchair, snoring.

Waking up, Edgar answers the phone and, after checking with me, suggests I return to hospital early the next morning. When he hangs up we sit staring into each other's eyes for too long and I feel my face soften into a smile. Patting the seat cushion, I make room for him next to me on the sofa and he sits down beside me.

'Who are you?' I ask his up-close face.

'Who am I to you?'

'Why did you make me your mission, that sort of thing?'

'I don't know. I guess it was to help Nelly at first, and then because I thought I could help you. But this evening in London I realised it was more than just that. I like you.'

I look at him hard. 'So have I gone crazy? I know I asked you once already, but everything feels crazy right now. I can't take it all in: Franz, my father and mother, and Tomas, the spot on my back, and now you and me …'

'Sometimes it takes a little time to separate reality out from the fantasy and denial, but it's all part of the therapeutic process,' he says, his hand warm in mine. 'Common sense says you were assaulted and injured in the flood in Prague. All that's necessary for you to do to be returned to health is to rest and recover physically. But my research and clinical practice suggest that things happen to us for a reason, and that this is especially true for our most difficult experiences. We learn lessons from pain, lessons about our past that help us to lead better lives in the future. So you're not crazy, I'm certain you're not. On the contrary, I really think you're getting there, you're doing incredibly well.'

I smile. Everything feels strange but nice. 'So it really is all about my childhood?'

'You know, I'd love to hear more about it some time.'

'You mean, give you the whole family history sort of thing?'

'Something like that.'

'Can it wait for another time?'

'Of course.'

Suddenly all I want to do is curl up on his lap, so I hold out my arms and ask him with my eyes. He pulls me to him and cuddles me close, stroking my hair and kissing the top of my head. I lean in; his hand stroking my head is light and slow, and after a while he stops and we fall into a long stare again, neither of us looking away. I kiss him quickly on the lips, and then I kiss him more passionately. I kiss him again and again and Edgar kisses me eagerly back, but when we break apart I immediately start crying.

'What's wrong?' he says.

'It's nothing,' I sob.

'Tell me, why are you crying?'

'I'm just a little sad.'

'Happy sad, or sad sad?'

'Sad sad. If you want to leave now, I understand.'

'No, I'm OK. Actually, I was just thinking,' he says and pauses.

I hold my breath.

'Maybe it's time you told me – what happened with Tomas?'

I pull him to me and hug him tight. 'I thought you were

going to tell me it was better for us to remain friends or something.'

'Everything's going to be OK,' he says, pulling me close. And, closing my eyes, I fall deeply asleep.

4

The grandfather clock strikes eight a.m. but otherwise it's completely silent; no birds stir outside. While it's been raining – the leaves outside are spotted with moisture – the rain has now settled into a heavy fog.

I've been talking for the last hour or so almost nonstop, telling Edgar all about Reed and arriving in Prague, about meeting Tomas, about the Deutsche Grammophon deal, about Nelly and the Rudolfinum, about my mother, and about trying to stop drinking and failing. I haven't got to the bit about the castle, though Tomas and I are just about to go there. I still can't bear to think about Reed and Sarah and their betrayal, but I already feel marginally better. It actually feels good to be talking about it all to Edgar at last; lighter somehow.

'Well,' Edgar says finally, stretching his arms and yawning. 'I'm going to make that pot of tea. Would you like some?'

'Yes, peppermint would be nice.'

'It's freezing in here,' he mutters, slipping back into his shoes.

'Here,' I say, handing him one of my blankets.

Draping the blanket around his shoulders, he stalks out of the room. As soon as I'm alone, though, my thoughts drift back to Tomas and Prague and the castle; talking about it all has stirred things up again in my mind. I'm trying to remember the name of that first nightclub in Prague, the one where I met Anna, something in Latin, when Edgar returns.

'So tell me,' Edgar says, handing me the tea and climbing back onto the sofa. 'Tell me about becoming a musician. Why music, for instance? Why not dance, or drawing, or writing?'

'I started out wanting to be a dancer but then I changed my focus to piano after I had a breakdown at sixteen,' I tell him. 'Piano was easy, I was instantly good at it. Then later, playing music well made me feel special. The rest of the time, when I wasn't playing, I felt ordinary, unimportant even. I remember my teacher congratulating me on my proficiency and how elated I felt. It felt good to be good at something so I practised for hours and hours alone in my room. It was that simple. I liked to feel special, that I was important in some way, so I played the piano more and more.'

'Your parents didn't tell you you were special?'

'They were inconsistent about it, particularly my mother. Sometimes I was the best person in the world, other times there was something very wrong with me and I couldn't be trusted to do the most basic thing.'

'I'm sure they loved you very much.'

I frown.

'Perhaps it's time to forgive them, Cathy?'

'For what?'

'For not being able to love you the way you needed them to.'

'I guess,' I sigh.

I pull the blankets up and we snuggle down with our tea. I don't want to talk about my parents at the moment. As the sun begins to burn off the fog, I resume my story about Tomas. Edgar listens with kind eyes, his face expressionless over the rim of his teacup. At nine o'clock we go next door and I return to hospital to continue my recovery.

'I'll pop by later,' Edgar tells me with a smile as he strides away.

After a nap I try to start Edgar's car again and this time it works straight away. I put the car in reverse, making the gravel crunch, and then follow the driveway around until I reach the lane. Then I turn right, heading away from London, and soon I'm motoring along nicely. It's like Edgar said: you've just got to get back in the saddle.

Soon high vine-covered walls close in on both sides of the road and suddenly I'm in the village, with shops built right up on both sides. When the road reaches a *V*, I take the left turn and then pull off to the side. The cafe … As I approach on foot – handbag, yes, phone, wallet, yes – I see that the cafe's closed. But, across the road, the pub seems to be open.

Just then another car pulls in and a mother and daughter get out and cross the road. Starving now, hoping for a pie or at least a sandwich, I take a deep breath and follow. I guess there always has to be a first time …

The front bar is closed but a second bar out the back is open, and when I enter it I see that the mother is already seated, sipping at a mineral water. I sit down at the next table and, studying the lunch board, my eye is caught by the girl. She's seated at an old piano in the corner which is partly covered by a dirty red cloth, and, without sounding the keys, is stealthily playing a song. I don't recognise the chord progression.

The mother looks up at me and smiles, and I realise I have to order at the counter. I stand up as the girl accidentally sounds a note.

'Come here,' the mother says.

Head down, the girl slowly closes the piano and walks back to the table.

'Hurry up and stop making a performance out of it.'

The girl sits down.

'Drink up …'

With a sigh, I order a cheese sandwich with pickles, a black tea and no alcohol. When I return to my table the mother and daughter are arguing.

'But we could put it in my room,' the girl says. 'Please. I measured, it'll fit.'

'But they're noisy, and expensive.'

'But my piano teacher said even a small electric one is OK until I save up.'

'And where's the money supposed to come from for all this?' the woman says, turning to me for support, but I meet her eye unwillingly. 'Piano lessons cost money, so do electric pianos.'

'But –'

Their lunch arrives, two servings of tomato soup and a pile of toasted white bread, and they fall silent. When the girl doesn't eat, the mother says, 'Eat up. It's not my birthday every day.'

Watching the girl nibble at corners of the toast in between longing glances at the piano, I can't stand it anymore. 'Excuse me,' I say.

The mother's eyes are frosty so I keep it quick.

'I couldn't help overhearing,' I say, then stop. The mother glares, but I press on. 'Do you live nearby?' I say, this time asking the little girl. She nods.

'It's just that I might know somewhere you can practise,' thinking of Edgar's unused piano, 'and I'd be happy to give you some lessons …'

But the mother's next look is unmistakable. 'No thanks, we're fine, thank you.'

I meet her eye and then look away as my sandwich arrives. But when the mother gets up to pay, I write my name and number on a napkin and sneak it to the girl, who pockets it just before her mother returns.

When they leave I call out, 'Don't forget …' and the girl turns at the last minute and looks at me shyly. I hope she gives me a call.

5

I pull up in front of a little slumped cottage and kill the engine. I'm in Devon, I think, and I'm supposed to be meeting my mother here. I knock on the too white painted door but there's no answer. When I push, the door opens, so I let myself in.

The heating is on and the large carpeted reception is cosily lit by two yellow lamps. The clutter of pine furniture is simple and modern. The bedrooms have chenille bedspreads and heavy curtains; there's a galley kitchen, and an old-fashioned pale pink and grey bathroom. But there's no car, no luggage, no toiletries in the bathroom, no dirty dishes: no sign of my mother, full stop.

The scene changes. It's a lovely sunny day with high, darting clouds. Green fields full of cows framed by untidy hedgerows lead down to a chaotic pile of rock which frames a long, deserted beach. Waves gently glide in and out. The hiss of the receding tide on the sand is delicious. So is the fresh sea air. Standing, shoes sinking, on the sand; the hazy light and spray from the water soften the contours of the headland before me. It's intensely familiar, though I can't quite place it.

I set off along the beach. The horizon to my left is clear of clouds, the sky above is faintly blue, and the water is a salty green.

Behind me, rocky mounds covered in heather and dotted with fir trees form a ridge which runs along the beach. After a while I decide to sit down and take a rest. Sleepy, I lie down on the white sand, my back to the warmth of the sun, the chill wind not enough to keep me awake.

I open my eyes to find someone standing over me, blocking out my sun: my mother. She's in her early thirties and is wearing a lemon pencil skirt and a matching cropped jacket. She holds a pair of black patent stilettos in her hand, and a white scarf is tied around her head.

'Mummy!' I cry, jumping up to hold her, 'I was wondering what happened to you – what took you so long? I've missed you so much.'

'I've missed you too, darling,' she says. 'I'm sorry if I worried you, I came as soon as I could. It wasn't safe to come sooner.'

We smile at each other. Impossibly, we're the same age; it's almost like we're friends. Strangely, too, our communication is somehow telepathic. I only have to think a thought and she answers it with one of her own.

Suddenly a campfire appears and we sit down beside it on a checked woollen blanket. I'm about to ask her about knowing Tomas but she jumps in first with, 'Listen, there's something I need to tell you.'

'About Tomas?'

'Yes.'

'I knew it. He lied to me.'

'But he had a reason. You see, I know Tomas too.'

This hits me hard: finally a confirmation, the truth. My answer is slow, tentative. 'You do?'

'I knew him when we were both dancers in Prague.'

Instantly I know without a doubt it's true: my mother and Tomas were lovers. She starts to explain, 'And there's something else you don't know. You see, the communists …' but, heart pounding, I'm already coming out of the dream.

I wake up drenched in sweat. It's seven p.m. and I've slept right through dinner. I can hear people talking outside, hanging around in the hospital corridor before the evening meditation. For once I don't join them and remain where I am, trembling and thinking about the dream. My mother and Tomas, lovers; Tomas, the man I saw trying to drag my mother out of the car; Tomas lying to me about it all; and now the communists are involved somehow, too. I make a note to talk through the dream when I see Isabella tomorrow.

LONDON

1

'Catherine?' Edgar greets me, his arms out wide. I've just returned from a visit to my father in the little second-hand Peugeot Edgar bought me for my birthday last week, and Edgar grabs me as soon as I walk in and pulls me into a passionate embrace. I barely manage to close the front door behind us before he drags me over to the sofa and mauls me shamelessly, George whining at us for attention. But when Edgar unzips my jeans I laugh and say, 'Shall we move upstairs?'

We walk hand in hand up the narrow stairs and enter the large sunny bedroom. The bed is made up with faded olive green and lemon bedding. An armchair draped with a colourful tribal throw and matching wooden bedside tables are the only other furniture in the room. We snog messily standing in the middle of the rug and then we inch over to the bed and lie down.

'Sorry,' he says, struggling with my bra strap, but I'm too impatient to wait for Edgar to remove my bra so I take it off myself. He's a good kisser; in fact everything he does is very gentle and nice, and when he reaches between my legs I almost come at once. He has a magic touch, but afterwards I start crying.

'What's wrong?'

'I'm sorry, darling,' I say, 'I don't know why I'm sad.'

'It's OK,' he says, kissing away my tears. 'Don't worry.'

Later, drifting off to sleep in Edgar's arms, I say, 'You really love me, don't you?'

'Yes,' he says. 'Do you love me too?'

'Yes.'

He pulls me to him again and holds me against his chest. 'I know you do.'

We're cooking Edgar's favourite meal, Moroccan lamb. I'm organising the vegetables, skinning and deseeding the tomatoes, while Edgar trims the lamb and lines up the spices. We need to put the meat on first because it will take a while to cook, and then later we can put on the rice. Earlier, Edgar went out for Turkish bread, hummus and vine leaves from the local kebab shop to eat with the lamb, and we've got baked fruit and a block of dark Green & Black's for dessert. As we cook, Mahler's First Symphony blares from the stereo; we take turns kissing and taking sips of homemade lemonade. Edgar wanted to invite Nelly and a couple of his old school chums along but I just wanted it to be us – oh, and George too, of course. Soon the lamb is bubbling steadily and while we wait for it to cook we sit down in front of the Channel 4 news.

Edgar sits at one end and I rest my head on his lap and stretch out along the couch. Edgar strokes my hair and, not listening to the report about the economic effects of September 11, I close my eyes and sigh. 'This is the problem with being happy,' I say, 'you never want to go out anymore.'

Edgar looks at me closely. 'Darling, are you bored with me already?'

I laugh, 'No. It's just the third night in a row we've spent at home in front of the telly.'

'Well, let's go out.'

'I'm perfectly happy here,' I say, but Edgar insists.

Taking advantage of the late summer light we end up walking over to Holland Park, where it turns out there's an opera on, and while Edgar is curious, I'm content to watch the peacocks preen and the rabbits sneak about in what remains of this year's bluebells. Eventually, I turn us back towards Kensington Gardens, still not ready to face the world.

'But you will need to confront these people,' Edgar says.

'I know. And I will, soon. I promise. There's Sarah's opening coming up.'

'So you're going to go?'

I nod. 'Why not?'

Later, in bed – Edgar is the quietest sleeper I've ever known – I lie awake for a long time. It's strange, I reflect, being happy like this. Unfamiliar, I guess. And I feel like I'm floating through life, as if my feet aren't quite touching the ground, as if nothing's really real.

I'm sitting in the armchair in the spare bedroom, my hands buried in George's fur as I ruffle and stroke his soft ears. 'I just love you,' I tell him. 'I love you so much.' George smiles happily back, his eyes shining and moist. 'Georgie Porgie,' I tease him, tickling his stomach as he exuberantly rolls back and forth, scratching his back on the carpet while licking my hands and rolling his eyes back in his head. 'We love living here with Edgar in Kensington,' I tell him. 'Don't we? We do, we do …' Then, sitting up, I admire myself in the floor-to-ceiling mirror and think how happy and healthy I look in my pink and camel, the colours flattering against my pale skin and strawberry blonde hair. People keep telling me how well I look and now, smiling at myself, I believe them. I should probably do some meditation practise but I don't really feel like it. I've only done one this week ... Maybe tomorrow? I don't feel like I need it at the moment.

Instead, I pick up Edgar's old guitar. He's given it to me on a kind of permanent loan until I'm ready to do more than just teach and actually play the piano again; I've started teaching the little girl, driving down with Edgar twice a week to Surrey and using the piano at the priory. Luckily there's a packet of new strings inside the case – the old ones are so old they've gone rusty – although I struggle to remember how to restring a guitar. It's been so long since I've thought about a guitar I've almost forgotten.

First I take off the two top strings, leaving the G string, and then I remove all but the bottom string. I leave these two strings on the guitar so I can use them as models for the new strings. Then I open the packet of strings and take out the first string and the fourth string. Am I doing it right? Once I restring the guitar, I want to teach myself to play lullabies.

I copy the way the G string is attached at the base, looping the B string through the holes and then twisting the end around. Then I pull the string tightly into place. Next I find the corresponding pin at the top of the guitar and wind the string around the pin, careful to push the string right down near the wooden frame. When the string is nearly all wound on, I insert the end into the hole in the pin and then double it back again, so the end of the string is securely tucked into the hole in the pin. I survey my work, lift the guitar up and turn it around. Then I tighten the pin with my left hand while strumming the string with the thumb of my right hand.

Once the string is up to a normal tension I hold the guitar away and examine the new string. Then I take out the E string and repeat the process, except that I leave the end of the string a little too short and it doesn't quite fit into the pin. I worry that this will mean the string will slip and come off, but when I tune it, tightening it slowly, it stays in place. I remove the G string and replace it with a new one from the packet in the same way.

Next I turn my attention to the lower strings. They work the same way as the other strings except that they're attached to the bottom of the guitar in a knot instead. I insert the end of the D string and try to copy the knot. To do this I have to turn the guitar upside down. I chip my nails trying to force the end of the string around and beneath itself so that the knot is secure. It's very fiddly and my neck hurts from leaning over. It takes much longer than the other strings. I sigh with impatience.

Finally, all the strings are on the guitar. The lower strings look white and clean. I tune the guitar to the piano downstairs. I feel quite satisfied just looking at the newly strung guitar, but I'm too tired to play it just now. I lie down on the sofa, cover myself with the cream mohair throw we bought last weekend at John Lewis and fall asleep; George is already snoring at my feet. I'm so tired. I'm still so tired, sometimes to the point where I can't think.

After breakfast – Edgar is working down in Surrey today and

I'm due to join him later to teach my student – I decide to try out the guitar to see how it sounds. It's a nice day outside and sunlight is streaming in through the windows onto the polished wooden floor in the lounge room. I'm not sure what to play at first but I start with songs I learned when I was at primary school. The first song I play is 'Top of the World' by The Carpenters. Somehow the chord progression comes to me quite easily and I still remember most of the words. I'm just struggling with the chords to 'Michael Row the Boat Ashore', probably the first song I ever learned, when there's a knock on the front door.

I almost don't answer it, despite George's barking. Thinking it might be the police again with an update on the Franz proceedings, I almost ignore it, but eventually I go to the door and say, 'Hello?'

'Tereza?' Tomas's voice is unmistakable.

'Who is it?' I say, even though I know who it is. Suddenly it's difficult to breathe.

'Tomas.'

Before I have a chance to think about what I'm doing, I open the door. 'Come in.'

The first thing I notice is that Tomas is holding an envelope with my name and father's London address written on it. I also notice that his hand is shaking slightly but that otherwise he looks well: his hair is freshly cut and he's wearing new clothes, a white shirt and beige jeans. George circles him once and stands looking at me, staring.

'Come in,' I say, smiling too much.

'Thanks,' he says, smiling too much back and preceding me inside. I watch him walk ahead of me, noting the way his ex-dancer's body fills out his clothes. Standing on the opposite side of the coffee table, I briefly meet his eyes and then offer him a cup of tea, though what I really want is a vodka – which surprises me because I haven't thought of alcohol for weeks now. Tomas asks for wine.

I leave Tomas seated on the sofa and hurry away to the kitchen, where everything takes too long. I put the kettle on, put a bag in a cup, pour some wine from the fridge. When the kettle finally boils I end up spilling the water on the bench while filling the cup. I start to wipe it up but throw the cloth back into the sink. I rush back with a cup of Edgar's green tea for me and some wine for him. What on earth does he want, turning up like this after all this time? Maybe it's time we became friends?

'So, I found you,' he says.

'You traced me through the hospital?'

'Hospital? No, I asked your father – he gave me this address.'

I try to meet his eye again but he looks away around the room, taking things in, gulping at his wine, patting George awkwardly on the head. Spying my guitar, he asks if I mind and picks it up. He strums a little, the beginning of 'Hey Jude', and then puts it down.

'And what made you want to see me again?' I ask, just as Tomas says, 'I'm sorry, Cathy, I know I really –'

We both stop and laugh.

'You first,' I say.

'I'm staying at the Hilton on Hyde Park and I've lined up a number of meetings with potential agents,' he says, gripping the letter in his left hand.

I study the envelope. 'You have an agent now?'

Tomas shrugs. 'I hope.'

'So what's in the letter?'

'Oh, that's just …' he begins, looking down, then looking back to meet my eye. 'Actually, it's for you – I mean, I wrote it for you and was going to deliver it but then, when I found out you were just down in Kensington, I decided I'd rather give it to you in person.' His sad hungry eyes stare into mine. 'It's just that,' he says, looking away again, 'I'm thinking about going into therapy, I know I really messed you around and I wanted to …' He pauses, studying his surroundings. 'Do you have a flatmate, or …?'

'No, actually,' I say, unable to meet his eye. 'It's Edgar's house, he lives here too, I mean –' I break off, not wanting to tell Tomas but feeling I have to; I owe Edgar that at least. 'Edgar's my boyfriend,' I add, a heaving feeling starting up in my stomach.

'I see,' Tomas says, his face blanching, then reaching again for the guitar and absent-mindedly singing, 'Hey Jude, don't let me down,' as his fingers fumble with the chords. He stops playing, looks at me and stands up, dropping the guitar to the floor with a rattle. He reaches for his mobile, checks it and returns it to his pocket. I avoid his gaze.

'Well, I'd better be going,' he says, picking up the letter and starting to leave.

'I'll walk you to the door,' I say suddenly, not wanting him to go. He obviously still likes me, not that I should care …

When he turns to me at the door his face is completely closed. 'I thought you wanted me to read that,' I say, pointing at the letter.

Tomas looks at it, frowning. I reach for it but he holds onto it. Then he kisses me stiffly on the cheek, and, taking the letter with him, runs down the mews towards Kensington High Street.

I watch him hurry away, my knees trembling. Then I go back inside and empty Tomas's half-drunk glass of wine into my mouth.

'I love you,' Tomas says. *'I'm so sorry I hurt you. I just want to be with you.'* I jerk awake, my head resting on Háta's book of fairytales. Even though I'm instantly alert, I can still feel the pull of the dream; it's almost as if Tomas is standing in front of me, pleading with me. I wonder what he was going to say?

I reach for the phone book and dial the number for Tomas's hotel but hang up before the receptionist answers. I pour myself a fresh glass of wine and run my hands around the rim of Tomas's glass. Through the window I watch a bird deliver a worm to a nest under the eaves of the mews house next door. The sunshine makes the green leaves dazzle.

The phone rings. I hurry to answer it, wine splashing the floor.

'Hi,' Edgar says. 'Are you OK?'

'Yes.'

'Weren't you due down at Surrey today?'

'Something came up.'

'I see.' There's a brief pause. 'Look,' Edgar says, sighing, 'I know I said I'd cook tonight but I've had a really tough day –'

'I haven't had a chance to –'

'Shall we eat out? Just somewhere local and easy,' he says. 'I'm too tired to even think about it.'

I agree and we hang up the phone. I mop up the spilt wine and pour another glass. Then, picking up Háta's book, *The Princess and the Magic Mouse*, I start to read from an English translation I find on the internet.

Once upon a time, two beautiful princesses lived in an old medieval castle near Prague. Princess Karla was sixteen and had long blonde hair, a lovely smile, a slender frame, blue eyes and pale skin. Her younger sister, Lucinku, was twelve and had hair that was so blonde it was practically white and a sweet, round, dimpled face. They were orphans.

All was peaceful and content, until one day there came a knock at the door. The two sisters looked at each other in surprise. Finally Karla answered it.

A handsome young prince stood before them. His name was Ivan and he needed their help. 'My car has broken down and my mobile phone has no coverage.'

Karla invited him in and the three talked over tea and cookies about what could be done about his car. Soon it was night-time. The prince was so nice Karla asked him to stay.

The next morning, even though Ivan had fixed his car, he still didn't leave, he liked being with the sisters so much. When a week had passed Ivan asked Karla to marry him. Karla said yes, and the three danced for joy.

However, on the night before they were due to be wed, the prince grew first pensive then sad. He refused to eat or play cards with Lucinku and sat in the parlour alone in the dark. Karla thought it was a case of prenuptial nerves and tried not to worry about it too much, but when Ivan came to her that night before she went to bed, her heart sank and she knew the prince must have some bad news.

'I'm sorry,' he said. 'There's no nice way for me to say this. So I'll just have to say it: I can't marry you after all.'

'Why not?' Karla said. 'We love each other. We are good to each other. Why can't you marry me?'

But no matter what she said, Ivan could give her no reason other than to say, 'It's a curse, I am cursed. I must go away and you must forget we ever met.'

He apologised profusely, told her he'd love her for the rest of his life, and ran from the house. He sped away in his car and Karla cursed her bad luck.

That night Lucinku and Karla both went to bed crying. Eventually Karla cried herself to sleep but Lucinku lay awake in the dark staring at a patch of moonlight on the floor, thinking about her mother and father and all the other things she had lost – which now included the prince.

I suspect there's some significance to the story, some hidden message for me lurking inside my mother's favourite childhood book, and I'm trying to puzzle it out when I hear Edgar call, 'Hello, darling,' and George whining downstairs. Swallowing the dregs of my wine, I shove the book beneath the bedclothes and hurry to brush my teeth.

On the way home from dinner we pick up a DVD. I want to see *Wuthering Heights* but Edgar suggests *Bridget Jones's Diary*. When I show no enthusiasm, wanting to avoid a lecture, he insists on *The Unbearable Lightness of Being*. While I'm initially quite taken with Juliette Binoche's Tereza, I'm unable to keep watching once Sabina appears and I excuse myself. I grab a bottle of sherry from the kitchen – Edgar says something about me drinking again, which I ignore – and stumble up to bed.

2

It's a beautiful summer's evening as I set out for the opening-night performance of Sarah's new protégé, Kaiselin Zhong: not too hot, not too cold, and the light is soft and pink. I'm wearing a new linen jacket to help boost my esteem, luscious red roses adorning a cream background.

I take the tube to South Bank and then have to fight my way through the tourists to reach the concert hall. While I manage to present a cool facade to the passing crowds, what's going on inside is far from calm. My mind is churning and my knees shake wobbly beneath me. Edgar offered to come with me but I wanted to face this alone, although I did promise to give him a call if I needed him. Suddenly the thought comes: *I need vodka. I don't want to be here at all.*

Seated in the second row, with no sign yet of Sarah or Reed, I watch my thoughts like Edgar taught me – now I'm thinking about a glass of champagne – and then check my watch. The performance starts in two minutes – too late for champagne now – so I sigh and settle into my seat; a lucky escape? I study the program and try to keep my eyes averted from the familiar faces that surround me. All I want to do is congratulate Sarah, say hi to Reed, and leave. Looking up quickly, I fail to avoid eye contact with the journalist from the *Daily Mail* who wrote the double-page feature about Reed and Sarah and who is smiling at me with lots of yellow teeth.

Thankfully the artistic director of the London Symphony Orchestra walks out onto the stage and all eyes turn in his direction. He waits for the applause to die down and begins, 'How many times in a lifetime are we touched by true genius? Once? Twice? Rarely, if at all. Perhaps every generation produces one?'

I squirm in my seat miserably; Sarah used to write the same introduction for me. But it's only when, to loud and prolonged applause, the tiny pianist walks out onto the stage – she can't be twenty years old – that I collect my things and struggle to my feet. I check once more for Sarah and Reed and then, not seeing them, I walk out, striding through the glass doors and onto the street.

Fuck!

She's not just replaced me, she's superceded me. The humiliation: it's not just the 'every generation has its genius' spiel – she's bloody younger than I was! It's only when I'm pushing through the crowds of tourists lining the river that I remember Edgar; I should call Edgar. I look at my mobile phone and dial his number but hang up before the call connects. I'm now standing outside a pub. I look at my mobile phone still glowing with Edgar's name and then I switch it off and put it inside my handbag. If I can just stick to wine, I'll be OK.

I straighten my hair and tramp inside.

I moved on to the Groucho long ago but now it's closing time and there's nowhere else to go. Maybe that undercover dive on

Lisle Street? As I stumble down the stairs, everything unravels and I end up on my arse on the floor at the bottom. A tall blonde, all lacy stockings and smeared red lipstick, giggles down at me and her date, short and bulbous-nosed, holds out his hand. I shake my head, making the lacy stockings blur. Eventually I make my way outside and join the nearby queue for mini cabs. 'Kensington,' I bark at the man booking fares.

As my head starts to clear in the cool night air I notice that my heart is aching painfully in my chest. But it isn't my career, or Reed, or even Edgar I miss. As my head slumps forwards onto my chest it's just Tomas – Tomas and his letter that I'm thinking of.

3

Edgar is asleep in bed by the time I stumble upstairs and into bed in the spare room. Completely stonkered – champagne blurred into vodka at the Groucho – I end up spilling my bottle of lavender oil all over the pillow. I swallow eight drops of Rescue Remedy with a glass of water but it does nothing so I take off the rubber dropper and pour the entire contents down my throat. I still can't relax, and in bed the room is spinning and I can't sleep. Switching the bedside light back on – God, it's four a.m.! – I notice Háta's book on the desk where I left it yesterday. I go to the kitchen, take a half-drunk bottle of chablis from the fridge, grab a wine glass and return to bed. Then I go to the computer and fumble my way through the rest of the story.

As the words dance and swim – I'm so drunk now it's hard to be sure I'm taking anything in properly – I think I discover that a magic mouse helps fix the curse on the prince, who then returns and marries Karla. Liking that idea, wondering how Mouse is going now she's living with Libuše in Prague, I return to bed and empty the dregs of the wine. Tomas's letter, the one he didn't leave … I stare at the number for his hotel. I pick up my mobile, five a.m., too early to ring. I think about the brandy downstairs and finally I pass out.

I don't get up until late. Edgar's gone to Surrey by the time I make myself a cup of tea and has left me a note: *Is everything OK? What do you want me to do about your student?* George's nose is cool against my legs.

I sigh into my bowl of muesli; I don't know what to do. I suspect it's never going to work for me with Tomas, but I can't help wondering about that letter and what's in it. I could forget all about him and go on with my day, drive to Surrey, teach my student and stop drinking again – I know that's what I ought to do – or I could call Tomas and …? I switch on my phone – there's a text from Tomas: *Sorry I had to run off – do you want to meet for coffee?* After a liquid breakfast (I find a six-pack of warm beer in the pantry), I get a crazy idea. Smiling, dizzy with the beer on an empty stomach and the remains of a hangover from last night, I get dressed in my white terry-towelling bathrobe and climb into my car. Suddenly I'm in a desperate hurry and the traffic positively crawls. Waiting at yet another red light, I text my student and cancel our class.

I can't find anywhere legal to park so I park illegally in a side street off Queensway. I sit in the car for a few minutes trying to decide what to do. Turn back, or go upstairs and ask Tomas about the letter and what he was going to say? I can't decide. Across the road I see a palm reader, a short man with grey hair and dark bushy eyebrows. Maybe this is a bad idea? Within seconds, I run into reception and ask the girl to call Tomas's room but she gives me Tomas's room number instead and points to the in-house phone which sits on a marble table in the corner. I dial his room. He takes forever to answer. Finally his cautious 'Hello?' comes down the line.

My stomach clenches. 'Hi, it's me.'

After a pause, his 'Hi' comes answering back.

'I was just around the corner visiting a friend and I thought I'd drop by,' I say, wincing at the lie. Then add, 'If I've got you at a bad time …'

There's another pause, and finally he says, 'No, that's OK. I'll come down.'

'Actually,' I say, 'it's probably better if I come up.'

His 'OK' is quiet.

He looks tired, and while the bed is made, it's messy with discarded clothes and today's newspaper. Tomas clears the surface and sits down in the armchair. I sit cross-legged on the bed. Then, without offering me anything to drink, he starts talking, but I can't concentrate on anything he's saying – all I want is to ask him about the letter. I'm trying to think of a way to work it into the conversation, but when he starts talking about Prague, my ears prick up.

'Perhaps it must start in Praha again, in Central Europe?' he says. 'The creation of a map for Europe's future … And perhaps we will be the ones to begin this new war, the war to humanise capitalism? To make free market economies democratic again …'

I look at him and frown. Across from me on the other side of the room, Tomas and his argument seem a long way away. We haven't seen each other for months, and with everything that's happened, he wants to talk about politics? When he mentions his flight back to Prague, I panic. 'When are you flying out?'

'This evening.'

Breathless, almost lost for words, I finally find my courage. 'Look, the real reason I came here is because things between us don't feel resolved yet,' I manage.

'No.'

I have his full attention now. 'The letter – my mother…' I say, watching his lips. 'When did you know?'

He looks me up and down and then our eyes lock. 'You really came here – in your bathrobe! – to talk about your mother?'

'Yes,' I say, laughing back.

There's a brief electric pause and then he's moving towards me and snatching me into a kiss. We study each other up close. His eyes are dark, unreadable, but watching me intensely. Finally, he releases me and laughs.

'While it's very *Flying Dutchman* of you, and quite appropriate given the circumstances – I've always felt kind of cursed – I think we need to get something straight between us first,' he says, undoing the belt of my robe and reaching inside.

I moan and kiss him harder. 'I've been reading this Czech fairytale which gave me the idea,' I start to say, before my words disappear as I bury my face in his chest.

I wake up alone in the bed. Sitting bolt upright, I only relax when I hear the shower running. I lie back down and, smiling, close my eyes. But when Tomas emerges from the shower he starts throwing clothes into a bag.

'What are you doing?'

'What does it look like I'm doing?' he says, not looking up.

'Do you have to go?'

'It's a non-refundable ticket.' He zips the bag closed.

I get out of bed, slide into my robe and take his hands in mine. 'Stay with me. Don't go.'

'I have things I need to do in Praha,' he says. 'I can't stay.'

'What about me?' I say, but Tomas ignores me. 'But we haven't talked!'

He looks at me. 'Let's talk over coffee downstairs.'

But I don't move.

'Come on,' he says, now offering me his hand. 'I've got to go,' he says, laughing.

'I'm in my bathrobe.'

'Yes, I know,' he says, pulling me towards him. 'But you know I can't do this, that I'm useless at relationships.'

'So you just, you just – *what?*' I say, pushing him away. 'Slept with me for, for …?'

'You didn't seem to mind just sleeping with me.'

'I wanted to talk. You're the one who wanted to –'

'OK then,' he says, looking at his watch and sitting down in the armchair. 'But I've got to leave in an hour.'

I sit down on the bed and try to relax. I take a few deep breaths but it doesn't seem to help.

'Do you want some coffee?' he says. 'Something to eat from room service?'

I shake my head, but he's gazing with concentration at the menu. 'My mother,' I start, twisting the belt of my bathrobe in my hand.

He turns slowly and fixes me with a hangdog look.

'Why didn't you tell me?' I say. 'You knew, didn't you? You knew all along.'

'Not in the beginning,' he says, frowning and looking down.

'Then when?'

'I don't know exactly,' he says, looking at me and then looking away. 'I think it was when you spoke about your mother, when you mentioned she was the principal of the Czech National Ballet.'

'And why didn't you say something?'

'I was frightened history would repeat itself,' he says, looking back. 'That I'd lose you, just like I lost her.'

'But it was your choice not to be with her and your choice not to be with me.'

'She was married. It wasn't the same in those days, it would have caused a scandal – not to mention communism, which made matters even worse. I could have lost my job and then what would we have lived on? Your mother wasn't always the most practical person.'

'But with us it would have been different!'

The silence yawns between us.

'You should have told me – as soon as you knew! You lied – I wouldn't have slept with you if I'd known!'

'You're one to talk,' he says, standing up and getting ready to leave. 'Won't your boyfriend be wondering where you are?'

'Look – Edgar's a nice guy, but it's you I want to be with.' I reach for his hands but he brushes me away.

He crosses to the minibar. 'Would you like something to drink?'

'Do you have any vodka?'.

Half a dozen vodka and tonics, a slurred conversation about his new agent and how he's going to do therapy and work himself out, and a parking ticket later, we pull up outside Paddington station.

'Well,' I say, smiling, slurring.

'I'll call you,' he says.

I want to tell him I'll be in Prague tomorrow, but I don't. I think about buying a bottle of vodka on the way home instead. 'Bye,' I say, as he starts to get out of the car. At the last minute he grabs me and pulls me close. He kisses me and then he's out on the street.

'Call me on the mobile,' I tell him.

He looks at me and shuts the door. I watch him disappear into the crowd. It's only then that I realise he still didn't give me the letter.

Back at home, Edgar's still at work, I crawl into bed in the spare room, where my recent conversations with Tomas play over and over in my mind. I'm so tense, the idea of meditating seems like a kind of sick joke. I push Háta's book to the floor and lie on top of the covers. I stare at the ceiling and swig from one of Edgar's bottles of brandy. After a while – Edgar will be home soon – I start packing up my things. I'll go and stay at my father's until Tomas has sorted himself out. I wonder if he'll move to London or if I should move to the Czech Republic? As he has the castle, it makes sense for me to go there, although I don't know what I'll do about work – but then my thoughts skip midstream. What if he just did it again, lied to me, used me?

I go into Edgar's room, our room no more, and sit on the bed. Edgar … Such a sweet, lovely man. I lie down on the bed and close my eyes. But as soon as I do, I'm instantly back in Tomas's hotel room and we're making love.

'How do you feel about me?' I say.

'I love you.'

'You do? That's good.'

'And?'

'I realised that if I didn't do something soon I'd lose the best thing that has ever happened to me. And I didn't want that to happen.'

'You could have fooled me!'

'You're so beautiful.'

'Am I?'

'I love you.'

'I love you too …'

While the fantasy lulls me to sleep, I soon jolt awake in the middle of a nightmare I can't remember. It's just after six. I shower, trying to wash away the bad dream, and dress in clean clothes: pink velvet trousers, a pink jumper, my camel suede coat. I pour myself a glass of wine and wait for Edgar, mobile on the table just in case Tomas calls.

At seven I flick on the TV and stare absently at the news. I check my mobile: there's a text from Edgar saying he's been delayed and to go ahead and have dinner without him, and Tomas still hasn't called. At eight I make myself a cheese and tomato sandwich and pass out after eating it on the couch with a glass of wine. I wake at ten, check my mobile and calculate when Tomas's flight would have arrived in Prague. Allowing for the one-hour time difference, shouldn't he be there by now?

I dial his mobile and get a recorded message in Czech and hang up. I try his landline. It rings and rings and there's no answer, no-one there and no answering machine. My stomach twists, my breath comes in shallow gasps, and my thoughts swim round in circles. I empty the bottle into my glass. The room swims a little. I try Tomas on his mobile again. This time the line is simply dead.

I call Nelly and get her voicemail and hang up on it. Then

I call Nelly back, still no answer. I open another bottle of wine and call Nelly's mobile a third time. This time I leave a message, trying to sound as sober as I can. I try Tomas once more with the same result, drink another glass of wine in one gulp, and then finally, Edgar arrives home. I pour myself a fresh glass which I finish instantly, though Edgar barely touches his.

'So how was last night?' he wants to know.

I sigh. 'I don't want to talk about it.'

'OK – well, what have you been up to today?'

'Reading.'

'What are you reading?'

'A children's story, a Czech fairytale, a present from my cousin.'

'And what's it about?'

'It's a love story about a princess and a prince, only they can't be together because of a mysterious curse. It's set in a castle.'

'Right,' Edgar says, scraping his chair as he stands up. He gives me a stern look. 'While it's not my place to make your decisions for you, I will say this. I personally feel you're wasting your time.'

I look nervously away, my gut hollow. He knows me so well.

He carries his plate to the kitchen and stalks upstairs. I hurry up after him but he closes the door to his bedroom in my face. I knock, open it.

'It's not what you think,' I try.

'Oh really?' he says. 'He's been here, hasn't he?'

I can't deny it, though I lower my head.

'That man's poison for you, Catherine. He's sick. And

you … ? This is the stuff of addiction. When you're ready to start looking after yourself again, I'm always here.'

And with that he turns away and walks to the window.

What to do? I can't leave it like this. 'Edgar,' I say, and tap him on the shoulder.

He turns around at my touch but then, looking past me, notices my bags out in the hallway behind me and then we both look quickly away. The pain on his face is like a physical blow.

I look at my watch. It's eleven-thirty and Tomas still hasn't called. Edgar sips at his glass of scotch and turns back to the window, staring out into the darkness, and I walk over to the bed and dial Tomas's numbers, landline and mobile, one last time. Please, God, please make him pick up … When Tomas still doesn't answer I can't take it anymore. I turn and look at Edgar, who's staring down miserably into his empty tumbler, and then I retreat to the hallway and stand beside my bags.

Edgar looks up. His ruffled hair and weary expression only make him look more beautiful in his navy linen jacket, blue jeans and lemon checked shirt. 'You off?' he says.

I nod. I just can't keep hurting Edgar like this.

'You probably shouldn't drive. Shall I call you a mini cab?'
'Yes please.'

He has to dial the number three times, he keeps getting the number wrong. For the first and only time I see Edgar lose his patience as he slams the phone in its cradle. 'Damn thing.'

'I'll do it,' I offer, but he picks the phone up again.

He orders the cab, giving my father's address as my destination. After he makes the call he stands up.

I check my mobile: nothing from Tomas. Edgar watches as I return my mobile to my handbag.

Seeing him there, his face so open, so sad, I realise that Tomas hasn't called me, isn't going to call me, that he's abandoned me again; that my fantasy has no basis in reality. It will always be like this with Tomas. But I also see that Edgar was right and that I've really hurt him, this lovely kind man.

'I –' I begin, and then I'm crying, sobbing hard. I walk back into the bedroom. 'I thought we could just be friends, but then he had this letter and one thing led to another … I'm sorry, I'm still really messed up –'

I want to run into his arms but he doesn't offer them. He just watches me, his expression not changing, calm but somehow distant. After a while I grow quiet.

He offers me his handkerchief, red with white checks, and sits me on the bed. 'I can't do this anymore,' he says quietly and starts to cry.

I stare at him.

'I've tried to help you, Cathy, but I honestly don't know where we can go from here.'

He picks up a pen from the bedside table, scribbles something quickly on the back of one of his business cards and hands it to me. 'They may be able to help you.'

With a mixture of numbness and relief, I pocket the card. I just need to talk to Tomas – why the fuck hasn't he called? Maybe if he does the therapy we might actually have a chance.

I need another bottle of wine. In the distance, I can hear George crying downstairs.

4

When I check in to rehab they confiscate my vodka and Valium and then leave me in a grey room to wait for my admission interview. I struggle to stay awake. I've never in my life felt so incredibly tired. My eyelids droop and my head slumps against the wall. My last waking thought is of marmalade and butter on thick toasted sourdough bread, which is strange as I'm not at all hungry and haven't eaten properly since – actually, I can't remember the last time I sat down and ate a square meal.

It's raining outside and I'm lying in my room listening to the rain. There are trees outside the window. I like the sound of the rain as it hits the leaves. Later I have to get up and go to my group therapy session. I look at the round white clock on the wall. The group meets in an hour's time. It continues to rain. My second day without alcohol.

Emily, my therapist, is in her late forties and has long grey-brown hair which she wears loose across her shoulders; an Aussie. Her eyes are blue and clear. 'How are you feeling?' she asks.

I take a deep breath but I can't speak, my eyes fill with

tears that don't fall. All I can do is shake my head while my shoulders heave. Dry, silent sobs.

After the session – we talk about the events that preceded my admission – I take a walk through the grounds. Walking between two beds of flowers, I can't stop obsessing about whether I should be with Tomas or Edgar but the fish pond cheers me up. Fat orange carp drift lazily through the murk. They sense me watching them and swim towards me, hoping for bread. 'Hello, fish,' I tell them weakly.

I'll keep some bread after breakfast and feed it to them tomorrow afternoon.

'Can you tell me why you're here?' Emily wants to know.

I take a deep breath. 'My drinking got a little ...' I begin, and then break off. I can hardly breathe but I force myself to take five deep breaths. 'Sorry, I'm just really anxious. I can't sleep and right now I can hardly breathe.'

'That sounds like withdrawal to me,' Emily says, looking at me with her keen eyes.

'Can you give me anything to help me sleep?'

'This is a rehab,' she says, shaking her head. 'We can give you Panadol, but that's all. In extreme cases a doctor might prescribe something else. But your case isn't extreme.'

'So what do I do?'

'I can give you some breathing exercises,' she says.

Emily takes me through an exercise that reminds me of the meditation I did with Edgar. During it I'm so tired that I almost fall asleep in the chair. I don't want to come out of it, to wake up, to come back to reality.

Afterwards we talk a bit about my mother and it's painful

but for the first time I start to feel sad about my mother's death. All those tears in Prague and Surrey … I thought they were about me, but now I see they were about my mother too. When my time is up I don't want to leave. Afterwards, I go feed the fish. Then I have group therapy. Later, before I go to sleep, I practise Emily's breathing exercise. It works. For the first time in weeks I sleep right through.

Bit by bit I tell Emily what happened. I tell her about Reed and Sarah, about Deutsche Grammophon and the Rudolfinum, about Tomas, about the castle, Anna and Franz, about New York, the flood and my injury. I tell her about Edgar, my mother, about my primary trauma, and then about Tomas again. Then one day Emily has a letter for me when I walk in. There are Czech stamps on it and it's addressed to my father's home address. 'This came for you today.'

'I don't know if I want to open it,' I say, holding out my hand, which trembles slightly. Emily passes me the letter. I look at it, and think, *Tomas*.

'Do you want to read it here with me?'

I nod, tearing nervously at the paper, my hands shaking, and devour the first lines.

Dear Tereza, I read before skipping to the end where I see *Love, Tomas*. I almost smile but go back to the beginning of the letter. 'I hope you're well,' I read aloud. Emily is watching me closely. 'I've been trying to write this letter for weeks now but I haven't known what to say. Anyway, I just want you to know that I'm sorry I didn't call you. I didn't plan it, it just turned out that way.' But I have to stop reading here as tears blur my vision and start streaming down my face.

'What does he say?' Emily wants to know.

'I can't read it,' I sob.

'Would you like me to read it?'

'No, I want to read it.'

I think about it for a minute and then, wiping my tears on my hand, then again on a tissue which Emily hands to me, I read:

I remember you were always asking me questions, why I couldn't have relationships, that kind of thing. What I didn't tell you is that I did once see a therapist in Praha who said the disorder I have is incurable, which means that I probably can't have a relationship with you or with anyone else, ever.

I know sometimes I act a little recklessly, and maybe I did with you, but I only meant for us to have a fun affair. But then you wanted more. I did think for a time that I could have a relationship with you but I didn't want to get your hopes up. I tried to change myself and think again about therapy but none of it felt right.

It just wasn't meant to be with us. Deep down, I feel completely worthless. It's not you, it's me. And of course, there was always your mother. She kept coming between us. I tried to tell you a couple of times about her and how I owe her my life – if it wasn't for your mother, I would have spent the best part of my life in a communist prison – but I always worried talking about her would mean I'd lose you. Maybe that was a mistake?

Anyway. Good luck with the music and keep crucifying Tchaikovsky, I think it's really working.

Love, Tomas.

'He doesn't love me,' I wail, unable to stop myself.

'No, Cathy, listen to me. I'm sure he has feelings for you.'

'He doesn't want to be with me!'

'What I heard is that he can't give you what you want. He wants to, but he can't.'

But at this point in the session, Emily, her kind words, the room, everything starts to fade. I can't talk, I can't think and, handing Emily the letter to read, disappear into a flood of tears.

At first Emily lets me sob and withdraw, but after fifteen minutes or so she tries to pull me out of it. 'Tell me about your music, why you don't want to play.' And when I don't respond, she says, 'It's very important for you, Cathy, your music. It's what you do.'

I don't sleep at all that night and the next day I tell Emily I'm leaving rehab. 'I need to talk to Tomas,' I explain.

Emily looks at me closely. 'Cathy,' she says, 'do you know why you're in rehab?'

'But what about the bit about the communists?' I say. 'In the letter – don't you see? This changes everything!'

Emily just keeps staring at me, hard. 'This is a rehab,' she says eventually. 'Everyone in here is recovering from some form of addiction.' She pauses.

'Yes,' I say, looking into her clear eyes. 'I mean, I know my drinking got a little out of hand at the end there …' I frown.

She raises her eyebrows.

'Are you saying you think I have an addiction?' I want to know.

She nods.

'I don't understand,' I say. 'What am I addicted to?'

'I think you're an alcoholic with dependency issues. You

also have post-traumatic stress disorder, your case notes say you experienced significant trauma during your childhood – the abduction scenario, your sister's death, we've talked a little about that, right? Also, there's a family history of trauma which includes a family member being imprisoned in Auschwitz and others being persecuted by the communists.'

'OK, I knew about the PTSD. But you said an alcoholic, with *what*?'

'When you were admitted here, we received a report from the hospital in Prague,' she says, rifling through her notes. 'The hospital where you were treated for your injuries after the flood.'

'Yes?'

'According to the doctor who admitted you in emergency, you had a blood alcohol reading of 0.2.'

'Is that a lot?'

'Where I come from you lose your licence if you're caught driving with a level over 0.05 …' she says.

I look down at the rug as my face flushes a brilliant red.

'Would you like to tell me about your drinking?'

'Are you saying I'm an alcoholic?' I say, my hands gripping the arms of the chair.

'That's ultimately for you to decide.' She shrugs. 'But going on this report, I think you have a drinking problem.'

'No, I don't think so!' I say. 'I hardly drink, I virtually stopped drinking when I came out of hospital. I only had a couple of drinks here and there during the weeks before my admission.'

Emily studies me, her face a blank.

'I mean,' I say, frowning, 'I might have had a slightly raised blood alcohol level when I was admitted to hospital, but I'd been drinking absinthe at this party the night before …'

Emily doesn't say anything.

'You think I'm an alcoholic? And a dependent … a what?'

'Have you ever heard of something called the addictive personality?'

I nod and swallow hard.

'The addictive personality can be addicted to many things,' she says. 'Drugs and alcohol, but relationships, too.'

The clenching in my gut matches the light bulb in my head.

'Addictions often run in families, and from what you've told me about your parents, your mother had affairs and your father drank – does that sit right with you?'

'I – did I say that?'

'Now, an addict by definition is someone who can't stop doing the thing they're addicted to,' Emily continues. 'Alcoholics, no matter how often they tell themselves they're going to quit drinking, can't quit, or they can't quit for long. People who are addicted to relationships have trouble leaving them, or once they do, with staying single.'

'But I did leave Tomas.'

'But just now you were about to check out of here so you could go back to him.'

'He said he loved me.'

'But he also said he couldn't have a relationship with you – at least, not the sort of committed relationship you want. We treat a lot of addicts here, people from all walks of life, and what we find is that despite their material and cultural differences, their stories are all remarkably similar: addicts aren't prepared to admit to their addiction, or to ask for help until they've lost everything. Their jobs, their relationships, their money, their health. Before an addict hits what's called a rock bottom, they usually live in a state of denial about their addiction.'

I look at Emily, my jaw clenched tight.

'Cathy, I really think you need help, and despite what you've just said, I actually think you're ready. You've lost enough to your addictions – next time you mightn't be so lucky. I'm telling you this because I don't want to lose you. And if you check out of here before I think you're ready, I'm frightened that's what might happen.'

I look away from her clear open face and stare at the floor. A clock ticks nearby. My thoughts skitter while tears prick the corners of my eyes.

Finally Emily breaks the silence to say, 'We have ten minutes left, Cathy. If it's OK with you, I'd like to talk to you about Tomas. Are you all right with that?'

I look up. Those clear grey eyes, the concern on her face.

'Yes,' I say, barely a whisper.

She shifts in her chair and looks at me, frowning slightly. 'How do you really feel about Tomas, deep down?'

'I don't know.' My mind is blank, my heart pounds harder.

'How does it feel when you're with him?'

I think hard. 'In the beginning it felt good, we seemed to have a lot of things in common, he understood about my work, we were inseparable to start with. I wasn't completely sure about him but things still felt OK. And then …'

'Yes …'

'Then at the castle, I don't know, things changed. I started to feel bad.'

'I see. And what is it you like about him?'
'I don't understand.'
'What are his good points? Is he thoughtful, kind …?'
'Um …'
'Do you share the same morals and values?'
'I'm not sure.'
'Do you want the same things out of your relationship?'
I stare at her hard.
'Not everyone wants the same kind of relationship, Cathy.'
I shrug.

'OK, putting Tomas aside. Can you tell me what usually happens for you when you start a relationship?'

'I don't know. If I like the sex I'll want to keep sleeping with them, then I usually want to marry them and have kids. But the men, they never want to marry me or have kids with me. Although Reed did, but he was –'

'And you want to get married and have kids with a man right from the word go?'

'If I like the guy, that's what I'll be looking for in the long term.'

'OK, that's all we have time for today. But for homework, I'd like you to write a history of your relationships.'

After therapy I walk back to my room and lie down on my bed, in shock. My mind churns and churns. How did she know? How come I didn't know? I can't stop thinking about Emily, and what she said, and what it means. I desperately need a drink, and when I catch myself thinking that, I suddenly know that what Emily said is true. That I'm an alcoholic, I'm a fucking alcoholic! Oh my God. I start to cry. Walking wounded all-bloody-right.

I rage and hit pillows and cry some more. It feels like I'll never stop being angry and sad. Then, gradually over days that turn into weeks and weeks that turn into months, my despair starts to ease. I still think about Tomas sometimes but somehow I'm able to forget about him for short periods of time too. I think about my addiction to alcohol, how I knew I had to stop but couldn't. I learn more about my PTSD. I see my denial about my addiction to Tomas. Edgar's words, 'that man is poison for you', finally make sense.

5

'Daddy?' I call, letting myself into his flat with the spare key, but there's no answer, he must be at the library. I leave my bags at the door, pick up and then straight away put down the letter from Reed's solicitor about our divorce proceedings, and wander through the empty rooms, the shabby old furniture making me feel sad, the grief for my mother heavy inside. I go into my childhood room and sit on the bed. Outside the window the tips of the branches are swollen with tight buds. Spring is here and I've been sober for ninety days.

I feel worse in this room. My old piano sits lonely in the corner – I'm still not ready to resume playing – and then I remember Emily's words: 'When you get home, find a therapist you like and work through everything that's happened to you.' I pick up my childhood copy of *Wuthering Heights* and flick through its pages, then put it down. A framed photograph of me with Bronte when I was three: my legs are wrapped around her hips, my arms grip tightly onto her neck and I hang, monkey-like, beneath her, my head tilted back and a bubbling grin for the camera.

I get up and make myself a cup of tea and drink it curled up on the sofa, the cup and saucer balanced on my knee. Hašek,

Havel, Kafka, Kundera ... I study the books on my father's bookshelves, the names all much more familiar to me now. Seeing them there I'm reminded of the trip my father and I are planning to make to Prague later this month to scatter some of my mother's ashes in the Vltava.

I glance through *The Guardian*. A tiny article about how the clean-up after the Prague flood has bankrupted the state. In the Arts section, the New World Symphony is playing at Festival Hall. I pick up the phone and dial Edgar's number. When he doesn't answer, I hang up. He's not my rescuer, or a romantic hero, he's just a really nice guy.

Then I hear my father's key in the door downstairs. 'Catherine,' he calls up the stairs, 'you're here.'

'Hi, Daddy.'

'I'm sorry I wasn't here to meet you when you arrived,' he calls up. 'I meant to be. Damn tube, there was a fire at Russell Square station ... Anyway,' he says, entering the room all smiles. 'Did you hear the message on the answering machine from Deutsche Grammophon? Your Janáček recording has finally got the thumbs up!'

Despite my smile, I feel myself starting to cry. I hold out my arms to my father for a hug just as my phone beeps with a text from Nelly – who's been incredibly supportive – sending me her congratulations. I guess this means I'll have to start practising again ...

Light dances on the River Thames. It's a beautiful Sunday afternoon and tourists throng the river's banks, although there's still a nip in the air and my nose streams slightly. While the branches of the trees are bare – the new leaves remain a distant fuzz at the tips of the branches – the clouds and winter rain are gone for today.

I'm wearing a three-quarter-length red velvet coat, a new pair of jeans and a navy embroidered jumper. A pink silk scarf clashes delightfully with the red of the coat.

Edgar is talking on his mobile when I arrive. He waves, I wave back. In his hand are two tickets for the Dvořák. I wait for him to finish his call.

'Sorry,' he says, tucking his mobile into his pocket.

We kiss hello and study each other's eyes. Today Edgar's eyes are green flecked with yellow. We link arms and, feeling like the sunny sky is inside me – so glad to be here with Edgar again – we hurry towards the auditorium. Aglow.

Acknowledgements

There are so many people, I hope this list suffices. Thank you all very much for your help and encouragement:

Mila, Libuše, Danny and Ivetta, Sylva, Mirela H, John Hamilton, Anna Davis, Piers and Cathy, Jo Kavena, Jill Dawson, Robert McCrum, Robert Potts, Kate Dennis, Nikki Gemmell, Cate and Andrew, Susan B, Mikey, Lyndon, Yvetta and Brian, Minna P, Cindy Mikul, Katya Kastner, Pepe, Sarah Sanders, Georgia de Chamberet, Alex Morely, Richard English, Sarah Sahardi, Lizzy and Richard, Bohumil, Tim B-M, Michel Hvorecký, Varuna, Amy, Dr Crumlin, Benython Oldfield, Fran Moore, Neil Mansfield, Dr Wu, Alena Jirasek, Barry Scott, Penny Goodes, Sandy Wagner and my family.

Praise for Justine Ettler

The River Ophelia

With an intoxicating mix of tough sex, violence and ink black humour, Ettler sticks it to the reader, with scant regard for those who might be offended by her hard-boiled prose.
Rolling Stone

Two Australian bestsellers about women's sexuality confronted readers in 1995. *The First Stone* by Helen Garner and *The River Ophelia* by Justine Ettler were so far apart in form and attitude that they came almost full circle on questions of sex and power, transgression and vulnerability. How, they asked, can women and men connect without someone being exploited? Eternal questions, still unresolved. Ettler's novel provoked, titillated, repelled and fascinated. Few recent novels have occupied critics more as they analysed the story of 'Justine' as postmodern, post-feminist, post-Freudian, internationalist, autobiographical, surrealist, parodic, pornographic, dirty realist, grunge ... Two decades later this daring debut novel and its author still have my respect. Ettler's book *should* be read as an x-ray of its hedonistic, anxious end-of-millennium days, and also as a timeless portrait of youth, because some things haven't changed.
Susan Wyndham, former literary editor of *The Sydney Morning Herald*

Picador—renowned for scooping up the best of experimental fiction—is so sold on her talent that it signed her to an unprecedented—for an unpublished author—two book deal.
The Weekend Australian

Sublime
The Mag

An impulsive, arousing and addictive read.
Voice Works

An electrifying cocktail of love, war and liberation.
New Woman

One of the acclaimed writers of Australian GritLit.
Rip-Up Mag

Sydney's Empress of Grunge.
Writing and Journalism

The *River Ophelia* places Ettler as a strong contemporary of female novelists working in the dark world of transgressive fiction. Significantly, with this novel she leaps beyond the nationalistic boundaries of Australia, her writing is best compared to Mary Gaitskill, Tama Janowitz or, at times, Kathy Acker.
Ariel View

In October 2017, after some years out of print, *The River Ophelia* was republished, and it's a novel worth re-examining during this moment of #MeToo, because it has significance beyond the 'grunge lit' classification. Set in inner-city Sydney, the novel focuses on a sexually violent relationship between literary studies student Justine and misogynist *Playboy* reporter Sade. ... *Ophelia's* importance also lies in the timing of its republication, which coincides with the rise of #MeToo. The women who have publicly spoken about experiences of abuse and assault under this title have collectively contested the myth that men's violence against women is rare, trivial and ignorable.

The shining of a spotlight on male violence and gender inequality that is crucial to #Me Too is also crucial to *The River Ophelia*. In the spirit of 'postmodern' novelists such as Kathy Acker, Ettler reworks canonical literary texts in order to highlight their (frequently dubious) sexual politics. Her novel's characters include the Marquis de Sade's Justine and Shakespeare's Ophelia. Even though these women live in the apparently woman-friendly 90s, they're still miserable as ever. The Justine and Ophelia of 1995 are still suffering at the hands of shitty men.

My point is that to classify *The River Ophelia* as 'grunge lit' and leave it there does the novel a disservice. Ettler's novel provides an unflinching examination of male violence – an issue that is as depressingly pervasive in the #MeToo era as it was in de Sade's day.

Jay Daniel Thompson, https://overland.org.au/2018/01/rereading-the-river-ophelia-in-the-era-of-metoo/

Marilyn's Almost Terminal New York Adventure

It [Marilyn] titillates, teases and bamboozles from beginning to end. It's a pepped-up punctuation-less prose-o-rama, zipping from page to page in a glorious onslaught of Hollywood glitz—this is Marilyn as you've never seen her before: alive, accident-prone and totally confused.
The Sunday Age

A modern fairy-tale.
The Age

Shuns realism in favour of a surreal, comically paranoid world in which Marilyn is Australian and lost in New York where she is trying to find the man who might cure her TV allergy. Her adventures are related with the barmy zest of an R-rated cartoon.
The Big Issue

Tumbling, rushing and spilling off the page … Ettler has constructed a mythical urban adventure peopled with archetypes. Marilyn is a female Don Quixote; her Sancho Panza is in the guise of the feminist heroine, Virginia Woolf … In a literary sense, Marilyn is the bastard child of the rollicking bawdy romp and John Travolta-style journalism: a cool, ironic tone that smiles, obsesses and notes but never gets involved.
The Sydney Morning Herald

Has unmistakeable echoes of 1980s New York novels such as *Bright Lights, Big City*, and *Slaves of New York*.
The Australian

Justine Ettler's second novel *The River Ophelia*, (Picador, 1995) was an instant bestseller in Australia and New Zealand and has been taught at University level. Her first novel *Marilyn's Almost Terminal New York Adventure*, (Picador) was published the following year to critical acclaim. In 1997 Justine was selected as one of six Australian authors to tour the UK as part of the New Images Writer's Tour, and subsequently moved to London where she lived until 2007. She worked as a book reviewer at *The Observer, The Evening Standard*, and *The Times Literary Supplement*, lectured in Creative Writing, and worked as a reader for the London literary agency, Cornerstones, as well as for The Literary Consultancy. In addition to her career as an author, Justine is an accomplished flautist who performed as a soloist at the Sydney Opera House while in her teens, taught flute at Sydney Girls High, who participates in amateur musical theatre, and who has accompanied members of the Australian band *The Go-Betweens*. Justine has a PhD in American Literature and in 2017 she published a new edition of *The River Ophelia*.